Quiet, Pretty Things

By Megan Stockton

Printed in the United States of America

First Printing, 2021

ISBN Trade Paperback - 979-8-9854017-0-7
ISBN Trade Hardcover - 979-8-9854017-1-4
ISBN Limited Edition Hardcover - Not for Public Sale

Any references to historical events, real people, or real places are used fictitiously.

Cover design by Dagan Boyd

Paperback and mass market hardcover printed and produced using KDP, an Amazon Platform.

Limited edition hardcover produced through B&N

Bad Luck Cat Publishing
Grimsley, TN
https://www.facebook.com/meganstocktonauthor

1
Quentin

Quentin Robichaud had been with the Whitebranch Police Department for fifteen years as of this past June. He had been a bit of an underdog at the Academy, a man of unassuming stature with a sharp tongue and penchant for sarcasm who was always stepping on the toes of someone far larger than him and therefore more equipped to kick his ass. He never did go down with any humility or grace. While you may have heard that he was a confrontational asshole, no one would have ever denied that he was also smart. He had a bachelor's degree and touted a 3.8 GPA, which he would say was only that low because he had completely failed Philosophy of Religion. Despite being as pleasant on the surface as a blender full of nails, Quentin was surprisingly quick to make friends and was loyal to a fault. He had been promoted fairly quickly at the Department, finding himself one of few detectives early in his career.

He hadn't changed much in the years since the Academy. His dark hair was streaked with a little grey, and his beard was flecked with the same grizzle. He held a cigarette between his teeth as he put both hands onto the wheel to guide the car over the bumpy terrain of the field. One substantial rut in the ground sent the ashen tip onto his black slacks. He put the car into park, getting out and dusting his pants off quickly, flicking the spent cigarette into the tall grass.

Another detective approached him, a man just slightly older than Quentin himself with cinnamon-and-pepper hair and narrow green eyes. He wasn't much taller than Quentin but was heavier by at least fifty pounds with a broad frame and a subtle beer gut. His name was David Polanski, and he was a transplant from up north who had moved to Whitebranch to appease his wife's need to be closer to her family. He was as abrasive as steel wool, and so he and Quentin had become fast friends even before they'd become partners. He chewed a wad of gum fairly obnoxiously, motioning in the direction of the sailing cigarette.

"Not quit yet?"

Quentin shook his head, "Nah, how you doing with it?"

"Still at a pack a day," he said, using his thumbs to pull his pants up an inch. "But instead of cigs it's this fucking nicotine gum. Tastes like drywall."

They started walking across the field together and Polanski began filling him in, "Dead woman, probably mid thirties. Owner of the field found her when his dogs wouldn't come back to him. They chewed on her a little, body looks fresh though."

"Who's the landowner?"

"Jack Clay. Guy's pretty shaken up."

"Is Paltro up here yet?"

Polanski scoffed, "You were late, Robichaud. Everyone's here but you."

Ahead he saw the yellow crime scene tape fluttering in the cool autumn air. On the ground were several markers and the body of the young woman. As Quentin and Polanski crossed the line, he took note that the girl was wearing shoes with heels, and she had on a tattered skirt and leggings. She was naked from the waist up, and several yards away he saw one of the bright markers lying by a pink top.

A man in khakis and a black polo was crouched down beside her body and stood slowly at their approach. He turned to meet them, pushing his glasses higher onto his nose with his wrist to avoid touching his face with his gloved hands. He was tall and slim, with richly dark skin and nearly hazel eyes. His name was Deen Paltro, and he was the county medical examiner. Quentin could always tell he kind of loved this type of excitement, in a morbid way.

"Paltro," Quentin said in greeting.

"Robichaud, how nice of you to grace us with your presence."

Quentin knew better than to engage in a battle of wits or insults with the younger man. Paltro would outdo him every damn time. There was something to be said about his passive-aggressive viciousness, the way he seemed to have an instant comeback for every single snarky comment, and the way absolutely nothing flustered him at all. He was calm, cool, and collected... All of the time.

"So, homicide obviously," Polanski interjected, stuffing yet another square of gum into his mouth.

Paltro nodded. "I suspect. Cuts on her chest are postmortem, I think. I'll confirm more when we get her back to the morgue. There's this though."

He pulled a sealed plastic bag out of his pocket. He hesitated, looking down at it before he finally extended his hand, letting the bag dangle in the air between them.

Quentin exchanged a sideways glance with Polanski, reaching forward and taking it from Paltro's hand. The plastic bag contained a small, bloody square of wood. It was probably an inch wide and two inches tall with a faded image of a flower. He nearly threw it down.

"Fuck," he muttered, letting Polanski take the bag out of his hand.

"There's no way," Polanski added quietly.

"Oh yeah," Paltro said with a solemn nod.

Quentin couldn't seem to stifle the jittery feeling that took over him. He reached to pull another cigarette out of his pocket, putting it in his mouth as he struggled to light it with shaking hands.

"Where was it?" he said between strikes.

"In the subcutaneous space of the laceration on her left breast. Tucked inside."

"It's him," Polanski said. "Nobody is saying it, but I know we're all thinking it."

Quentin took a deep breath before he exhaled a long stream of smoke into the air. He didn't want to think about this. Six months ago, another young woman had shown up dead in a field not unlike this one. She had been dating a few different men online, and it was always suspected that one of them had murdered her. The case had wracked the small town with horror, and the lack of answers had put a lot of pressure on local law enforcement. There had been no trace of anyone else. No fingerprints, no DNA evidence. Animals had scavenged some portions of her body before she'd been found, and a heavy rain had washed away any sign of tire tracks or footprints... but the thing that had puzzled them the most was a little wooden game piece, just like this one. It had been found in the victim's mouth. It had a different floral design on it, but it was the same style. The case was still open, but they had nearly given up on finding the girl's killer. All of the guys they interviewed were scumbags, but they all had alibis that checked out. Most of them hadn't even been in the county when the girl was killed, and even fewer had ever met the girl in person.

"Now I think saying 'him' is getting ahead of ourselves, just a little," Paltro stated quietly, "But I don't think it's a coincidence."

Polanski smacked his gum once and then looped his thumbs in his belt loops. "Well, where do we go from here?"

Paltro shrugged, motioning over his shoulder. "You tell me. There's a shoe print, they're making a cast of it right now. Other than that, we don't have much yet. I'll let you know what I find when I do the autopsy."

Quentin nodded, carefully walking around the scene to take in all of the small marked evidence stations. The body first: pretty woman with red hair and green eyes. Her skin was ashy pale, and he imagined that it had not been much more colored when she had been alive. She was probably in her late 30s, if he had to guess, not much older than that for sure. She had been dressed to go out and have a good time. This had clearly not been the afternoon she dressed for. Judging by the mud caked on her heels and the way the knees of the leggings were torn and muddy, she had at least tried to run.

He moved over to the discarded top, which had been carefully preserved. Either she had removed it or her murderer had taken great care to not tear the fabric when they did. Next, the shoe print, which he could not examine as the cast was still being prepared. And finally... tire tracks. The soft grass was just barely depressed by the weight of the vehicle, and there was no sign that he'd left in such a hurry that he'd spun or torn up the ground. In time, the vegetation would spring right back up, and there would be no sign he'd been there at all.

Polanski approached him and said, "No one comes down this road that doesn't live here. Someone had to have seen the vehicle."

"Maybe not, if it was dark," Quentin mused.

"I'm going to ask around anyway."

"Yeah, nothing else to do until we find out who the girl is and get some more information from Paltro."

"You probably need to go touch base with the chief before the media swarms her," Polanski suggested. "I'm betting Mr. Jack Clay can't keep a secret to save his life. He's probably called half the county before you rolled out of bed this morning."

2
Polanski

The police cruiser bounced through a mud-filled puddle as it turned into one of the gravel driveways down the road from the crime scene. A rusted metal single-wide trailer lay at the end, obscured by an overgrown yard and long abandoned child's playset. In the backyard, a dog barked at the end of a long chain, having run a dirt circle around his dog house. It wasn't an oddity, there were houses just like this one all over the poverty-stricken county.

He put the car in park and walked up the rotting steps and across the algae-stained porch to the door. He rapped his knuckles against it, pulling his pants higher up on his hips before someone answered. Even with a good belt, he never could keep his pants up. He recalled the name on the mailbox to smooth his introduction as he heard someone walking across the floor inside the trailer. The door cracked open and a young woman with dark circles around her eyes peered at him through the opening. Her blonde hair was tousled and on top of her head in a messy bun, and she was dressed in heavily worn, blue-and-pink cartoon mouse pajamas.

"Mrs. Phillips? I'm Detective David Polanski, I'm with the Whitebranch Police Department. Do you have time to answer a few questions for me?"

Her brow furrowed with deep concern, and she chewed on the inside of lip.

"There was an incident last night," David explained, hoping to ease her fears of speaking to him, "Just down the road. I'm just wondering if you heard anything."

She seemed to relax a little, even pulling the door open just a hair more, revealing behind her a toddler in a bouncer, chewing on the crust of a piece of a pizza.

"It ain't Phillips, this is my boyfriend's place. Nathan Phillips. I'm Mallie... Debrot. What happened?"

"Miss Debrot. I can't give out any information as to the nature of the crime just yet, but I need to know if you heard or saw anything suspicious yesterday or last night. Maybe a vehicle coming down the road you didn't recognize, shady characters, anything at all."

Her eyes wandered to his feet and then back up again. "The dog barked. He barks a lot, I mean. At anything that moves, but last night he started barking about... six thirty? Seven? It was after dark but it wasn't real late. I peeked out the curtain and saw a car driving down the road kind of slow, but didn't think nothing of it."

"Do you know what kind of car it was?"

"No, but it was light colored. White or silver maybe."

"Did you see the car leave?"

"No."

"Did the dog bark again later?"

"He never stopped barking, so I never looked out again."

David nodded his head, turning to glance down the road before looking back at her, "Is there anyone else that lives down the road that might be helpful?"

She twisted the corners of her lips and shook her head, "I don't think many of them will be much help. I don't know how far down whatever happened, happened, but maybe talk to Jackson Clay. He owns a lot of the property around here."

"I'll be sure to talk to Mr. Clay. Thank you so much, Miss Debrot."

She nodded at him, seeming hesitant about closing the door, but she did so. David descended down the stairs, sliding once on a particularly slick portion of green wood.

"Well, that was a waste of time..." he muttered to himself as he backed out of the driveway and got back onto the road. He knew she was right; none of the other residents on the road would be of any more help than she was. Jack Clay's property stretched all down the south side of the road.

Still, he found himself driving back down Moorehead Road to the mailbox with a bold "36" in faded print on the side. He hadn't asked Jack much. The man had been red-faced and flustered. He was sweating even in the cool autumn air, panting and wheezing so intensely that Polanski had thought he would burst every button off of his too-tight shirt. He had sent Jack away as soon as the man had taken him to the location of the body and told him how he'd discovered it. Jack had headed back home before anyone else showed up on the scene.

He didn't even have to get out of the vehicle, since Jack came out of the house with the screen door slamming obnoxiously behind him. He was still panting, but had removed the overshirt and now exhibited only a sweat-stained wifebeater.

"Officer Polski." He waved as he came down the steps and approached the window of the cruiser.

"Polanski."

"Sorry, Polanski. Did you find him? Did you catch the bastard?"

Polanski's brow furrowed and he jerked his head back like he'd hit a wall, "What? No."

"Ah, you will. You will." Jack Clay seemed like he had watched one too many crime shows, where the case was always cracked in a half hour... Full hour if you were watching the pilot or finale.

"Listen, I had a few more questions for you. Do you have any kind of surveillance on your property? Security cameras, anything?"

"No, we don't have nothing like that. We rotate cattle out of that field, where the girl was. Just rotational grazing."

"Gotcha. A girl down the road said her dog was barking at a car coming through here last night, about six-thirty or seven. Do you remember seeing anything?"

"No, I don't recall hearing anybody. Some boys drive down here to drink sometimes. Just drive down, drive back. Good kids, you know."

"Is there anyone who knows their way around your property well? The entrance to the field is kind of off..."

The little section of road that led to the field was a sharp turn to the left between some old trees and a hay barn. It barely looked like a road, with grass that had grown up around the gravel, and was only distinct from the surrounding vegetation by the flattened grass from frequent use. He may have never noticed a road there at all, had Jack not told him exactly where to turn.

"I have some farmhands, but they wouldn't do something like this."

"Do you have their names and addresses?"

"Well," Jack fumbled. "I guess I could get those for you."

"You do that."

"Can I ask why you might think it was one of them?"

"I don't think that, Mr. Clay. I just know the killer had to know his way around. He knew that little road off to the side was there. I barely saw it myself. Just seems like an odd path to take if you didn't know where it was going. No room to turn around or anything."

Jack seemed to be thinking about something, and he said, "They also knew the gate would be unlocked, I guess. It's only been unlocked the last three or four weeks. Before that, we'd always kept a padlock on it. For safety, you know. Get somebody back there hunting or joyriding and tear up the good grass."

This only lended suspicion to, perhaps, the perpetrator being someone who lived down this road or someone directly employed by Jack... *or* Jack Clay himself.

Of course, David had no suspicions beyond that. He didn't think it was Jack Clay, judging by the very real reaction the man had to seeing the dead woman even at a distance. The way he couldn't look at his beloved dogs because they had nibbled around on her. Not to mention that girl would've outrun Jack, even in her high heeled shoes in the mud. As of right now, he had no leads on it being anyone else there either. There just wasn't much to go on. He would wait for some better evidence from Paltro.

For now, he needed something to eat. Something greasy, deep fried.

3
Quentin

The Whitebranch Chief of Police was a fifty-something year old woman named Pat Welch. She was more leather than flesh, heavily tanned with a headful of nearly white hair and dark eyes. She ran a tight ship but was easy to talk to, and beneath it all she cared about her staff more than she would let on outloud. 'Pat' stood for Patience, which Quentin always found to be the most interesting name choice. He wondered if her parents regretted the name or laughed at the irony as Pat grew into a young woman. She was anything but her namesake.

Quentin watched her shoulder her way through a mass of reporters nearly two feet taller than her, jaw set so tightly that her teeth ground in her ears. He stood at the side of the building as she came up the street and he moved to join her as she ascended the steps of the department. He turned around, arms up as she entered the door.

"Alright, you'll get your chance later. Get out of here." he snarked, flapping his hands as though they were birds.

"Detective, is this murder at all related to the murder of Lola Simmons earlier this year?"

"We don't have..."

He was cut off by another reporter, "Detective!"

"No comment," he said, turning his back on the group as he went inside. If they weren't going to let him talk, he wasn't going to fight to give them a few shreds of information either.

Inside he saw a few officers peering out the windows at the reporters like children on a snow day. One of them ran to his side, wringing his hands together nervously.

"What about it, Robichaud?"

"What about what?" Quentin asked, irritated. He watched as Pat made a beeline for her office and slammed the door shut. He winced at the sound and the accompanying rattle of plaques on the wall. He turned to look at the young man beside him, frowning. He could sometimes barely stand to be in the presence of the rookie detective that he'd been forced to take under his wing. Torres was baby faced with a bad haircut and dark circles under his eyes. He wasn't cut out for police work. Quentin wouldn't put him on traffic duty.

"They're saying another murder. The reporters have been asking about it all morning, we couldn't even go get lunch, they just swarmed us at the door."

"You'd know what was going on if you'd showed up."

Torres opened his mouth but only stammered.

"I called, went straight to voicemail."

Torres pulled his phone out of his pocket, flipping it to the call screen, "I didn't get a call..."

"Are you calling me a liar?"

"Of course not... I'm sorry. I must've been in the shower or something."

"Not my problem."

Quentin had not really called Torres that morning because he had been running quite late himself. He watched as the young man's cheeks darkened with embarrassment, and he returned the phone to his pocket. He reached up to scratch the back of his head nervously.

"Yes," Quentin filled in. "Murder. Young woman. Another game piece in her body."

"A game piece?" Torres repeated softly in confusion.

"Like Lola Simmons. Same type of game piece."

His jaw dropped but he quickly closed it, clearing his throat. "Do we have any leads?"

"None yet... Paltro will get back with us soon."

"Do you think it's the same guy?"

"Don't know."

Torres chewed the fingernail of his pinky nervously. "Let me know what I can do."

"You can start by getting them away from the fucking windows. You'd think they'd never seen a reporter before."

Torres nodded and turned around, going back over to gossip with the others, and Quentin took a deep breath before he headed over to Chief Welch's door. He knocked gently and heard her voice from the other side telling him to come in. She sounded calm, he noted thankfully.

"Hey," he said, slipping inside and shutting the door behind him.

"Sit down."

He obeyed quickly, easing himself into the plush armchair across from her desk.

"What a shitshow." she mused, putting a pair of reading glasses on her nose as she started scrolling through the list of unread emails on her computer screen.

"I know. Lot of excitement. It'll die down."

"I don't know about that, Robichaud. I'm worried this isn't a one off."

"What do you mean?"

"Just me being paranoid, maybe. Maybe not. Paltro said there was another little block."

"Yeah, the game piece. Some matching game, with flower tiles."

"What do you think?" she asked, voice softening with some sort of authentic curiosity. He looked up at her, putting his hand over his mouth to be sure he didn't betray himself with any kind of emotion before he decided how to respond. They watched each other for several seconds, and then she quirked a brow to goad him on.

"What do I think?" he parroted.

"That's what I asked. I'm not asking you to lay out a case... I'm just shooting the shit with you. Just me and you. What do you think about this?"

Quentin knew that she was hoping he would ease her mind. He also knew that despite the way she tried to make this a personal and amicable conversation, he would have to tread lightly. Pat was a good woman and, honestly, a great boss and coworker, but she could be ruthless. Anything he said right now would be stored away in her brain for later use, and he knew he had to see this as an opportunity to mold the way she *thought* he viewed this situation.

"I think we need to be careful what we say about it, to anyone. I don't know if I think it's related to the Simmons girl, but we don't want to give anyone the idea that it *is* right now."

"You don't think it's related?"

"I don't want to make up a problem that doesn't exist. It could lead us away from what really happened to that girl today."

"Why do you think the game piece showed up again then?"

"You remember how people got excited about it the first time. We should've locked that shit down. No one should've ever known about that detail until we understood its significance."

"Small town... you know nothing stays quiet. This won't either, people will talk. You think someone is just throwing this in there to lead us astray, then? You really don't have concerns that it's... something bigger?"

He shrugged his shoulders. "No, I don't have a reason to think that yet. Let's focus on the problem at hand, go from there."

She was reluctant, he could see her picking at a tooth with her tongue to avoid saying anything else. She nodded. "Okay. We'll see what Paltro comes up with. Keep your phone on you."

"Always do."

4

Paltro

Deen Paltro had been the coroner and medical examiner, serving the entirety of Delton County, for nearly ten years now. This was his dream job: not glamorous by any means, but it was fascinating. He always had a morbid enchantment with the dead and a great eye for detail, a little bit of creative spark that did not offer much in the way of artistic talent but did plenty for him in the realm of forensics. He also loved the quiet, the peace, the solitude. He occasionally had an assistant, an EMT named Tresa Hughes (who he was actually quite fond of), but most days he just liked to sit by himself and enjoy the silence of his work. Tresa had called and asked if he needed help today, almost sounding a little hopeful. He had declined, but suggested she could come over for dinner. She had in turn suggested she was busy but would check her schedule.

The morgue was adjacent to the now defunct hospital, whose owner had gone bankrupt years prior and left it abandoned. Several investors inquired about the purchase of the hospital, but it had remained abandoned for so long that it was now in a serious state of disrepair. The nearest hospital was about a half hour drive from the majority of the county, in nearby Last Bend. The ambulance used to deliver the bodies to the morgue, even after the closure of the hospital, but county funding changed and it was determined that they had too few ambulances to risk missing a life-or-death call because someone was tied up transporting a dead body. They danced around for months, making it very frustrating to get anyone who needed an autopsy to him, until he finally offered to use a personal vehicle to transport the bodies himself. He traded in his little Honda Civic towards a Ford Transit: a more practical vehicle for transporting dead Delton County residents.

By this point, the red-headed woman from the crime scene had been laid out on the stainless steel table, her insides opened up completely. Deen spread several photographs on the countertop and opened the dictaphone software atop of the victim's file. He turned on the dictaphone and began speaking, watching as the words filled the screen to make sure everything was in working order before he began walking slowly around the body.

"Decedent's name is Olivia Charlotte Brown, caucasian female, age thirty-five. Type of death violent, suspicious and unnatural. Discovered by one Jackson Clay on private property owned by the same Jackson Clay on 36 Moorehead Road in Whitebranch. Body was partially clothed. Investigation taken over by Whitebranch City Police Department, headed by Detective Quinten Robichaud. Victim's eye color is green, hair color red, weight is approximately one hundred and thirty pounds, length of body five foot and five inches. Body temperature at time of autopsy was eighty-five degrees fahrenheit. Time of death estimated to be between seven and ten pm last night. Rigor mortis still present. Livor mortis present, but I think some of the significant petechial hemorrhages on the neck and petechia on the inferior tarsus OU are not postmortem changes. Body was found face up, and the rest of livor mortis does not suggest that she was moved after death. Fingernail impressions on both sides of the neck suggest that she tried to pry her attackers hands from her throat. There is skin and blood underneath some of her fingernails. Awaiting results, but I expect it to be her own..."

A sound, a small tapping, took Deen's attention away from Olivia's body, and he turned to look at the door behind him. In the small window, he saw Torres' face peering inside. He smiled and held up a plastic container. Deen forced a smile and nodded, motioning for him to come inside. He shut his computer and sat down in the rolling chair by the countertop, removing his gloves and tossing them into the waste bin.

"Hey, Paltro."

He had two plastic tubs, stacked on top of each other, in his hands as he scuttled through the door and popped it away with his hip.

"Torres. What are you doing out here?" Deen knew exactly what Torres was doing out here, of course. While the young detective was nice enough, and more genuine than half of the police force, he always came to Deen to do snooping so he could try to get ahead on a case. Deen tolerated this because he didn't really blame him. The rest of them were hard on him, especially Robichaud. Deen appreciated that Torres had potential, and he'd do what he could to help him get ahead when possible.

Torres sat down on top of one of the trashcans, handing Deen a plastic container and a plastic fork. Inside was a generous slice of chocolate cake with fluffy icing.

"Mom made me a cake, thought you might like a slice of it."

"Thanks. I do love sweets."

They ate quietly for a few moments, and Deen noticed Torres get antsy in his seat. Sometimes he liked to see how long it took him to get the balls to ask about the case, but other times he felt guilty about letting it linger in the air like this. Today, he was feeling generous.

"You wanting to ask me about what I've found?"

Torres feigned surprise, putting his hand up to cover his mouth as he spoke through the cake, "Oh, no. I was just thinking... You know, like you could get some of those little air fresheners for in here. Those little plug ins, like some Tahiti Breeze or something."

Paltro nodded slowly. "Uh-huh."

"Just thinking... but I mean, since you brought it up... What *do* you think?"

He rolled his eyes, putting a single chocolate chip he found in the icing between his teeth with the fork, "I haven't got into my organ assessment yet, but I think she was strangled."

"When did it happen?"

"Last night."

"Has the family been notified yet?"

"No idea. We found her purse with an ID in the field. She must have dropped it when she was running."

Torres nodded.

"Did Robichaud tell you anything?"

"You mean the game piece? Yeah."

"I think it's too much to be a coincidence." Paltro spun around in his chair, grabbing the baggie that contained the piece and handing it to Torres to examine.

Torres would recognize the game, something his mom had on a shelf in the foyer for years. He didn't think he had ever played it, but he could still remember now that she would pull it down and sprawl the tiles out on the table some nights with a mug of hot tea. She toiled over those tiles, all flipped face down, turning each over two at a time to try and gain a match. He thought that the flowers had to have some kind of significance, assuming this was the same murderer. Would he do it again? Six months from now? A year? All of those little game pieces on the table, now representing dead women.

It was just a little flower, and the pale wood it was imprinted on was stained dark red now. Just an innocent flower, a white thing with a yellow center and a gently curved stem.

"Just a flower," he said.

Paltro shrugged. "In my line of work, nothing is ever 'just' anything."

Torres thought maybe he was right. He handed the bag back to him, "Was the piece from that other girl, Simmons, the same flower?"

Paltro 'hmmm'd in his throat for a moment and then shook his head. "No. It was purple."

Torres stood up and reached out for the container in Paltro's hands. He stuck the plastic fork in his mouth and replaced the lid before handing it to him.

"Thanks for the cake. I really appreciate it."

"Think about the scented plug ins, they have some really nice fragrances," Torres insisted with a smile.

"Yeah, I'll think about that."

He watched as Torres shuffled out the door, trying not to look at the dead woman on the table as he did so.

5

Rion

Whitebranch was a sleepy little town that seemed to shut down reliably around 9 p.m. The shops started slowing down, the lights went off, and the traffic became nearly nonexistent. The townspeople either went home to be with their families, or they went somewhere quiet to bask in their drug of choice. There were a grand total of three intersections with red lights in the middle of town, with a few scattered in the smaller towns and unincorporated areas in the surrounding county. The pavement illuminated red and green as the lights went through their regular routines, with or without drivers to follow the cues.

A little station wagon drove through Whitebranch on this autumn night, passing through all three lights on the way out of town, obeying their every signal with dedication. The driver coasted across the two lane highway out of town, maintaining exactly two miles under the speed limit the entire way. Homes grew less frequent, and sprawling fields spread on either side. Some were full of sleeping cattle, sheep, and goats; others had signs listing them for sale or foreclosure. He knew all of these fields, the hundreds of acres of desolate countryside.

These fields had become a favorite place for him to fantasize about dumping the bodies of the young women he had, and would, kill. He thought it was poetic in some way, like blowing the seeds of a dandelion to the wind. They became another little treasure for someone to find amongst the wildflowers and golden wheatheads. People love finding a body, although they might deny it. There was always a stir; always a little glimmer of excitement. It was all people would talk about for weeks at a time. He loved walking through the grocery store, staring too long at the peanut butter selection, so he could hear the murmur and thrill in the voices of the people. He was always proud that *he* did that.

He turned down a little sideroad that sliced through two identical pastures. A large white dog lying among the sheep raised its head as he drove past and, had he not flipped his lights off, it would have barked. An elderly woman lived there. Her husband had passed away and left her with the farm. She had sold all of the animals except the dog, who seemed to come and go as he pleased. She claimed she didn't even feed him anymore.

Rion had performed a fair bit of reconnaissance to scope out these isolated locations. He knew that this particular woman was hard of hearing and had a strict routine. Once, he had even ventured as far as to stop by her house to introduce himself, explaining in immense detail that he was part of a local missionary group. She had asked him, with great interest, where he was from and who his parents were. Everyone here knew everyone, so it was one of the hardest places on earth to keep to yourself. People were nosy and trusting of familiarity. Too trusting. Rion had sprawled a story out in front of this old woman. He told her about the parents who had spent a majority of their youth in Uganda, where he was born. Rion told her he believed there were plenty of lost souls right here at home. She nodded her head deeply at that, holding her palm to the sky.

Of course, none of this was true.

Rion's father had been dead nearly two decades now, from a heart attack. His mother was in an assisted living home in Foster's Hollow, a town in the neighboring Heresy County. She had crippling dementia and most often did not seem to recognize Rion at all. He still sometimes visited her, finding something comforting about her presence even when she was not able to engage with him. He had never been one for meaningless conversation anyway; small talk and the like. Sometimes when she slept he thought about suffocating her with one of the little embroidered pillows that sat in the recliner he often found himself in. He would toy with the tulled edges of the pillow as he watched her, sleeping with her mouth open to reveal nothing but gum and palate. It would really be a mercy, he thought. Maybe that's why he never did it.

He had always recognized some sort of *difference* in himself. He realized that he wasn't alone, however. A lot of people had this same deeply seeded awareness that there was something not quite right in their brain. Not a flaw or a handicap, Rion didn't like to think of it like that. No... just a variable. He thought of himself as unique, even among the other outliers. His variable was something primal, bred out of the civilized human long ago. Where the world seemed to foster cooperation and restraint, Rion lacked certain inhibitions that seemed to make humans... human. Less than, he would argue. Some people tried to get help when they realized they had these desires and cravings. Medication, distraction, suicide... but he had chosen to placate the demon. He indulged. It was a curious thing; he never set out in the beginning to start murdering people, per se. It wasn't really about the pain. It was the excitement, the fear, the chase. The attention. Everyone likes attention, and Rion was just exceptionally good at getting attention. He was becoming famous, *infamous*, revered.

Lola Simmons had opened up this world to him, something new and fresh and exciting at the time. He had started stalking her, and it had been easy. She was in her late twenties, on every dating app imaginable, with no discretion on social media. Rion liked to snoop around on those apps and look at all the pretty, desperate girls. It just so happened that Lola worked in the store adjacent to the garden center that Rion worked for, and so she was easily accessed. He watched her eat lunch on the patio with friends. He watched her walk to her car every evening. She never even looked up from her phone as she strolled across the dark parking lot, completely unaware of her surroundings. He started by sending her a bouquet of lilacs, anonymously. He left them wrapped and sitting on the window of her car one evening with a note that said it was from a secret admirer. It was a symbol of first love, and he watched as she admired them with surprise, checking her phone every opportunity she had over the next few days for some hint as to who may have sent them to her.

His initial plan had not been to kill her, or to even hurt her. He didn't know that was what he was actually needing all along, he had no way to know until things seemed to go so wrong. He stalked her one night, following her to one of the small dive bars in town, where she had met up with some man she didn't know. He had watched her through the window from his car in the parking lot. She had chosen a great seat, right by the large window with the name of the bar across the front. It was warm enough inside that he did struggle to see her beyond the fog, but he was focused intently. He was almost a little envious of how they, and so many other people, seemed so easily amused and satisfied with just... being with other people. He never felt that same contentment with conversation or relationships. Why did any of those meaningless conversations *matter*? What real, tangible benefit did they hold? People were so desperate for companionship. The longer you spent with someone, the more you noticed those flaws and bad habits. The more you realized how imperfect they were. He tried to fake it, many times before, but he found it wasn't worth the effort. He did wish that he could gain satisfaction and pleasure from something so simple and trivial.

The woman had left without her date, standing outside the bar with her phone in her hand. She looked down at it expectantly. He sat there at least fifteen more minutes, watching her wait, before she finally started walking down the street. This was a safe town to do so, even alone, usually. No one was out this late and anyone who was often drove home drunk or not. People were just reliable here. You didn't worry about things like walking alone at night.

Rion pulled out of his parking space and drove to the old hardware center, parking around back where he knew there were no security cameras. No one ventured back into the old part of downtown, other than teens looking to get drunk, do drugs, or have sex. It would be little patterns and expectancies of small town life like this that would make it so easy for him to get away with these murders.

He shoved his hands in his pockets and put the hood of his jacket up on his head before he started walking down the street behind her. He maintained a distance that he considered not suspicious, but the woman seemed to sense someone behind her.

She turned around once, and he offered a smile that she returned. It wasn't lost on Rion that he had been blessed with good looks, but even so it seemed like people always picked up on something 'off.' Maybe some sort of sixth sense, an extension of self-preservation when you encounter something just a little dangerous.

She turned her head once, acting like she was looking up at one of the old buildings, but he saw her eyes move to look towards him. He noticed that she started walking faster, and he also picked up the pace. His heart was pounding, and he didn't know what his plan was yet. At what point did he head off down an alley and back to his car? Not yet, he wanted to see her face again. One more glance of uncertainty, of fear. That would be enough for him.

Instead, the girl had started sprinting and before he knew it she had pulled out her cell phone to call someone. It was in this instance that he had to become a little physical. At first, he just jerked the phone out of her hand, but when she started fighting back, he found himself holding her down on the ground, and then his hands found their way around her throat. It wasn't something he had consciously decided on, but it felt so right. It was like his own instinct had taken over and said 'here, let me show you.' She struggled against him, arms just slightly too short to reach his face as she clawed at him. Her fingernails dug into the fabric of his jacket, and he felt them pinch against his skin through the layers. She screamed, and he found that if he both applied downward pressure and squeezed harder simultaneously that she could no longer make noise. Instead she croaked a little, making much quieter sounds. Her hands turned into fists and she began beating them into his chest, but they were faint thumps. Then she went limp.

It was this: a moment he considered so intimate, where he realized the girl was *perfect*. She was beautiful, she was flawless, she was frozen in time in a moment of perfection. He had held her neck tightly for several moments, feeling her pulse change from a furious flutter to slow, long throbs before it finally stopped altogether. He had exhaled, realizing he had held his breath the entire time... but he did not feel any remorse. He was thrilled and enthralled. This was what he had been after his entire life.

In the car now, Rion exhaled again after thinking of that first girl. He had wanted so badly to take a piece of her with him, a locket of hair, something... but he had thought of all of the ramifications. He had dragged her body off of the sidewalk and into a swampy alleyway before pulling his car to the back and loading her inside. He had chosen to dump her in a field on a whim, but it had been ideal. She was so peaceful among the grasses, staring up at the sky. He had meticulously cleaned a game piece from a floral matching game, a lilac just like the bouquet he had sent her, and he stuffed it into her mouth before her jaw locked up. He remembered her still, vividly, but six months later he found himself craving that rush again.

This had been why he had killed the second girl. There was already a stir about her in the town. He had heard people talking, making theories. He was a little disappointed that no one had yet mentioned the game piece, but he thought it would happen eventually. He had to be patient. He had stood outside the police station with the media as one of the detectives had gone inside. He was a little bit older than Rion, or maybe he just hadn't aged as well. Slim, not quite the body type he imagined contributed well to a physical career. He had a confidence about him though, an air of arrogance and conviction, and Rion felt somehow struck by him. This was the Magnus to his Cesear. The thought that someone would be looking for him, trying to find him, just made him even more excited to leave another gift for the community.

So tonight, girl three. He didn't know her name, he didn't know any of their names until the news reports came out. After that he remembered them. It seemed like an irrelevant detail until they were immortalized.

He turned and smiled at the girl in the seat next to him, still alive. She was pretty enough alive but there was something about the dynamic motion of life that seemed to mute the vibrancy he sought.

"So where is this romantic place we're going? You said you have a cabin?"

Rion answered dryly, "Yeah. It's kind of off the beaten path, you know."

"I'd say," she laughed. "I didn't think there was anything back this way but farmland. I swear I went down some of these roads in high school."

She probably had. Her excitement and slight intoxication from a little heavy pre-gaming had her throwing caution to the wind. She had found Rion to be charming, albeit a little weird. She chalked it up to him being nervous about their date. He bought her a beautiful pink peony, which she'd taken inside and placed in a vase of water before she got into his car and they'd headed out to eat dinner. He had insisted they get food to go, and said they could eat it at his place. He described his little cabin in great detail to her, and it sounded wonderful.

"So are you going to take me back home tonight?" she asked.

He really wished she'd stop talking. He kept a close eye on the gates of the fields adjacent to the road, knowing one further back was always open, as the rusted gate had fallen off the hinges and remained unrepaired.

"I can, absolutely. No problem. Let's just see where the night takes us."

"Oh," she giggled. "I guess I *am* a little overdressed. I thought we'd be going out."

She pulled her shoes off and strapped them together, laying them in the floorboard. She was too comfortable, he thought.

"Are you disappointed? We can always turn around."

"No, no. I'd love to see your place! It sounds amazing, and the food smells so good. I'm starving."

Rion had been simultaneously thinking about how nauseating the mixed aromas of their dinners smelled in the cab of the car, combined with her overbearing perfume (lightly fruity) and the chemical scent of her hairspray.

The open gate loomed ahead and Rion pulled in, car making a muffled sound against the tall grasses as he drove through them. His headlights illuminated just a small portion of the field ahead of them at a time, insects flying through the brightness.

"Is it out through here?" she asked quietly.

"Yep."

"Have you considered a driveway or something?"

"Nah."

He stopped just short of a large oak tree and stared forward at the trunk that was visible in the darkness. The car rumbled quietly. He could see her slowly turn to look at him out of his peripheral, but he continued to look forward.

"This seems like a good spot," he said, touching his jaw with his thumb thoughtfully.

He heard her try to giggle again, but instead she cleared her throat, "For what?"

Rion looked over at her, noticing a glimmer of uncertainty in her eyes. She wasn't scared yet. She probably thought she had no reason to be. Trust was the hardest thing to get past, and it really shouldn't be. She didn't know him; she never should've gotten in this car.

"I'm going to kill you."

He did not notice that switch to fear, instead she murmured, "What? Aren't we... going to your place?"

"I am going to kill you."

"Wh-... what do you mean?"

"Oh, fuck it..."

He reached down to unbuckle his safety belt and the girl opened the door and dove out of the car in one smooth movement. Rion followed, getting out and walking around the car. The old oak had deposited a generous amount of acorns on the ground, and the girl's flight was hindered by her bare feet as she stumbled across the hundreds of tiny seeds.

She reached down and grabbed a fallen branch, swinging it at his head with a feral snarl. He managed to dodge the first swing, the second swing, but the third struck him in the shoulder and the rotting branch exploded into shards of wood and lichen-covered bark.

It didn't *hurt*, of course. The branch had been too weakened by weathering and decay to cause any damage upon impact but the eruption of debris had gotten into his right eye. He squinted it closed, feeling the contact lens roll up and stick to itself. So with the one eye clamped shut he started towards her as she backed away from him, skidding against the acorns under her heels.

6
Quentin

Quentin accepted the canned soda from the puffy-faced woman before sitting on the edge of the floral couch. She seated herself on the matching loveseat, rubbing beneath her eyes, although the tears were long dried up. Her face still itched and felt dry, and her eyes burned. Quentin offered her a sympathetic smile, setting the unopened beverage on the end table beside him. On the adjacent seat, Torres noisily sipped the soda that had bubbled around the lip of his own can.

"Mrs. Brown," Quentin started, pulling a small notebook and pen out of his pocket. "When was the last time you talked to your daughter?"

Torres pulled a notebook out as well, struggling to hold it and also hold his drink, poised with a pen for her response.

Mrs. Brown took a long breath and then exhaled it for a similar length of time before speaking, "Oh, probably Tuesday afternoon? It isn't... wasn't uncommon for us to go a couple days without talking."

"Did she mention meeting anyone new? Was she seeing anyone intimately?"

"No, hadn't met anyone new that I know of. She was a little discouraged lately with dating. Thought she was getting too old to find anybody. I told her it would happen... one day."

Torres interjected, "Was she using any dating apps that you are aware of, Mrs. Brown?"

Quentin shot the younger man a look out of the side of his eye. Not that he necessarily thought it was a bad question, but because Torres was there to observe... not to ask questions.

She nodded her head. "Well, isn't everyone?"

Torres shrugged and nodded reluctantly.

"Do you know of anyone who may have wanted to hurt your daughter? I know that is a terrible thing to consider, something no one wants to think of. But can you think of anyone she has had a recent altercation with? Someone she maybe disagreed with?"

"No, not my Livvie. She didn't have enemies; she was friends with everyone. Anyone. If anything she was too hard to argue with. She was very agreeable, even when she knew you were wrong."

"Did she work anywhere?"

"No, she was studying accounting at Delton Community. All of the classes were online this semester... This is just so hard. I don't know how much more I can talk about this right now. When can I have some of her things?" Mrs. Brown then asked, looking between the two men. Her eyes glossed with tears.

Quentin watched as Torres leaned forward and clasped the woman's hands with one of his own. "We will give you a call, in the meantime if you need anything..."

He cut in, "Yes, Mrs. Brown. If you need anything or think of anything that may help us find your daughter's killer, do not hesitate to let us know."

He gave Torres another sideways glance, and the younger man nodded. As far as Torres was concerned, this was a woman who had just lost her daughter. Any extension of respect he could offer was worth the mutters of insubordination from Quentin. It wasn't that Quentin was necessarily uncaring, but his stoicism did not allow for much coddling, Torres acknowledged that.

"Thank you for your time, Mrs. Brown. We will be in touch with you again. Once again don't hesitate to call." Quentin extended a bland, white card between his index and middle finger. She took it, looking down at the stiff black font, which reflected the detective's personality in fair accuracy.

They left the house together, standing on the stoop as they surveyed the neighborhood. Torres pulled a cigarette out of his pocket and placed it between his lips. It was slim and black papered, and as he lit it up, it smelled like a fucking pumpkin pie candle. That fake, overdone spice combination that made you think of an old woman's house during the holidays. Torres motioned towards Quentin with the lighter, and so he pulled out his own and allowed the younger man to light it.

"Thanks," he said.

"No problem," Torres muttered, following him to the car parked on the street.

Quentin stuffed his notebook into the center console and fixed his hair in the rearview before turning the key in the ignition and making a u-turn in the road.

"Where to now, boss?" Torres asked, buckling his safety belt long after the car had begun motion.

"Don't call me that, please," Quentin said. It made him feel like they were in some kind of vapid western movie. Sitting on their horses, looking for clues in the dusty west.

Torres turned to look at the window at an extreme angle, like he was pouting. Quentin looked over more than once to see nothing but the back of his head and his shoulder. Torres busied himself with other thoughts. The face of Mrs. Brown and all of her little knick knacks: the little bronze boots, ceramic cats, and biblical verses on cloth fabric between photos of her family. Photos of Olivia Brown alive and bright and warm.

"Going by the girl's place again," Quentin said, flipping the turn signal up with the back of his hand.

"What are we looking for?"

"Nothing. Just want to get a feel of who she was, where she may have been, who she may have been with."

"Sorry about the whole dating app thing," Torres said, scratching the back of his head. "I thought maybe... maybe the guy is finding the girls on one of those apps."

"Even if he was, there are thousands of users on those things, and most of them don't verify identities. It would be impossible for us to gather any information from that."

He could tell by the way Torres shifted in his seat, tapping his foot against the floorboard, that he disagreed. He knew he wouldn't argue back or verbalize his disagreement. He was respectful and typically quiet, rarely insubordinate... at least, not to Quentin's face. He was sure that behind his back Torres might talk a big game. That was fine, everyone needed their own stage.

The apartment complex where Olivia Brown had lived was not far from her mother's neighborhood. Granted, the availability of housing in the small town was fairly sparse. They were two story, dingy little buildings that looked like they may have once been an old motel. The entrances for the apartments were all outside, and there were doors on every surface, suggesting the living spaces were quite small.

He parked in one of the resident spots, and the two men entered the complex through the narrow, dark alleyway that housed a set of stairs onto either side of the complex. It was damp inside, with thick, slick slime growing on the brick walls. Quentin thought that it might also smell lightly of urine, which was not unsurprising. He had more than once gotten a call to remove a drunk man from the stairwell or investigate a squatter.

Apartment B24 was signified by chipping brass alphanumerics on a red door. There was a crumbled piece of paper taped to the door that read POLISE OFFICALS ONLY. MEDDLARS BE FINED - MGMT

As Quentin unlocked the door he noticed a curious resident two doors down peeking outside her door. He smiled and nodded at her, and she continued to stare on, not returning his friendly gesture of greeting. They entered inside, and while Quentin went straight to the living area, Torres was quick to lock the door behind them.

The apartment was fairly cold, Quentin imagined they had shut off the heat in order to conserve energy costs. Above him a light flicked on and off, and he turned to see Torres moving the light switch.

"Power's still on," he said.

Quentin resumed his examination of the small living room, which was the same large room as her dining area and kitchen. Off to one side was a single bedroom.

"I don't think they can shut off power to a single apartment. They probably already have someone lined up to rent this place out as soon as we give them the okay."

The bedroom had a light and airy feel. The curtains were a sheer white with light blue accents in little, fragile swirls on the surface of the fabric. The bedspread was the same light blue with golden and white birds, matching throw pillows, and a large stuffed bunny sitting in the center: waiting for Olivia Brown to come home. On her nightstand was a planner, stuffed full with sticky notes and receipts. It appeared she was meticulous about keeping up with spending. Quentin flipped it open to the night of her suspected murder, and saw that it had a single entry scribbled. Date Night with Misty.

Quentin pulled out his phone and snapped a photo of the entry and also of the closed planner. They hadn't talked to a Misty yet, and if she had made it to their date night then Misty could have been one of the last people to see Olivia alive. He looked at the pictures on her walls of her and her mom and friends, one of her in scuba gear at the old dam.

"Hey, Robichaud?" He heard Torres speak from the living area.

"Yeah?"

There was no response.

He walked back into the room, seeing Torres standing solemn and staring at the dining room table. Quentin was puzzled, approaching slowly as he looked at the various opened bills and mail lying on the surface. Nothing caught his eye immediately. He glanced to the table and from Torres' face several times before finally saying, "What? What is it?"

Torres, a hand to his mouth, truly looked a little green around his eyes. Quentin briefly wondered if he would vomit.

"Torres. What the fuck is it?"

He motioned to the table in front of him. "The flowers, Robichaud."

Quentin hadn't even paid attention to the modest vase sitting in the center of the table. They were wilted and dying in browned water. Several crunchy petals were already scattered around with the papers.

"What about them?"

"It's the same flower from the game piece."

Quentin remembered the game piece, stained with blood and etched with the faintest impression of a flower on its surface. These flowers looked *nothing* like the flower on the wooden block.

"Torres, I think you need to take a break. Just step outside and wait on me. These flowers aren't even the same color as the one on the game piece."

"They're the same. Daffodils. Do you think he had been here? In her apartment?"

"No. They've dusted everything for prints, came in with the light. The apartment owner was very cooperative and has cameras outside. No one was in or out of her apartment except her."

"How did they get here?"

"It's a coincidence. Tons of people have flowers in their houses."

Torres shook his head, "No. They're the same."

Quentin rolled his eyes and sighed, putting his hands on his hips, "I found an entry in a planner. She met a girl named Misty the night she died. A friend, it sounded like. Let's go find out who Misty is."

He started walking towards the door, but noticed that Torres had not moved from his place in front of the table.

"Torres. While you were staring at home decor, I did some actual work and found something that could help us. Let's *go*."

He reluctantly looked away from the flowers and followed Quentin outside.

7
Polanski

David walked through the front door of his home with the two white paper bags tucked against his chest. He kicked his work shoes off at the door, where his wife always demanded they be kept. He tossed his keys in the glass dish on the entry table and went into the kitchen.

"Leah?" he called.

His wife came around the corner with a full basket of clean towels. He could feel the warmth as she passed by and set the basket on the couch. She helped herself to one of the bags, unpacking a hamburger that dripped with grease and melting mayo. She ate it as delicately as one could, sticking her pinkies out so that the drippings fell onto the wrapper on the countertop instead of her fingers.

"How many times do I have to beg you to lock the front door when I'm not home?" David asked, opening his own bag.

She shrugged. "It's the middle of the day, David."

"Do you really think people don't break into houses in the daylight? They're criminals, not vampires."

She rolled her eyes at him but smiled, reaching out to pinch his elbow. "What's got you worked up?"

"Nothing," David insisted. He could feel her eyes on him as he unpacked the food from his own bag. He usually overshared what happened at work, all the details that his wife liked to hear. It wasn't that she enjoyed those terrible things, it was because she didn't look at them like they were something real. She had a disconnect. He knew that while Chief Welch thought the slip to the public about cases came from within the department, it was a good possibility that Leah gossiped with her friends, or worse, with her sister. David couldn't keep information from her when she asked, though. It was against his marital ethics. At least, that was always his claim.

"Did something interesting happen?"

"You could say that," he admitted between bites.

His work phone started buzzing around his waist and he reached down to pull it off of his belt loop. 'Robichaud' scrolled across the screen as he held up a finger to Leah to pause the conversation before putting the phone to his ear.

"Yeah?"

"Hey, busy?"

"Of course I am."

"Stuffing your face?"

David swallowed a mouthful of his sandwich. "Maybe."

"Me and Torres did some digging and found out Olivia Brown had met up with a friend before she died. Talked to her mother and Mrs. Brown says her name is Misty Rockwell. I called her up and she's coming down to the station in thirty minutes. Will you talk to her and see what she knows?"

"I'm home, I just got here."

"I know. I've just... I've got some things I've got to do."

"Like the fuck what, Robichaud?"

Leah smacked her palm on the counter top and snarled her lip at him silently. David flapped his hand in the air between them.

"Just do it, Polanski."

"Fuck you. *Fuck you*, and fuck your mama."

David dropped the phone trying to slam his thumb on the button to cancel the call. He knew that he would go in, and so did Robichaud. The phone clattered to the countertop in the midst of his frustration and Leah looked at him with an expression of disappointment.

"What now?" she asked, combining her wrappers into the original paper bag to deposit in the trash can.

"Gotta go to the station for a few."

"You say no, but you always let him run over you."

"I don't let anyone run over me, but especially not Quentin Robichaud," David insisted grumpily.

Leah knew that, on the contrary, David let everyone run over him. *Especially Quentin Robichaud*. David liked to play the tough guy role, and as he had become a gruff old man, it had likewise become a more convincing persona. In reality, however, he was soft and maybe even compassionate. She had always loved the way he melted in a puddle around baby animals, and how he would vehemently deny that he cried at his own wedding. He was on speed dial for half of the neighborhood when they needed anything at all, whether it was car repair, lawn work, or when Janice Taylor wanted him to do a walkthrough of her little home when she got home from buying cat food after dark. David was always there to do those things, although he would moan and groan about it.

She had always liked Quentin. He was David's closest friend and had literally saved his life on multiple occasions. When something was tough, she knew that Quentin would have David's back and was there to hear him out if he needed to talk. What she did not like about Quentin was the little bit of a superiority complex that he had. His time was always more valuable than David's, and he took advantage of the knowledge that David would do anything he asked him to.

"I'll wait up for you," Leah finally said, putting a hand on his shoulder briefly as she passed by.

"Okay," David responded, standing up to watch her walk over to the couch. She sat with her legs folded to the side, where he would usually sit and hold her socked feet. She flipped on the television and began scrolling through the channels as he walked out the door.

The drive to the station was fairly short. David had purposely selected a home in their neighborhood for its close proximity to work. Maybe this would be a fast in-and-out type thing. He would have a few minutes to get settled into his desk, look professional.

Quentin had said she'd be there in thirty. Why was he surprised when he walked in the door and she was already seated at the chair in front of his desk? He straightened his tie, licking his thumb and smudging a mustard stain adjacent to a button on his white shirt. He tried to pull the tie over to lie across the stain, but the strip of dark fabric did what it wanted to and ended up under his left armpit before he made it to his seat.

He bent down to sit, extending a hand across the desk with a smile. "Ms. Rockwell. I'm Detective David Polanski. I'm just going to be asking a couple of questions."

She smiled at him, taking his hand awkwardly and giving it one downwards shake. She was a young woman, younger even than Olivia Brown, he suspected. She had black hair with blue underneath, thick rimmed glasses that made her green eyes twice their original size, and tattered feather earrings that nearly reached her shoulders. She was wearing a light jacket over what arguably could have been a pajama outfit: some sort of ruffled one piece thing that was made of mismatched patterns.

"You were friends with Olivia Brown?" he asked, looking up at her as he put on a pair of reading glasses and opened the file that Quentin had put on his desk for him. A sticky note presented itself on the first page, it just said

"Thank you" in Quentin's handwriting. David crumpled it tightly in his fist and dropped it into the waste bin beside him.

When he looked back up, he saw the girl was patting underneath her eyes with her coat sleeve, glasses shoved up under her bangs as she tried to dry her tears. He rocked back in his chair briefly to grab a box of tissues and handed them to her.

"Thank you," she muttered quietly, grabbing a tissue.

"Take your time."

"Yes, we are best friends," she choked out, making a loud squeak-like hiccup that echoed in the station. David regretted not closing the door to the office behind him. He saw the curious eyeballs of coworkers as they huddled around the water cooler.

"Did you meet up with her the night that she..."

Misty Rockwell burst into tears, so upset that she was spitting saliva from her lips. David cleared his throat, pushing the tissue box even closer to her encouragingly.

"Am I in trouble?" she asked. "The other cop said that you guys knew we hung out before she died. How did he know that?"

"You're not in trouble, Ms. Rockwell. I just need to know everything about those hours before she died. Anything you know may help us. We just want to do right by her."

"We go out a lot, I mean we don't do anything crazy. Sometimes we just go to a movie or something."

"What did you two do that night?"

"We just went to eat, and then we walked around a few shops. We were going to go to a movie, but the one we wanted to see was sold out. I had to run to the garden center to get potting soil for my succulents. Then we went to get junk food at the grocery store for this weekend. We were going to have a night in and invite some other friends."

"When did you last see Olivia?"

"It was probably around... Seven? Eight? I don't really know. It was early. I took the ice cream home so it wouldn't melt. I could look..."

She pulled out her phone. As she did, David scanned over some of the information in front of him. The estimated time of death in comparison to when Misty expected she parted ways with Olivia meant that the killer had worked very quickly, unless she was mistaken.

"I sent her a text at 7:45 when I got home and asked if I'd left the marshmallow fluff in her bag."

"She had her car?"

Misty nodded slowly. "She rode with me, but I dropped her off at her car after we got done at the store. She parked it on Miller street across from the post office."

"Did she respond to your text?"

"Yes, all she said was 'no.' I didn't talk to her again the rest of the night." The color had drained from Misty's face as she laid the phone between her legs. She was looking at David, but not *at* him. He knew this conversation was about over; she was mentally checking out.

"Was Olivia seeing anyone, or do you know if she planned to go home afterwards?"

"No... She said she was tired."

"Okay, I think that's everything. Thank you for taking the time to talk to us. Do you need a ride home?"

She shook her head, "No, I had my boyfriend wait in the parking lot. I didn't think I could drive home after this."

"I understand. If you think of anything else, please call. Here's my card. Any time of day."

She took the card and whispered something, maybe it was thank you. She hurried out the door and David grabbed his notebook. He had a list of things to do now. Find the car, find her phone. Maybe the post office had some kind of surveillance outside. He scooted up to the computer and booted it on so he could start logging the new information he'd obtained from Misty Rockwell.

8
Torres

Lucas Torres would have normally been excited to have been sent on *any* assignment alone, but in this instance he couldn't help but feel like this was busy work. He had developed a distaste for busy work in school; when the teacher had run out of things to teach the class they would give them sprawling worksheets of repetitive work. He rarely ever finished it. When Quentin had called and told him to go to the city post office and check in on a car that would've been parked there, he took the instruction with feigned enthusiasm.

He walked into the post office and straight past the walls of silver mailboxes to the manager's office. He had noted when he pulled up that no car matching Quentin's description was parked parallel on the street, so the car had been moved. This was encouraging, he thought. Either the killer had moved the vehicle or the girl had, which would give them more clues as to where and how she had been abducted.

"Detective Torres?" An elderly man met him just inside the doorway, grasping Lucas' hand with his cold fingers.

"Yes, that's me," he responded awkwardly.

"What can I help you with? On the phone you said something about an ongoing investigation."

"We're investigating a violent crime, and the victim's car is currently missing. The last known location was here on the street..."

"The little red one?"

"I'm sorry?"

"The little red car?"

Lucas nodded, "Yes. Did you see it?"

"I did... I had it towed. It sat here overnight and then the next evening it hadn't moved."

"Dammit," Lucas muttered.

"We only have a couple of spaces for customers. People have to walk across the street sometimes to get here. I hope having the vehicle towed didn't cause any problems with your investigation."

"No, no. That's fine. At least we know where it is. Who towed it?"

"Jenny. On the north end of town. Picked it up last night. Sorry I'm not more help."

"You've been a lot of help, thank you. I'll get with Jenny about the car. Do you happen to have any cameras on the street where the car was parked?"

"I do, but they're mostly for show. They pick up the opposite side of the street near the hydrant, not even sure her car would've been in the shot."

"Can we take a look? Do you have time?"

"Of course..." he waddled over to his desk, squinting as he searched for the app for the cameras on his desktop. Lucas saw it nearly immediately but didn't say anything as he leaned on the desk and waited for him to find it on his own. He clicked it about five times, and the computer made a grinding noise as the fan kicked on to try to accomplish the simple task. A single, grainy, black and white image showed up with a play button. A timeline appeared beneath it, spanning back the course of the week.

"Here we go," he said, scrolling back to the day that Olivia Brown disappeared.

He clicked 'play' and touched the screen with his finger as just the front of the vehicle pulled into view. The hood of the car and part of the windshield were visible in the corner, but it was not the focus of the camera's view.

"Here's where she parked... Looks like she's getting in with someone?" He looked back and up at Lucas.

"A friend," Lucas confirmed. "They went out to eat and stuff."

He thought that maybe he detected a little disappointment in the man's face as he turned back to study the computer screen, hoping he had single-handedly found the one who had taken the girl. He skipped on to later that night. Lucas stared at the car, puzzled.

"What's on the hood of the car there? By the windshield?"

"I... Don't rightly know. It wasn't there before. It wasn't there when I had it towed either."

"Can you skip back and see where it came from?"

It took them several minutes of sifting through the hours between to find the brief moment when a figure appeared and laid the item on the windshield before disappearing out of the frame again. It was too grainy to make out any details other than it was likely a man with a hood on his head. Torres still could not tell what was lying on the car, but it was sizable and not heavy. Narrow on one end and fanned out on the other. When they watched the end of the night, time stamped at 715, Olivia Brown walked up to her car, opened the door and put a bag inside before she grabbed the item off of the hood.

"Flowers," the man whispered.

"What did you say?"

"Flowers. That's a set of flowers. A bouquet. Whatever you call it."

Lucas' heart skipped a beat. Was it the flowers from her apartment? He stood up, tucking the back of his shirt back in where it had rode up.

"Thank you. I'm going to go touch base with Jenny. I really appreciate the time you've taken with me. Can I have you make a copy of that video feed? I can come back by and pick it up this evening, or you can drop it off at the station."

"Yes, sir. Absolutely."

"Thank you again."

"Yep." He beamed.

Lucas was shaky as he descended the stairs and skipped across the street to the police cruiser. The car was stuffy inside and smelled like the tiny pine tree hanging in the windshield. He couldn't wait until he had his own vehicle to use, but for now this was what was given to him. He backed the large car out of the spot and headed across town. Just as the buildings would start becoming fewer and fewer, a long dirt road on the right led to the lot where Jenny kept all of the towed vehicles. Lucas had been there a couple of times before and didn't bother worrying about formalities this time. He had gone to high school with Jenny, so there was a degree of familiarity and comfort.

He stopped the car in a whirl of dust, rolling the window down prematurely and starting to choke on the aerosolized red clay. A pit bull on the end of a long chain barked half-heartedly at him, tail swinging wildly behind it as it danced on its front feet.

A man exited the small building, wiping his hands on a dirty white rag. He waved a hand at Lucas, who took the signal as a welcome. He turned the vehicle off and walked inside, giving the dog a wide berth. He entered the building, which was no more than four plywood walls and a slab of tin on top. He imagined it worked well for what Jenny did and served as his small office attached to the old garage.

"How's it going, Lucas? Been awhile," Jenny said, seating his wide frame in what looked to be a too-small, dusty office chair.

"It's going, Jen. Good to see you."

"You here for Olivia Brown's car?" he asked.

Lucas looked at him in surprise. Jenny had always been an unassuming character. He was a huge man: standing at least six and a half feet tall and nearly three hundred pounds, but somehow seemed so unthreatening. He had been given a hard time when they were kids, until he started growing and never seemed to stop. He had taken it upon himself to defend some of the smaller children (Lucas included) and took in stride all of the insults thrown at him about his size, his name, and his mother's reputation. Nothing seemed to get under Jenny's skin. He was one of the best people Lucas knew. He admired him and in some ways envied him. Even here in his junkyard, where he towed and fixed cars, Lucas thought about the pleasure of a simple existence.

"How'd you know?"

Jenny flipped open a sudoku book, picking up a blunted pencil as he started slowly solving another square. "Heard she showed up dead. Recognized her car when they had me come pick it up. Keys aren't in it, but it's unlocked. I checked the door, with a glove, but I didn't look inside. Figured one of you guys would eventually be up here for it."

"Can we take a look at it together?"

Jenny nodded but continued writing until he'd finished a section. Lucas didn't interrupt him. When he was done, he stood up and pulled one of the straps of his overalls onto his shoulder, and headed back outside. They walked down the lot of totaled cars and parts to a gate in the back where Jenny unlocked a padlock and led Torres inside. There were fewer cars there, some that had been towed, repossessed, or were simply in for repairs. He walked with dedication to the car at the end of the lot, and motioned to it.

"That's her. I got some gloves I use to clean carbs sometimes. Will that work?" He retrieved a pair of black latex gloves and handed them to Lucas, who slipped his slender fingers inside the too-large sleeves. He opened the car, feeling a cold sweat overtake him. Inside he saw a bouquet of wilted flowers, nearly browned, and wrapped in pink plastic with a large bow. A card was folded and tucked inside a little envelope, Lucas removed it to see that it read: *Hello, pretty thing. I've been watching you.* He laid it carefully back into the seat until he could call someone. It was handwritten, but had the name and address of Roots and Shoots gardening center across the top in type.

He opened the back seat to find two plastic bags of groceries and a can of marshmallow fluff on the floor.

9
Quentin

Quentin had been coming to Cecilia Norrington for therapy over the last eighteen months. He wasn't sure that it helped him any, but it was sometimes nice to just have someone to tell all of his frustrations to. Cecilia was very no-nonsense, she had a disposition that made Quentin think of his grandmother. He could recall her now, and how as a child she had intimidated him in a way that had taught him the true meaning of respect, and how it required a certain degree of both fear and gratitude.

As the man across from her removed a pack of cigarettes from his pocket, Cecilia raised a brow and laid her pen down heavily. The sound made him look up at her as he placed it between his lips. She raised her brows at him, motioning towards the pack in his hands.

"Quentin, you know you can't smoke that in here."

He nodded, leaning back in his seat and crossing one leg over the other, "I know. It just relaxes me some."

She nodded, she understood the anxiety he sometimes came to her with. He had started coming to her, reluctantly, after a stressful experience on the job nearly two years ago. This quiet town didn't have much in the way of excitement, even for the police. A man, well-known, had killed his wife and children before turning the gun on himself. Quentin had arrived after the wife's distressed phone call, and the man killed both of the young boys in front of him. The wife was dead before he got there.

Something had clicked, apparently, because Quentin never stopped coming. He was here at least once a week, every week, without fail. He never acted like they were getting anywhere, but Cecilia knew that he wouldn't come if he wasn't finding value in their sessions.

"You know," she started softly, lifting the pen again, "If you aren't ready to talk, we can wait."

"No, I'm ready."

Quentin retrieved a lighter from his pocket, putting it up to the cigarette in his mouth and shielding it with his hand as he lit it. His face was briefly illuminated by the flicker of light on the tobacco paper. Cecilia sighed, but she didn't say anything. Her building was under renovations and so she was crammed into a too-small space without a smoke detector anyway.

"A young woman was murdered a couple of days ago... and there's something that suggests it's the same guy that killed a girl a few months ago."

Cecilia listened quietly. She did not ask questions or suggest he elaborate on his stories. He already shared too many details, and she often had to remind him to be discreet. Even though it was against her oath to tell anyone any details, there were things she just didn't want to know. When work ended, she had to take things home with her, but she couldn't bring things she didn't know.

"How does this make you feel? Does it make you feel anxious again?"

Quentin nodded, scratching above his brow with a thumbnail. He looked at her in a nervous way, as though he wanted her to reassure him somehow. She watched as his shaking hand removed the cigarette from his mouth and he tapped the ash onto his sock.

"You do not have control over these criminals, over these accidents, over murders, over suicides, over robberies. All you can do is try to uphold justice, and to help people along the way."

Quentin rolled his eyes, taking a deep inhale before extinguishing it on the arm of the chair.

She frowned, thinking, *Why do I put up with this bullshit...* before checking her watch for the time.

"I know that. This isn't about me being a control freak."

"I've never called you a control freak, Quentin."

He laughed, knowing that she probably wanted to. He wasn't sure, but maybe she was right about his need for control. Was that really what it was all about? He had always been fine with policework, always recognized that he couldn't save them all. He had always been able to neatly box up those human reactions to the shit he had to deal with, stuffing them in a compartment so they couldn't keep him up at night. He would use a little bit of that protective apathy, disconnection, isolation. After the family murder-suicide, Quentin had found himself lingering and dwelling on his inability to *stop* that man before he killed those kids. Allowing himself to feel that guilt, to see their deaths play over and over in his head, caused him to open that box of neatly packed trauma... And it had overwhelmed him since. Everything was a failure, someone he had let down. If only he'd been a better detective, if only he had trusted better instincts, if only he could focus more on work, if only, if only, if only...

"Have you thought about taking some time off?"

Quentin shook his head. "I can't do that. They'd fall apart without me. I definitely can't now that this case is reopened."

"I'm not undermining your importance to the force, but they would get along just fine while you took a little break. A vacation, not retirement. They could hold it together until you got back. You could function better as a detective *and* a human being if you gave yourself just a little room to breathe."

The thought of being at home with nothing to do, or even at some resort his wife picked out, made Quentin shudder. He saw the opposite of relaxation: too much time to think about the things he was trying to forget. If work wasn't there to keep him busy, he wouldn't know how to cope. What did people do with all of that time to think?

"I'll look into taking a vacation day or something."

"What about your trainee? How is he doing? Surely it helps to split the workload between yourself, him, and your partner."

Quentin considered how he had thrown Polanski into interviewing Misty Rockwell the night before last. He had avoided it to instead sit in his car in his own driveway and drink beer, smoke too many cigarettes, and listen to podcasts. He didn't want to go inside and encounter his wife, where he was also failing, but he didn't want to work anymore either. Cecilia was right, he needed a break, but it was the kind of break you only got when you were dead.

"I did send him to retrieve the victim's car yesterday. Alone. He was calling me by the end of the day. If I send him to do something, I just worry about him doing it right the entire time he's there, so it's really useless to try and delegate to him."

"And your partner?"

"I try to give him a break. He has a family, other stuff going on in life."

"So do you."

Quentin shrugged. He didn't like talking about his marriage here, even though sometimes when an argument arose he thought about how Cecilia would want him to handle it. His marriage was possibly beyond repair now, and he knew it was his fault. He wanted to do something about it, but he just didn't. Cecilia was accustomed to him dancing around the topic, and she didn't push it. She never pushed it. She had a good feeling about how his marriage was, just by knowing how he was handling everything else in his life. It also didn't help that he wasn't as honest as he should be with Cecilia, but he sometimes had trouble admitting he was wrong.

His phone buzzed in his pocket and he slipped it out far enough to look on the screen to see the caller. It was Emily. He muted it and put it back into his pocket.

"Do you need to take that?"

"No," he said.

Cecilia looked at the other phone around his belt and tilted her head, "It was your personal phone. Do you often ignore your wife's calls?"

Quentin sighed, "No. I wouldn't say that."

"What if it is important?"

"She'll call again if she really needs something." He checked his own watch, "That's it for today, I guess."

He stood up and started walking to the door without giving a formal goodbye. Cecilia called after him, "Just remember that even your smallest actions and decisions have consequences, Quentin. Sometimes we have to take small steps towards change."

"See you next week, doc."

Quentin didn't want to go home, but he didn't have much of a choice. He always thought the air there was heavy and tense, and he anticipated an argument before he ever laid eyes on Emily. He shut the door quietly behind him and followed the small hallway to the kitchen. He opened the refrigerator to retrieve a bottle of water. When he closed the door, he saw Emily was standing on the other side. He jumped and put a hand over his chest.

"Scared the shit out of me."

"Where were you so late last night?" she asked, ignoring his comment.

Quentin shrugged his shoulders, "Got a tough case at work. It's going to be really time consuming."

He almost couldn't stand to look at her. Guilt overwhelmed him as she studied him with her luminous eyes. Even when she was angry they seemed to hold an effervescence that glistened with life and joy. It was hard for him to see her look at him the way she did. It always made him want to work for her love and happiness like he used to. Sometimes it made him wish he didn't love her so damn much. It would make things so much easier if he didn't.

He swallowed, finding that his mouth was dry.

"Where were you this morning?"

"Again, work."

"David said he hadn't seen you."

"Well I was with the rookie. He went yesterday to find a car and we were going over evidence. Ask him if you want."

She shrugged. "I've never even met him. I don't even know his name."

"Torres. I've told you that before. His name is Torres."

"There's no reason to be hostile, Quentin."

He wanted to respond with a denial of the hostility, but he knew he would only deflect and start an argument. He needed to admit a fault. He needed to apologize, *even if he didn't really feel like he was wrong.*

"I'm... I'm sorry. I just have a lot going on. I'm stressed out, okay?" he cracked the seal on the bottle of water, putting it up to his lips to take a drink of the crisply cold water. It had no flavor, and it did not seem to moisten his mouth. It went straight down his throat and into his gut, leaving a cold and unsatisfied trail in its descent.

Her brow seemed to soften immediately when he apologized, but she didn't say anything else. Instead she shuffled past him to the table and sat down next to a stack of shiny newspaper and her craft basket. Emily had always been this bright and shining soul. He had watched her change over the last couple of years, a result of his own internal crumble. He didn't mean to let it affect her. He had promised her that he would never bring work home, when they were still trying to have kids. He had told her that it would never be anything other than a job, which had always been a lie. This job took over your life sometimes. There were days he was glad that they never had kids, and it always made him sick that he felt that way. It was best though, he would always say that, even though he kept a single pink baby sock in his glove box for the last five years. A gift from his mother-in-law before they lost their only unborn child, he would never admit that he had kept it after all of that time.

He followed the same path she had taken to the table, leaning hesitantly against the back of the chair adjacent to her, "Can I sit too?"

She made a noise in her throat, one without any assurance that she was permitting him to be there. She snipped one edge of the paper aggressively, allowing the strip to fall onto the table top silently. He pulled the seat out and sat down, pulling his sleeves up as he took an extra pair of scissors out of her craft basket. He used a single finger to drag a sheet of the coupons towards himself. His eyes scanned over the various foods and household products. He was sure they used some of the stuff, but he couldn't remember the last time he had been to the grocery store.

"Which of them do I clip?" he asked.

"Things we need," she retorted.

He nodded, twisting his mouth around in disappointment as he tried to look again. He felt her turn her eyes up to look at him, but he didn't dare look back at her.

Her voice was condescending, "Oh, I forgot. You barely live here."

He frowned, “Maybe... uhm... let’s see... Toilet paper?”

“For all your bullshit?”

This time he did look over at her, just in time to catch her stifling a smile.

He smiled back at her and went on, “Buy two get one free.”

There was a moment of silence between them, but silence of a different kind. Quentin didn’t mind this, the sound of the scissors cutting through the thin paper. There was something less venomous about the way she sat there now, more relaxed. It wasn’t natural for her to be so angry, and he knew it could be hard for her to try to be like this.

Quentin shrugged his shoulders, picking up another newspaper sheet, “Paper towels?”

“Yep.” she said, voice now calm and clear.

“Got any of these for take out?”

She laughed again.

10
Rion

Things had a particular order. If things weren't in order, there was a likelihood that a certain element of surprise could develop, and Rion did not like surprises. It wasn't the desire for perfection, or an obsession with tidiness or refinement; it was a need to avoid chaos. He needed predictability to some degree. Which was one of the many reasons why he was such a valued employee at Roots and Shoots: Whitebranch's premier, locally owned gardening center. He had a great attention to detail, he was quiet, he was non-confrontational, and he always showed up for work. Some of his coworkers thought he was a little weird, but no one ever said anything to his face. No one except Evan Walsh.

Rion hated Evan Walsh with a passion. Even today, as he carefully positioned the tiny succulents on the display counter, he imagined what it would feel like to kill him. He often had to reel himself back in to avoid following Evan to his car at night, or getting too curious about where he lived and if he ever travelled anywhere alone on foot. Evan wasn't worth his time or attention. In fact, the thought of touching Evan at all nearly made him nauseous. Maybe he could hit him with his car, like he did animals on the road. Nice little bump, and all done. He imagined he'd pop like a roll of prepackaged hamburger meat, or a tube of toothpaste.

He heard the gentle ding of the bell on the front counter and he leaned back to see the back of a young woman as she waited expectantly. He initially ignored it, returning to his work of precarious plant arrangement. Evan was standing by the window on his cell phone, running a hand through his stringy hair as he spoke. He should've been a used car salesman, Rion thought.

The soft sound rang again, and Rion saw that the young woman was still waiting. Evan turned around to make eye contact with Rion, who tightened his fists around a plastic planter so tightly that the plastic crumpled. Evan motioned towards the counter, shrugging his shoulders. Rion looked down at the plants on the counter as he set down the crushed cup, watching as it slowly expanded to regain some semblance of its previous shape, before he headed up front to assist her.

"Oh, hello!" the girl said with a smile.

Rion approached the other side of the counter slowly, dragging his palm across the surface as he looked at the girl.

"How may I help you?" he said without greeting, giving her a soft smile.

She was pretty. Very young, lacking much confidence. He could see all the little cues that she was rehearsing what she would say in her head. The way her eyes focused on his and the way her jaw clenched, causing her cheeks to quiver. She swallowed once before she spoke, making a small click in the back of her throat as she started speaking just a little too soon.

"My name is Mary Allen, I'm a member of the Delton Church of the Fellowship. We are putting up these flyers around town to invite people to our revival..."

He interrupted her, "I'm sorry, they don't allow us to put up flyers."

He watched as Mary's expression melted into a look of disappointment. She even lost just a little color, starting around her nose and mouth, a little pinkness found its way onto her cheeks. It was in that moment that he struggled to stifle all of the vivid fantasies of putting his hands around her throat like he had the little plastic pot. How could he have her? He needed her. It was his turn to swallow back something in his throat, but it wasn't the same as her dry-tongued nervousness. He had a tingle in his salivary glands so intense that it crept up under his eyes.

"I'm sorry I've interrupted your work," she went on, smiling at him but eyes now finding a focus somewhere between them on the countertop.

He extended his hand with a comforting smile, "I'll talk to them though, I'm sure they'd be happy to help advertise the revival... Sometimes they just need a little encouragement."

She beamed at him, but he somehow preferred the downtrodden expression she'd just shed like old skin. She handed him the flyers, and he thought maybe she brushed her knuckles against his palms on purpose.

"Thank you, we're hoping to get as much of the community involved as possible. Brother Rudy says the county is really in need of a revival right now."

Rion nodded, "Oh, absolutely. I hope you have a great turn out."

She backed away from the counter, tucking a strand of hair that had fallen loose from her ponytail behind her ear, "Well, thank you again. You should consider coming out too, if you want."

He shrugged his shoulders, as though he hadn't considered it before then, "You know, I might do that."

She smiled, still awkwardly backing away before raising a hand to wave bye, and then she ducked out the door. Rion watched her leave, and then turned to watch her walk across the parking lot. He noted that she had gotten into a car with an older woman, and was not driving on her own. He wondered if she really was as young as she looked.

He tossed the flyers into the waste bin beneath the counter and returned to his succulent arrangement briefly. Evan strolled over not long after his return, slipping his cell phone back into his pocket as he started setting plants on the counter *completely wrong*. Rion stared at the crooked plants, placed in such a way that they had no pattern or aesthetic appeal.

"So, did you hear?" Evan said quietly, raising his dark brows at Rion.

Rion reached over to turn an owl planter around so that it faced the customer's point of view, "Hear what?"

Evan looked around as though he were sharing a dirty secret and then said in a hushed voice, "Cops were here earlier this morning."

Rion stopped what he was doing, looking at Evan now with interest, "Cops?"

"Yeah," Evan laughed. "Apparently, from what I hear, they found a note on a dead girl's body from the shop. Girl's name was Olivia Brown."

"A note... from the shop?"

"You know, one of the address card things. From whoever, to whoever, with a message?"

"Oh." Rion said as though he finally understood, nodding. Of course, he knew that the note was in fact *not* found with a body. He wished people could keep their stories straight. "So what? Do they think Mrs. or Mr. Rice were involved?"

Evan scoffed, "This bitch's head was cut off and her guts were strung around all over. I don't think they think the eighty year old Rices are involved. They asked if we kept records of who all bought those cards blank. Mrs. Rice told them we don't keep a log like that."

"Maybe we should." Rion said. He was infuriated at the way Evan described the girl's body, and the way he called her a bitch. She had not been a bitch, such a vulgar term that was undeserving of the young woman. She had done everything he had expected her to do, she had not disappointed him. Of course, Rion had not desecrated her body in such a way either.

Now, when they found the girl under the oak tree... He might let Evan call *her* a bitch.

He shrugged the conversation off, sidling around the table to get away from Evan and encourage him to move on to do some kind of work.

"Whoever did it is a psycho. Cut a girl up like that."

"Just stop." Rion snapped quietly. "Stop talking about it."

Evan raised a brow, looking both offended and surprised at Rion's sudden impoliteness. This only pressed him on, "Pussy."

Rion turned his back on Evan completely, ears humming from anger. Evan thankfully did not follow him, although he echoed the insult through the store again loudly. An elderly woman popped her head out of the soil aisle to scowl at him over the golden rims of her glasses. Rion made a dedicated line for the timeclock, punching out for lunch and heading to his vehicle. He usually just ate outside so he could watch people on the streets, imagining their little lives and the things they did. Sometimes he imagined them dead, changed, suspended in time. Today he would retreat to his car to avoid Evan. Since he had started indulging in violence, he found it harder and harder to withdraw from the desire and hold himself back. Granted, he wanted to kill Evan in quite a different way than he did the women. They were beautiful things that he was preserving, like pressed flowers dried and placed between glass. Evan was like a rat you find in the pantry: a pest that deserved all the suffering and humility of dying for a dab of peanut butter.

He settled down in his car at the back of the parking lot, locking the doors. As he turned the key one notch in order to allow the AC fan to kick on enough to stir in the air in the vehicle. It still had a "new car" type of smell and was totally free of debris or trash in the front seat. In the back seat there had recently been the slightest amount of dead leaves crunched into the carpet. He had spent hours vacuuming and then taking a toothbrush to work loose the remaining crumbles and debris. It was now spotless.

He opened his plastic bento box of fruit, crackers, and pepperoni. He took a clean, disposable fork out of a plastic sleeve and started eating them one item at a time. He didn't like to feel the texture of the foods on his fingers, when he did it seemed to be more noticeable when he placed them on his tongue. He had once eaten pizza by hand, but the feeling of soggy cheese on the crust and grease running down his fingers led him quickly to vomit as he became acutely aware of all of the conflicting sensations in his mouth. Now he ate his pizza with a utensil. He knew exactly how many bites it took to get each item to a swallowable state: two for the white grapes, four for the pepperoni, eight for the wheat crackers.

Rion found himself lost in thought, however. He thought about the police officer that he had seen going into the station. The man who was going to try to catch him. There was a desire there but in a different way. He had snooped around social media to see if anyone was talking about the murders. They had not found the girl beneath the oak tree yet. He would risk driving past the field again tonight to see if anyone had been around. Maybe he could somehow drop a hint, give them a little help. Work both sides. It was a little dangerous, but he wanted this to last.

He read some news reports and gossip columns about the cop, one Quentin Robichaud. Married, no kids, seemed to keep out of the public eye usually. Involved in a bad murder-suicide about two years ago that people talked about for months. The photos of him seemed to age almost instantly, his eyes were colder, surrounded by dark skin and lines. He'd lost some of his soul along the way, and Rion wanted to introduce a little spark back into his life. The internet was a wealth of information, and he found himself saving pictures of the detective and screenshots of his presence in the news.

He hadn't noticed that he had finished his food, safe for one lop-sided grape that he would be discarding, and was sitting lost in thought. His eyes were looking somewhere far beyond the parking lot of the garden center. In addition to the detective, there was someone else he couldn't stop thinking of... Mary Allen.

It was later in the evening when Rion finally got off work. He had punched out without much outward enthusiasm, and sauntered to his car like he didn't have any plans for the afternoon. On the contrary, he had intentions of going somewhere very specific.

He drove out of town and down the long stretch of desolate highway to the little road where he had left Lisa York underneath the fruitful oak tree. On his way down, however, something else distracted his otherwise determined journey.

He first took note of the dented metal mailbox that was bulging with notices and bills. The old woman had always walked out to check her mail with dedication. She would trudge across the sloppily paved sideroad in her thick, pink floral nightgown and open the creaking door to take the papers, important or not, inside. She shuffled with the grace of an 80s cinema zombie, gnashing her worn gums together as she did so.

Curiosity got the best of him, and he pulled his car into her driveway. Dusk was approaching, his headlights illuminated the little leaning house with a mellow butter hue. He watched the dead porchlight with intent, knowing that although the woman was nearly blind and would not be able to tell who he was from a distance, she would flip on the light before she came to the door.

Three minutes, no movement.

Rion shifted in his seat before shutting the car off and killing the lights. He walked around the side of the house, peering in each hazy window until he finally came to the bedroom window... He knew immediately, mostly thanks to the screen in the window that was once used to offer some air circulation to the old house, that she was dead. The saccharine odor wafted from inside, the smell that you somehow instinctively know belongs to the deceased. The prickling sensation that there could be some sort of danger afoot, something murderous or otherwise vile. He cut the screen out with his pocket knife before hoisting himself inside, falling inside the window and onto the floor with a clatter.

He found her body fairly quickly, in the hall that led from the bedroom to the kitchen. There was not much left at this point, her body had already swelled and burst, and now remained nothing but a deflated remainder of what little there had been of her before. A larger, dark shadow stained the floor around her where all of the fluid had oozed into the carpet. He walked around her body, admiring the advanced state of decomposition. It was not often that he saw a body at this stage of death, he liked to see the girls he killed when they were still lifelike. They were like realistic dolls, sometimes still a little warm even after their faces turned porcelain cold.

He then roamed around the house, looking at all of her belongings. The kitchen floor sagged heavily in the center, the counters were covered in a fair layer of dust. A candy jar was filled with golden butterscotch disks, and little beetles shifted around in a tub of flour.

As he passed into the bathroom, covered in rust and mildew, he was surprised to find an orange cat curled up in the sink. It yawned and mewled at him, curling its paws in the air as though it were not at all surprised to see him there. Rion did not like animals, but he did appreciate the domestic cat for being independent and... not so domestic, afterall. The marbled red cat was wearing a blue leather collar that had a dangling bronze tag that read: REGRET. He had not noticed any food dishes for the cat, and he assumed it must come and go as it pleased. It could exit the window now, with the screen removed. Maybe, being the tiny opportunistic carnivore that it was, it had engorged itself on the body of the old woman.

Rion saw a deep freezer in the utility room, empty and cold. He thought of all the things he could put in it. All of the precious memories he could save.

11
Torres

Lucas felt like he was onto something which was not a normal feeling for him. Usually he just felt like he was in the way, doing something wrong, or a glorified errand boy for Robichaud and Polanski. But this was different. It was such a *good* feeling that Lucas was sticking to his guns, no matter how much shit Polanski gave him.

"So you think this psycho is sending flowers to the girls." Polanski repeated dubiously.

"I think so... or something."

"I think you're stupid, or something."

Lucas put his face in his hands, leaning over the cafe table heavily. Polanski was paying more attention to Lucas' plate than his face, and he motioned towards it, "You going to eat your sausage?"

Lucas shoved the plate at Polanski a little roughly, causing the congealed pepper gravy to jiggle enough that it sloshed onto the crisps of hashbrown.

"Hey, hey," Polanski said, cradling the plate in his hands. "Careful with the goods. The breakfast here is a delicacy."

"Sorry," Lucas said quietly, the apology sincere. "I just feel like no one is taking me seriously."

"I get that you think there's some kind of connection. I know. You're a creative type, like Paltro... and, you know, that suits Paltro just fine. You have to be creative to do a job like that. It's like... I don't know, reading signs in dirt or something. Requires a little imagination. But you're not a Paltro. You're a cop, you're a detective. It doesn't suit us."

"The girls had gotten flowers before they died. That's too big of a coincidence don't you think? And then the game pieces... They have f-..."

"What type of flowers did Lola Simmons get?" Polanski interjected, looking at the tip of a sausage link on his fork lovingly. "Was it daisies? Was it... petunias?"

Lucas swallowed back his mentally prepared presentation on The Significance of Flowers in the Murdered Girls of Whitebranch and picked at the metal edge of the tabletop, fighting the blush against his cheeks, "I don't know."

Polanski popped the sausage in his mouth, chewing with his mouth open, "I know everything about the Simmons case. I lost a lot of sleep over it, spent a lot of time trying to find the bastard that killed her. I don't remember any flowers, other than the ones at her funeral. I will admit, yes, I think this is a single killer. I think the flower tiles are his calling card. I do not have any reason to think that these girls have dated their murderer."

"I didn't say that. I didn't say they were all romantically involved, just that they got flowers from somewhere."

Polanski waved his hand in the air dismissively.

Lucas shut down his attempts to convince the older detective. He thought it would be easier to persuade Polanski to humor him, help direct him, or at the very least give him some sort of permission to do his own thing. Lucas was beginning to think he may have to give himself permission to go a little rogue instead. He wouldn't deny that being able to say he knew it all along would feel great, but more than that he felt this urgency to prevent another girl from this same horrible fate. He felt like he had a good hunch.

"I'm going to head out," Lucas said, pulling money out of his pocket and laying it on the table.

"Where you going?" Polanski asked, scraping his fork across the plate.

"Mom's. Don't want to spend the day off with you." He smiled warmly.

"Alright, mama's boy." He slid Lucas' money back over to him. "I've got breakfast, you didn't eat it anyway."

Lucas said his thanks, stuffing the money back into his pocket as he left the small diner and got into his vehicle. It was an older model Olds, rusted and it ran loudly. The air conditioning didn't work, and the heat was unreliable. Windshield wipers, even if they had been replaced like they should, smeared the water around and scuffed the glass, but didn't clear for a good view. If you looked at his car and his modest apartment (in what could be considered the 'bad' part of town, where most of the drug addicts and down-on-their-luck young adults seemed to congregate), you might think he was broke. He got paid a decent salary and worked hard at his job, but he paid his rent plus his mother's rent and purchased all of her groceries. She had been in the same house since he was a kid, but his dad had borrowed a lot against it in a reckless manner before he'd taken off and left his mother to deal with it.

She had not wanted to lose the house, and had worked until she couldn't anymore. In just a few years from now, she could have it paid off, but her body was breaking down. She had stopped working a couple of years ago when the arthritis prevented her from using her hands like she used to. He took over her payments for her, exaggerating his pay and comfort financially. He would never let her know it was a burden to him, even when she questioned his decision to keep the old rustbucket he drove around.

His mom lived in a little town about an hour away called No Business. It was a little unincorporated farming area in neighboring Heresy County. Heresy County had quite the dark history. If these murders had happened there, people may have not batted an eye. The county was known for the rich stories of witch trials, desecrated sacred grounds, mysterious disappearances, and even hauntings. Of course, many people who lived there would deny any of that. They would say it was a nice, quiet place to live.

He pulled into the narrow driveway of his mother's house, walking through the slightly overgrown lawn. He made a mental note to mow it on his next day off. He went straight into the house through the creaking screen door. It clattered shut behind him and from the kitchen he heard his mother's raspy voice, "Lucas?"

"Yeah it's me, Mom," he called back, walking across the peeling linoleum to the kitchen. She was sitting at the table with a fork, eating a pickle straight out of the jar. She still wore thick eyeliner underneath her wrinkled eyes. They glistened with a bright, vivacious flicker and were only a shade apart from her olive skin. He came over and kissed her thinning hair before sitting beside her.

"Pickle?" she asked, sliding the unlabeled jar towards him. He nodded, reaching in with his fingers to pull out one of the sweet, crispy spears. She slid a napkin under his chin as it dripped onto the tabletop.

"How is everything in Whitebranch?" she asked.

"Everything is great. I'm working extra hours because I'm getting to be involved on a big case. Real big case."

"Oh, what kind of case?"

"You know I can't tell you that," he said with a wink.

She smiled, rocking back in her chair as she put her palms together. "I am so proud of you. When are you going to take me to see your house? And meet that handsome Detective Robichaud?"

Lucas laughed, "Maybe after all of this blows over."

Of course, Lucas would have to find a house. Maybe he would have enough in a few months to rent a little place that was better than his current apartment. He didn't think he would introduce her to Robichaud anytime soon, though. She liked seeing him on the news, hearing him on the radio. She was thrilled when she heard that Lucas was his 'partner' (nevermind that he had told her multiple times that his partner was Polanski, and he was just training underneath the two senior officers).

"You want me to take you to the store today? Get some groceries?" he asked, standing up and wiping his hands on his pants.

"I do need a few things," she said as she placed the lid back on the pickle jar and made her way over to the refrigerator. He heard her replacing the jar as she looked through the shelves, and he moved to the curio cabinet in the corner.

On top of the cabinet was a maroon cardboard box, a board game with the golden title across the side: *Love in Bloom*. He reached up to pull it down, swiping a thin layer of dust with his palm before sitting the box on the table. A dramatic representation of a Hispanic woman reaching towards a hyper-masculine white man, positioned suspiciously like The Hand of God. His mother used to ask him if he thought she looked like that woman. The game itself was ridiculous, a pastime of old women who smelled like cheap perfume and menthols. His hands were shaking as he opened the lid, peering down at the scattered game pieces inside the box. These were more faded than the ones that they found at the crime scenes, but also less sinister. They lacked the dirt, residue, blood. The clues that they were part of something more macabre.

"You wanting to play?" his mom asked, making her way over to the table.

"No. Just curious. I remember you playing it when I was younger."

She would sit in front of the television, watching predictable soap operas where everyone had died and come back at least one time. She would set the little tiles up and start pairing them up and picking them off one by one...

"Used to be the game to play, when the books was popular."

"I remember those books, you used to read them so fast... They were sitting all over the house." He could remember seeing them, with the scantily clad women on the covers and the man with the perfectly chiseled body. The spines were worn out, the pages dog eared.

He cleared his throat awkwardly as his mom slipped on her shoes, "So tell me about the flowers in the game. What's that all about?"

"Just made up for the game, I think. It came with a little pocket guide that explained the meaning of all the flowers."

"Do you still have that guide?"

"No, it's lost by now."

He moved back over to the cabinet, running his fingertips along the backside. He felt a number of gossamer cobwebs, the long-since-dead carcasses of ladybugs, and...

He pulled the yellowed book down, pages curled and withered, cover faded. As he flipped the pages, too quickly to read anything specifically, he saw pictures of flowers along with their names and symbolism. A little cloud of dust arose in the air, glistening as it caught the light.

She walked over to him, "Look at you... Finder of lost things."

"It was up top, just out of reach," he explained.

She frowned. "I need to dust up there, probably. Think I could reach it standing in the chair?"

Lucas looked at the old kitchen chairs, which were wooden with wicker seating. He imagined she might fall straight through the sagging seats if she tried to stand in the middle.

"I'll get it for you," he said with a smile. "If you'll let me borrow your flower book."

12
Quentin

Quentin sat adjacent to Polanski as they stared at the white board in front of them. Neither one looked very impressed; it was arguable which was less engaged. Torres was writing words on the board like LILAC, DAFFODIL. Holding a musty-smelling book in one hand, using the squeaky marker in the other. Quentin rubbed his hand over his face in exasperation, and started to stand up. Polanski swatted at him, scolding him with his furrowed eyebrows.

He knew Polanski felt the same way about this *bullshit* but he was much more tolerant. Quentin swatted back and got up, walking over to stand behind Torres who had not noticed him get up and was still rattling on.

"So," Torres went on, "Lola Simmons was the lilac, which is symbolic of first love. Olivia Brown was the daffodil, which is representative of a few things but... Maybe unrequited love? Maybe she wouldn't come with him? Maybe..."

He turned around, starting as he noticed Quentin standing behind him. Quentin reached up and smacked the book out of Torres hand. It flew up and nearly hit the young detective in the face before flopping on the floor.

"Maybe this is a huge waste of time," Quentin finished for him.

Torres reached down to pick up the book, bending a page back into a proper position, "I'm onto something here, Robichaud."

Polanski stood up to interject, "Listen. This guy might as well be a ghost. We have *zero* leads on him. So... Let's not argue about the flowers. I've got something else that could be related. Was... on my desk this morning."

Quentin already knew, but he didn't say anything. He watched as Polanski retrieved the thin file folder and brought it over, laying it down on the conference desk near the whiteboard. Torres moved over a little more enthusiastically than Quentin, although now he was clutching his scorned book against his chest protectively.

"Young woman named Cat Ji-su was reported missing by her parents this morning. They haven't heard from her in forty-eight hours as of last night. Ji-su still lived at home with her parents. They have been trying to find her since she didn't come home after a party. I don't have the location yet, but the parents are expecting one of us to come and talk with them at home this afternoon. They're getting access to her laptop, hoping it'll give us something."

"When are you heading out there?" Torres asked.

"Well, I was thinking you two lovebirds could go. You need to bond a little bit anyway."

Quentin looked down at the sparse information they had so far, pointing at the girl's age, "Eighteen years old. That's a little young for our guy, if that's where you're going with this."

Polanski shrugged, "It's a missing girl. Chief wants to assume everything is related until we prove it isn't."

Torres muttered to himself, "Two girls is hardly enough to find an age preference."

Quentin snapped his head in Torres' direction, "What was that?"

"There's only been two girls, how do you know this girl is too young?"

"You're one to talk, Mr. Fucking Flowers. Olivia Brown and Lola Simmons were both in their mid to late thirties."

Torres didn't respond, but Quentin made sure to stare him down to make sure he didn't get another burst of insubordination. He didn't know what had gotten into him lately. He wasn't the type to act out like this. To voice his opinion. If Quentin weren't so on edge, he might've thought 'good for him.'

Polanski rolled his eyes, "Just both of you shut the fuck up. Go talk to the Cats, don't ask about flowers. See what they've got as far as electronics. Don't act like this is a homicide. Her mom's real uppity right now. This is just a missing person, nothing more."

Quentin motioned to Torres, "I'll meet you in the car."

Torres reluctantly left, and Quentin turned to Polanski. He studied his face, which was gleaming with a little perspiration as he gathered his small stack of papers back up. Quentin put his hand on Polanski's shoulder, giving it a light squeeze.

"What's going on, man?" he asked quietly.

Polanski made a grunt in his throat, "What do you mean?"

"You wouldn't throw me under the bus like that... sending me off to deal with a missing person *with Torres*. We've got too much on our plates right now to deal with a teenager who's probably just running around with friends. Have you seen the news?"

He shifted, papers against his side under his arm as he turned to face Quentin. "Ji-su is a friend of my daughter's."

Quentin sighed, "Shit. I didn't know. I'm sorry."

"They aren't best friends or anything, but they've gone to school together since the first grade. I'm just... I'm afraid to get too close to this. You just go talk to them and let me know... you know. Let me know what you think."

Quentin nodded slowly, patting Polanski on the back with the most comforting gesture he could muster.

Mrs. Cat handed the tablet to Quentin. Although Polanski had described her as uppity, he noted that she was far more collected and calm than Mrs. Brown had been. Stoic. She had her black and silver-streaked hair pulled back in a tight bun, and her clothes were neatly pressed. He noted the dark circles beneath her eyes, somehow shining blue through her foundation, the only clear sign that she had not been sleeping. Mr. Cat stood behind her chair, face drawn and concerned. Behind his small glasses, his eyes seemed to glisten still with tears, and his jaw and lips quivered.

"This is Ji-su's tablet. She has a messaging app that we unlocked. The code is 0713."

Quentin nodded at Torres, who was jotting the number down.

Mrs. Cat continued, "She was messaging someone about the party. None of her other friends were going, no one knew about the party that we have talked to. Can you somehow... trace the messages?"

Quentin swiped up on the tablet, and was scrolling through the messages as he responded, "We have some guys that should be able to trace the IP, so we will know where this guy was using his device. It may take us straight to his house, this is very helpful."

"We did not want her to go to the party," Mr. Cat explained. "She never went to parties. The invitation she had suggested it was a very small party, and she said friends were going. She lied to us. None of her friends even knew about the party. She never lied to us before."

Quentin did not have children, but he suspected that Mr. Cat was ignorant to the ways of the teenage girl.

Torres interjected, "Has anyone had any contact with Ji-su since she left for the party?"

"She responded to messages from my husband that night, just saying she was having a good time. She was not home the next morning and none of our messages have been read."

Quentin saw the string of messages between Ji-su and another person named 'Mr. Right.' She had been talking to him for weeks now. He didn't read every word. Most of the early conversation was innocent, casual. He began to grow uneasy as Mr. Right started pushing Ji-su to meet up with him. She seemed uncertain, hesitant about meeting someone she didn't know face-to-face. She said she enjoyed their friendship, and he made her feel less lonely. She talked about her overbearing parents, and how she was rarely allowed to do anything even though she considered herself an adult. She could not wait to leave for college. At the end of the messages he suggested they meet up at the quarry, where the old dam was. He told her there was a party, even included an invitation with the date and time, and it said 'by invite only.' He said it was very exclusive, and she could make a lot of friends there. She agreed. That night she said, "Are you here? Where is everyone?" and there were no further messages.

Quentin cleared his throat. "Can we take Ji-su's tablet to the station?"

"Absolutely, anything you need." Mr. Cat responded.

Quentin had the sinking feeling that they would not find Ji-su alive. Plenty of people, especially young people, went "missing" and showed back up. It was usually either just a miscommunication, or lack thereof, or a little harmless, albeit frustrating, rebellion. Everything about this was too eerie. Too unsettling. He had this cold fist in his gut. It was too late for Ji-su, if this was their guy... It seemed that he wasted no time.

"Thank you, we will be in touch. If you hear from Ji-su or have anything else for us, please let us know."

The walk back to the car was tense. Torres started talking as soon as they got into the vehicle, and Quentin slung the tablet into his lap.

"I'm sick," Torres admitted.

"Pull it together," Quentin muttered.

"Do you think something happened at the party? Abducted?" Torres asked.

"There was no party. This invitation was fake, he probably threw it together and she never checked into it before she went. It seemed legit, and she was comfortable because there were supposed to be people there. By the time she realized, it was probably too late."

"So you think she's dead," Torres said, voice monotone and flat.

"I didn't say that... just... don't say anything to Polanski, alright? This girl is a friend of his daughter's."

"Oh, shit."

"Yeah. Let's head down to the dam, have a look around. See if anyone has seen anything."

"Alright," Torres agreed, buckling himself in.

Quentin reached over to put the car into reverse out of the driveway, when he saw something resting on the windshield.

"What is that?" he said quietly.

Torres blinked, leaning forward and squinting at the small object on the windshield wiper.

"What the *fuck* is that?"

"I... I don't know."

"Get the fuck out and look!" Quentin snapped, hitting Torres in the chest with the back of his hand.

Quentin put a hand to his mouth as he took a deep breath, composing himself as Torres scrambled out of the car clumsily to get the item. He already knew what it was. The small wooden block was nearly too miniscule to be seen, if not for the accompanying piece of paper. He watched as Torres' face paled, thin fingers plucking the game piece off of the glass and then the paper. He unfolded it, peering down at whatever lay on the other side. Quentin banged on the windshield with his fist and Torres jumped.

"Right, coming," he said, coming back into the car as quickly as he could, fumbling with the door.

"It's..."

"I know," Quentin hissed, as though someone could hear him through the car. His head was fuzzy and his heart was pounding.

"Are you alright, Robichaud?"

"What's the paper say?"

"Nothing."

"Nothing?"

Torres stammered, "I mean nothing. It has a picture of a nut on it."

He turned the paper around to show Quentin a pen sketch of an acorn, with crosshatched shading and a tree above it.

"That's an acorn."

Torres flipped the paper around to squint at it, but didn't argue. He looked at the game piece then in his shaking hands, flipping it over and over before he muttered, "It's a new flower."

"What?"

"It's a different flower. Not the same one as the two before."

"Stop with the flower bullshit, please." Quentin said quietly, but without the same aggression as before.

"Do you think *he* did this? Do you think it was him? No one knew we were coming here but Polanski..."

Quentin put the car in reverse, backing out of the spot as he responded, "It's just a joke. Someone is fucking with us. If this *is* our killer, he wouldn't know we were here... he wouldn't risk getting caught by putting this on our fucking cruiser in the middle of the day."

"So you think it was one of the guys?" Torres asked, surprised. "You really think any of them would stoop that low?"

Quentin didn't believe it was a joke, and he knew Torres knew that. The case had all of them stressed, although not as much as those involved directly with it. Knowing that someone was out there, still setting his sights on young women.

"We're all a bunch of sorry bastards."

13
Rion

Rion was giddy for today. He had gotten up this morning and put on a nice set of slacks and a blue button-up shirt. Tonight was the revival that the girl had left the flyers for. He looked up church attire online, and the consensus seemed to be that it was business casual. He even found a tie and trimmed his beard. He stood in front of the mirror and feigned interest and excitement, watching his features carefully to be sure they looked as authentic as possible. He had several hours, nearly twelve, before the revival was slated to start, but he was going to make sure he was ready early on. He planned out his day: picking up his check from the garden center, cashing it, going to the grocery store... But first, he visited the Whitebranch Police Department.

He parallel parked his car across the street, leaving it running as he made sure to look fairly busy. He even brought along a book and some envelopes, so that he would have two different excuses as to why he was loitering. He watched as Detective Robichaud arrived, late as usual, and entered the building. He looked tired. Stressed maybe. Rion had noted that the word of Olivia Brown's murder had reached the news outlets. It was everywhere. No one had thus far connected it to the previous murder of Lola Simmons. Not yet, but the seed was there. Some mentioned the fact that two young women dying so close together was rocking the small town. Rion wasn't above giving the media a little nudge if needed, but for now he would wait. He still had a few tricks up his sleeves. He had been scoping out a few new girls using dating apps and Find a Friend type sites.

Sometimes he pretended to be a woman, sometimes he just pretended to be another guy. Some of the girls weren't panning out to be attainable, but some had the potential to take the bait… one of those girls being Ji-su. He had been setting her up for weeks. She played hard to get, getting all she wanted from him in terms of conversation and digital affection, but Rion made it clear he wanted something a little more. He used a little passive aggressiveness to make her feel guilty when she would shut down his invitations to meet up for coffee or a movie, when he needed someone to help him pick out a gift for his mother, when he went to pick up dining room chairs. But the party invite, that's what had gotten her.

She had arrived at the quarry, noting that there were no party goers, but she had still gotten out of the car. He called to her from the water's edge near the old dam, and she walked over. She was dressed head-to-toe in pink and sequins. It was pretty clear that she hadn't been to many parties. He told her everyone was inside the old dam, but she was hesitant. She went as far as walking three steps through the old door, noting the desolate state of the decrepit building. He tried to convince her to come inside farther, but she immediately tried to retreat. He hadn't wanted to kill her so quickly, but women could be flighty and unpredictable. Rion had been prepared and blocked her exit, first trying to choke her with his hands but resorting to a new toy he had picked up. It was a flexible piece of wire sleeving. He had been enlisted to repair the irrigation system in the greenhouse and was immediately inspired by the durability and flexibility of the sleeve. He cut off a good size piece and stuffed it in his pocket, and now he had the opportunity to try it out.

He used his larger form to force her onto the ground. She fell to her stomach and tried to crawl away, screams echoing in the building. He had a small sensation of fear, the sound multiplying and rising through the stone structure. He wondered if it were as amplified on the outside as it sounded inside. He lay on top of her as he wound the two ends of the pipe covering around each hand once. Her screams were muffled under his weight alone, and he used his forearm to hold her face on the debris-ridden ground.

He pulled it around her throat, twisting it tighter and tighter. He could feel her chest's movements slowing beneath him, and she started to struggle out small breaths at a time from her throat. The elasticity did exactly what he'd hoped: it dragged out the suffocation. He was able to savor it just a little longer. What he didn't like was the fact that she was face down, he wasn't able to watch that climax to death. The way that her features would become still and relaxed all at once. The way that her pupils fell open into a dense vacuity. When he was done, he propped her up against the wall and admired her, then he threw her into the water.

Bringing himself back to the present and out of reliving the thrill of murdering Ji-su, was the sound of the department door banging shut. Rion's curiosity was piqued, as he had anticipated his little 'stake out' to have lasted much longer. It had only been an hour, maybe two, since he had parked here. He noted that he had his younger partner with him.

Detective Robichaud's trainee had as much aptitude for police work as a supermarket door greeter. He had this displaced arrogance, Rion thought, although anyone who knew Torres would suggest that he was quite the humble young man. Rion could empathize with how the rookie looked up to Robichaud, but he felt as though he did not treat the older detective with the respect that he deserved. Rion had a strong dislike for Torres. He thought perhaps it was a little tinge of jealousy.

He followed them to the house where they were greeted and went inside. Rion parked a few houses down, in front of a home with a FOR SALE sign in the yard. That would be the least suspicious place, he supposed. He walked down to the house where the police cruiser sat, popping the black mailbox open and pulling out a piece of mail. The addressee on the front read Cat Beom-seok.

Oh, this was *exciting*. Did they know she was dead yet? No... surely not. He thought there would be more of a stir if they did. Now was his chance to leave his clue for Lisa York, while they were tangling up in the affairs of Ji-su... He was going to have them going in four different directions. If they were so flustered after two girls six months apart... Well, he had something really fun in store for them.

He jogged back to his car, retrieving a piece of notebook paper where he sketched the acorn, and then he retrieved Lisa's matching tile from his pocket. It was personal. This was the matching piece, the other half of the cloven soul.. But he had to give it to Robichaud, he needed to give the baby bird a push out of the nest.

He walked over to the car, laying the piece and paper on the windshield as quickly as possible, passing around the passenger side to notice the copy of *Love in Bloom* in the seat. It had been in the hands of the rookie detective when he'd left the building.

Rion found himself pausing, almost a little too long, before he retreated back to his car.

That night at the revival, Rion saw Mary notice him from across the sanctuary, and he smiled and waved at her. She raised her hand shyly in response. The revival was loud, and in any other scenario Rion would have been so overstimulated by all of the shouting and violently moving bodies that he would have been heading out the door. Tonight, however, he kept his eyes on the young girl. She was much more controlled than all of these heathens... how ironic that his mind procured that specific word to describe the people in the church. What was it that made her less enthusiastic? No, that wasn't it... it wasn't a lack of enthusiasm or excitement. He noticed now the way that her hands quivered when she put one into the air and bowed her head gently, whispering an agreement to whatever the preacher had said.

He couldn't wait to be near her alone, he found himself shifty in his own seat. The old woman he was seated by reached over and squeezed his knee, nodding as though she understood. Oh, if only she did. Sometimes artistry was a lonely place that no one understood, a place guarded by complex locks with a key from your own flesh.

He found the time passing quickly as he kept his eyes on her through the crowd of other worshippers. When it was all over, everyone stood and held hands with those around them, and they sang together. It gave Rion the creeps, and he didn't enjoy holding the hand of the elderly woman beside him, although he pretended it was the highlight of his evening. When he was done, he shoved the dirty hand into his pocket to be sure it was washed before he touched anything valuable with it.

The crowd started dispersing, spreading throughout the sanctuary as the murmur of conversation grew and a song was put over the speaker for ambience. Rion tried to casually approach Mary, but indirectly. He saw that she was only a few feet away. She caught sight of him when he was looking at a painting on the sanctuary wall. He could see her looking at him in his peripheral vision, but he did not look back at her.

She approached, tucking her hair behind her ears, "Hey! I am glad you got to come. We had a good turn out, didn't we?"

"Yes, looks like there's a lot of people here," he responded, finally looking over at her.

"He's a good preacher, isn't he?"

Rion nodded.

"Do you like the painting?"

"Blake."

"I'm sorry?"

"William Blake. It's one of his paintings."

He could tell by her silence that she didn't know who he was talking about, which was fine all the same. He wasn't a fan of Blake anyway, although he was fascinated by some of his work.

"Do you do any missionary work?" he asked.

She seemed to brighten up all at once, turning her body towards him, "Yes. I mean... I haven't gone on an official mission or anything, but I like to visit some of the local homeless people and take them bibles and food. You know."

Rion wasn't sure how many 'homeless' people lived in Delton County, but he couldn't imagine the number was that great. He thought perhaps the people who Mary Allen considered homeless might have just been druggies... or at this point, anyone standing outside of a residential building.

"I do a little bit of that, too," he admitted.

"Do you?"

"Yeah. Actually... I've been helping this elderly lady... Her name is Mrs. Harrison. She doesn't have anyone left. Her entire family is dead."

That sounded a little morbid, in hindsight, but she reacted just the way he expected. She covered her mouth and gasped, and her eyes might have even glistened with tears. Rion continued, "She always looks forward to my visits, but I think sometimes she wishes... well, she misses her daughter the most. Died in a car accident."

"How terrible. Can I add her to our prayer list?"

"Of course." He looked down at his watch, "I actually have to go over there tonight so I better get out of here."

"Let me send some things for her... We have care kits put together. Do you think she'd be offended if you took one?"

Rion scoffed, "No, of course not. She would love that."

He followed her to an office near the entrance door, where she picked up one of a dozen boxes and handed it to him gingerly.

"You know, you could come with me and give it to her yourself," he suggested. She started to protest and he went on, "It would mean a lot to her to see someone other than me. She is always telling me how lonely she is, and how she feels like the town and the church abandoned her when she became homebound. People send her things all the time, but no one takes the *time* to see her. No one except me."

"That's so terrible..." she whispered, looking back over her shoulder at the people who still grouped together to talk.

"I could drop you back off here if you want to ride out to her place with me. I pass the church on my way home anyway."

"That would be nice," she said, voice still hesitant, but then she spoke with a sort of resignation: "Yeah, I would like to meet Mrs. Harrison."

Rion smiled, glad that she had taken the bait, but he knew he still didn't have her just yet. It wasn't unlike fishing. Casting out over and over and over, and *usually* not getting anything, but when something nibbled... it was hard not to get a little ahead of yourself. He needed to be patient and make sure he had his hook in there before he started dragging her to suffocate in his hands.

"Well, let's head on out before it gets too late. She'll be in bed."

He watched as she looked back over her shoulder again, and for a moment he thought she might insist on telling someone where she was going. People seemed to take that precaution. Normally he didn't mind, but in this instance he knew she would explain how she knew him. A guy from the garden center, and she knew his name. She instead followed him dutifully to the car, even opening the door for him as he carried the box.

He got into the car, sitting with his palms against his thighs until she got in. He heard her buckle her seatbelt in, and she shifted to get comfortable. He used a dollop of hand sanitizer, filling the inside of the car with the odor of alcohol and aloe. Then he turned the key in the ignition and put the car in drive. The doors automatically locked and he smiled. He pulled out of the parking lot, onto the road, and headed out of town.

"I want to travel to do missionary work," she said as the car rolled down the road.

He 'mmhm'd in his throat but noticed in the silence that she started to shrink away towards the car door. She was not used to the lack of conversation, and he was not ready for her to be prematurely fearful. He stifled the little bit of irritation that rose up from having to talk to her, aimlessly, and he cleared his throat to be sure he sounded pleasant.

"You'll like Mrs. Harrison. She doesn't say much these days, but she could really use some prayer and some company. I can't be with her all the time."

"You're so kind to be there for her," she said with a smile, laying her soft palm on his knee not unlike the old woman had during the ceremony. Of course, this made him feel quite different.

Rion took his eyes off the road only long enough to look at her hand and then over at her face. She was smiling expectantly, so he returned it with a smile of his own.

"Do you like working at the plant store?" she asked.

He nearly winced at it being called 'the plant store,' but he didn't correct her and gave a simple response of: "Yes."

"Do you believe in God?"

He didn't respond immediately, and in the silence she quickly filled in, "I'm sorry if that's too personal."

"I think God is different for everyone."

"What do you mean?"

"Everyone worships something... the idea of something."

"So you... Like you don't..."

"Ah, there it is," Rion interjected quickly, turning the car into the driveway of the old woman so quickly that Mary gripped the side of her seat.

Rion shut the car off, getting out to open her door for her. He would have forgotten the box of care items had she not retrieved them herself from the backseat and placed them into his arms. The light inside illuminated the shadow of the aptly named cat, and Rion led her to the locked front door. He rapped on the door heavily with his knuckles and he could hear the cat shifting around inside.

"Mrs. Harrison?" he called.

He waited for a moment, leaning to pretend he was looking through the window.

"Do you think she's alright?"

"I'm going to go in the back door. Just wait here."

Mary nodded.

He walked around and crawled in through the broken window, acknowledging the foul aroma that emanated within. Although he had cleaned up the floor the best he could before temporarily disposing of the old woman's body, the scent remained. He left the carebox in the bathroom, sitting on top of the toilet seat, and walked through to open the front door.

Mary was waiting quietly and stepped inside. He closed the door behind her, both locking and deadbolting it, but she did not seem concerned about that. She *did* seem concerned about the odor.

"Oh..." she said as she entered the house, putting a hand to her mouth and choked out, "What's that smell?"

Rion explained calmly, "Her freezer went out a few weeks ago. Can't get the smell out. Everything went bad. Do you want to leave? We don't have to be here."

He reached out to grab her hand, just barely grasping her pinky with all of his fingers. She didn't pull away, but instead her entire body seemed to relax.

She shook her head, "Oh, no... It's fine. Where is she?"

He motioned to her and led her through the kitchen and then let her go ahead of him into the laundry. When she entered, she realized nearly immediately that it was a dead end and the room did not have another outlet.

He leaned across the doorway, using his body to block her exit. He erased the fake smile from his face as she turned around to face him. She seemed frightened now, already. Distrustful, where she previously had not.

"I lied to you," he admitted, quietly.

"You did?" she asked, taking a step away from him and further into the room.

He walked forward, putting his hand on the freezer.

"Yeah, her freezer isn't broken."

She laughed, smiling, "Oh, that's all?"

He opened the lid, yellow bulb inside illuminating the interior, which by now was soaked with red, and the bottom had a two inch thick layer of frozen juices. Mrs. Harrison's frozen body was crammed into such a position that he was almost surprised that Mary recognized it as a human corpse at all.

But judging by her scream, however, she most certainly did. It was almost amusing, but he didn't take the time to laugh. He'd add that to his bucket list: *take the moment to enjoy laughter.* She dove past him, and he was too slow to catch her. He threw his entire body in her direction but only managed to barely bump her with his hip. She hanged her side on the rusted edge of the old freezer lid, and he could even hear the tearing of her top as she stumbled out the door.

She was heading for the door but tripped over the cat and was down onto the floor as both her and the animal screamed in surprise. Rion was on top of her almost immediately, holding her hands together with one hand and using his other to push her hair out of her face.

"Shhhhh, shhh," he hissed. "It's okay. It's okay. Why are you running?"

"Just, please..." she begged, wiggling against the floor.

"You said you wanted to see Mrs. Harrison. Poor old lonely, forgotten Mrs. Harrison. I didn't lie about that part. She died in here. Actually, right... here."

He gently poked a stubborn stain on the floor, and from above you could still see the pale outline of her bloated carcass, now bleached to a faded umber. She squirmed more, tears pouring so heavily from her eyes that they ran down over her ears and pooled around her nose.

"How ironic," he said quietly, lifting himself as the wound on her side soaked through his own shirt. He took his finger and parted the torn fabric. "A wound not unlike your savior's, isn't it? Like Thomas, I can hardly believe you're here. With me. That I'm in your presence."

He stuck his index finger in the wound, blood gushed around it as he forced his way inside. He put the finger between his lips, both sucking off the metallic flavor of blood and moistening it to reenter the gash. She screamed, even as he put his free hand over her mouth, feeling her teeth just against his fingers.

"I've read the Bible," he assured her. "I have. You know, you just asked me earlier in the car... Do I believe in God? This is where I feel *closest* to God."

She snipped at his hand with her teeth and he put his arm instead across her throat. He could feel the slight crunch of cartilage against his skin, "Shhh, let me explain. Have you noticed how man struggles to define the angel?"

He waited for a response, raising his brows expectantly as he nodded at her, leaning closer to her face. She reluctantly shook her head from side to side. He noted the vessels in her eyes expanding, rupturing with pink and purple under both the pressure of his weight and the stress of the situation.

"The descriptions are terrifying. Unreal. 'Do not be afraid,' they have to say that. They have to tell man not to be afraid. Why?" He laughed, and he felt her startle beneath him. "This ... beautiful creation from God, a messenger, has to tell us not to fear them. You see... when you become that perfect thing, in death, most people won't see that beauty either."

She squealed a protest, jerking her knee up so harshly that she nearly toppled him over, but he continued, "They won't understand. You have to have some kind of... godliness to see an angel and comprehend its beauty. Do you understand? Do you? Are you ready for that? Don't worry, I will cherish you and your perfect image."

14
Polanski

David woke up late. He never slept in anymore, he always had something to do or somewhere to go. He would have still been sleeping this particular morning, however, if not for the sound of a neighbor's mower starting up somewhere nearby. His eyes snapped open, dry and crusty, and he had drooled on his pillow. He sat up groggily, rubbing the bridge of his nose between his eyes. He couldn't tell if his head was throbbing because he had slept so hard or if he had a sinus headache coming on. He had some trouble with alcohol years ago, and hadn't touched a drop to drink since he had gotten sober. Last night, however, he had taken a long swig of his mouthwash. He could still taste the hot flavor, and guilt, on his tongue. Guilt was good, he told himself. Guilt meant that he hadn't sunk back in yet. Not yet.

He got out of the bed and shuffled into the kitchen, where he could hear the static-buzz of bacon in a pan. Leah was standing at the stove in one of his t-shirts and a pair of paint stained jogging pants. Her hair was tossed up in a wild, frizzy bun that was lopsided and on the verge of falling to pieces. He stood and watched her as she busied herself at the stove, and had the refrigerator not groaned slightly as he leaned against it she may have not noticed he was there at all.

"Hey," she chirped. "You slept awfully late this morning. You okay?"

He rubbed his arm, moving over to pick up his work phone from the island and put it up in the cabinet. He left it there for just a moment before he retrieved it again, laying it back onto the countertop. She watched him curiously before putting the bacon on a paper towel to drain.

"It is your day off," she reminded him.

He liked to put his phone up some days, so that he couldn't be called for work related instances. Of course, with the recent events he had started keeping it on hand in case he was needed. This was different though. He even knew that, if needed, they would call his personal phone. If he was *really* needed... but it still didn't feel right.

"I know," he said. "I just want to know if they find Ji-su."

Leah looked past him, around the corner, and then nodded. "Any leads on where she might be?"

David swallowed back a sour taste at the back of his tongue. "They're dragging the lake."

The color seemed to drain from Leah's face and David immediately regretted telling her. He regretted knowing. He wished he hadn't known. Robichaud and Torres had gone out to talk to the man who owned the property at the lake, and talked to some of the people who rented property there. No one had seen or heard anything suspicious, but sure enough Ji-su's car had been parked in the lot when they arrived. One woman had seen a second car leave there in the early hours of the morning. Her dog had the shits, and she'd groggily noted the station wagon pulling out of the parking lot. A young man had even waved at her from the window, she'd said. She didn't remember what he looked like, dark hair maybe, but he was wearing a hoodie. She didn't get a plate number, but maybe it had started with a Y. She had assumed he was another renter, or she claimed she would have paid more attention.

"So you think she's...?"

David reached over to grab a piece of bacon, holding it up as though he would take a bite. The grit in his throat suggested that the saltiness would either quelch his need to vomit or elicit it. He shook his head from side to side. "Don't really know. Quentin is the one that jumped to dragging. He wants cadaver dogs out there too. I think he might know something... I don't know."

Leah didn't immediately respond. He could tell by subtle cues in her face and neck, and the way her blinking speed increased just a little, that she was trying not to cry. He tried to give her a minute before he went in, biting the bacon in small pieces without any enjoyment.

"Listen, I don't know if all of this is related to... stuff that's going on. We need to be a little more strict with Anna for a while. Where she's going, who she's with."

"David, that's not how we parent. She's sixteen years old, we have always agreed that her freedom and independence is very..."

"Leah," he said, a little more harshly than he intended. "This isn't about us being helicopter parents. This could be life or... this could be life or death. Just until we get some shit sorted out. Until I know this isn't some psycho after girls. You need to be careful too, please. Start locking the damn door. Carry your gun with you."

"I always carry it."

"I mean actually *have it with you*. There's a difference in carrying a gun and *carrying a gun*, and you know it."

She grabbed a piece of bacon, crunching it somewhat aggressively, "You're scaring me a little."

"I'm scared," he admitted. "I've got this really bad feeling, and it isn't because it's the Cat girl missing either."

"I'll talk to her about it, I promise."

He nodded, reassured some.

"Anna thinks she's run away," Leah said. "She told me that Ji-su had been talking about how she couldn't wait to get out of Whitebranch."

David just shook his head. "I don't think she ran away. I hope she did but I don't think that's the case."

"So tell me everything you know," she said, getting another piece of bacon.

"Leah, it's not a good idea for you to know everything. If anything gets out..."

"I won't tell anyone. I just want to know what you know."

David tried to pause so that it at least seemed like he had considered not telling her. He wanted to tell her, and she knew that. It was easier when he shared this burden with someone other than his coworkers, and Leah had a way of comforting him just by her presence and empathy alone, "She was talking to someone online. He told her about a party, one that didn't exist. Sent her this invitation that was fake. Ji-su's car was parked where the invite sent her, where she met him. She was nowhere to be found."

"At the lake?"

"Specifically at the levee. The old dam building."

"Why would she go there by herself? With someone she'd never met?"

"She's just a kid... like Anna. Kids don't think sometimes. They think they're untouchable. They think bad shit can't happen to them."

"That's usually true in a town like this... I grew up here, David. "

"I know. Hopefully we can take care of this pretty quick. Quentin and Torres are going to try to pin down where the guy was chatting with her from. They got an IP from Ji-su's tablet."

"Good. I hope she's just off fooling around with whoever it was. I'll take bad decisions over fatal ones any day. I don't even want to think about it. God, I don't even want to think about it."

"Have you talked to her mom?"

Leah shook her head. "No. She called but I couldn't answer. I didn't know what to tell her... what I *could* tell her."

"Don't tell her anything. Just... just let it work. We'll all have answers, hopefully soon."

His phone made a noise on the counter and both of them looked over at it, face down and now silent.

"They'd call if it was important," David assured her. "Let's get out of here. Matinee?"

"Yeah, what's on?"

"Doesn't matter. See if Anna wants to go with us."

David knew that she would have no interest in watching a movie with her parents, but he wanted to extend the invitation all the same. He wished she would go, even if she saw a different movie, but perhaps she would be safer here with the doors locked. His real goal, of course, was to get Leah out of the room for just a moment.

Leah walked into the hall, calling Anna's name as she did. As soon as she was out of sight, David grabbed the phone and flipped it over so he could see the screen. It was a message from Paltro. His hands were cold as he swiped the message open with his shaky thumb. It read:

Not good. Call me.

15
Quentin

Quentin hadn't gotten the return he'd hoped for on the IP of the person Ji-su had been chatting with. All they could tell him was that the messages were sent from a computer at the county library. It wasn't that clean shot that they had wanted, but at least it was something. It was further along than they had been before.

Quentin hadn't been to the library in years, although he felt some fairly fond memories of sticking his nose into every criminology and criminal justice book that he could get his hands on. The building seemed smaller, quieter, more dingy colored. He seemed to remember it buzzing with a sort of kinetic energy, the walls were stark white, and it seemed like the shelves had expanded into endless rows. Funny how things changed, even when they didn't.

As the two detectives entered the building, the atmosphere seemed to become more tense. A young man in headphones reading some manga in a recliner even got up and moved to the other side of the room. The police were still a fairly respected presence in this small town; it was the perks of being in a rural area. That didn't stop some people from avoiding walking on the same street as you, or in this instance, sitting on a chair in the same vicinity.

A small woman behind the counter turned her chair to face them, large brown eyes made twice as large behind her thick glasses. She could barely be seen over the counter from her place in her chair. A young man came out of the office behind the desk and she handed him a stack of papers and shooed him away as they approached.

"Good morning, Mrs. Gutierres. I'm Detective Quentin Robichaud and this is Detective Torres of the Whitebranch Police Department. We've got a few questions for you."

"Ma'am," Torres said in greeting.

"What can I help you with?" she asked.

Quentin continued, "Someone might have committed a crime, and they used the internet service here at the library five days ago, on the eighteenth. We were wanting to check your cameras to see if we can get an idea of who may have been using the computers here during that time."

"Cameras?" she asked.

"Yes, like your security system."

"We don't have a security system. I'm sorry I can't be of any help there."

"No cameras?" Quentin asked dubiously, looking back over his shoulder as though he could have seen them hanging from the eves from where he stood inside now. "You don't check IDs, nothing?"

The librarian snarled her lip at him, standing up although still a foot shorter than he was. She leaned towards him, using her palms flat on the desk to bring herself closer to his face.

"No. This is a library, officer. We have never had any need for cameras."

"Detective," he corrected coldly. "You never have any issues with vandals? Thieves? Kids just causing trouble?"

"Not enough to justify the cost of a security system. And anyway, if someone wants to steal a book, I'd say they probably needed it. They can have it."

"I appreciate your generous spirit, Mrs. Gutierres," Torres interjected politely, putting his shoulder in front of Quentin and forcing him backwards with it. Had they not been in the middle of something here, Quentin might have decked him right in his babyface. Stupid rookie.

"Do you have any record at all, maybe a log of sign-ons, for the computer systems or internet usage?"

Mrs. Gutierres immediately relaxed, shoulders moving down, growing smaller somehow and less venomous. Was he really in this deep? Although part of him really wanted to think that she was only relaxing because she identified somehow with the young Hispanic detective, some sort of racial solidarity... he knew it was because Torres was being polite, his body language was not aggressive, and his voice was kind and quiet. It wasn't forced either, Torres was just a nice guy. *Great, Robichaud. You're a dick.*

Quentin took this opportunity to also come off of the defensive, taking a breath as he told himself he needed to chill out. Torres was right, he was getting too wound up in this thing. Growling and snapping at librarians was going to get them nowhere, and he knew that. What was wrong with him?

"Yes," she responded, exhaling all of her negativity at once. "Yes. To use the internet services, they must sign in on the book, and sign out when done."

"Can you see who was using the internet at approximately 2pm on that day?"

She put her glasses on the end of her plump nose and started flipping back through the pages, moistening her thumb with her tongue to get better traction on the paper. She nodded her head.

"Easy enough, only a dozen people online that day and only one at that time."

She scanned down and suddenly paused, her brow furrowed and she tilted her chin down so far that it multiplied.

"Mrs. Gutierres?" Torres asked quietly, turning his left ear towards her.

She looked up, but not at Torres, instead fixing her eyes on Quentin as she slid the book towards him.

The checkout line read, "Quentin Robichaud :)".

"Fuck me," Quentin whispered, walking away from the desk as briskly as he could without seeming too urgent. He could hear Torres talking to the librarian again, but he didn't stop walking. He went straight into his cruiser, cranking the AC on like it was the dead of summer. He found himself glancing in the back seat just to be sure.

Torres joined him soon after, refusing to look over at him as he said quietly, "You okay?"

"No. I'm not okay."

Torres nodded. "That's alright too."

Quentin's phone rang in his pocket, and he withdrew it to see Paltro's name on the front. He looked over at Torres, who watched expectantly. Quentin needed a moment, just a fucking minute to process what had just happened. Instead, however, he found himself answering the call. He knew that if Paltro was calling him, it was already bad news. He might as well not delay the inevitable. He could tell by the way that Torres turned away from him, leaning against the door, busying himself by pretending to look out the window, that he knew too. He turned the air down so he could hear better, then answered the call.

"Hey, Robichaud. How did the library pan out?"

Quentin rested his forehead on his hand, propping his elbow up by the window, “Well, it didn’t. This son of a bitch is playing with us. He signed the fucking computer out *under my name.*”

“With a smiley face,” Torres interjected, as though this were valuable information.

“I’m afraid I don’t have good news either,” Paltro said, voice quiet. “We found the girl.”

16
Paltro

He hadn't been surprised when the dogs picked up the girl's scent and led them down to the water's edge. The boats hadn't even left the dock yet, it had taken more time than anticipated to clear the waters and area of civilians. The dog descended the hill, tail waving above it like a solemn flag. It wagged only for balance correction, and it seemed like even the animal took no joy in this. Not until he found the body and was rewarded with a tug toy and a ruffle around the neck. She had washed up among some of the largest rock debris from the old building, Deen expected.

He had initially thought that perhaps she had been tossed out from a higher elevation and the gentle current had slowly placed her here to be found. Her hair was matted with leaves and dirt, but she was remarkably intact and unharmed. Deen saw the signs of strangulation immediately, even without taking the time to really examine her. This was no drowning accident, and he suspected she might have indeed been a victim of the same man as the other two girls.

He had them load her into the back of his van. He had taken the time to text Polanski (the polite thing to do, since it was his day off) and call Robichaud. He didn't like to be the bearer of bad news to Polanski when he should be enjoying time with his family, but he knew this was one of those situations when he would want to know as soon as possible. A call in response to his text came in shortly after the girl had fully ascended the bank on the stretcher.

"Hey, sorry I don't have better news," Deen said, looking out over the still lake water. It was like a sheet of unpenetrated glass, black and cerulean and green.

"Can you at least tell me it was an accident?" he asked quietly.

Deen shook his head, and although Polanski couldn't see the gesture over the phone, he felt the silence was answer enough.

"Shit," Polanski said. "Shit, shit, shit."

"I know. I haven't left yet, but it looks like she was strangled or hanged. Can't tell for sure yet. She was in the water."

"Is Robichaud there?"

"Not yet, but they're on their way. Apparently the library might have been a bust. I'll get back with you. Do you want to tell the family? I know your daughter is close."

"No," Polanski responded, almost desperately.

"That's okay, I can have..."

He cut him off, "I mean... Yes. Yeah, I'll do it. It's better they hear it from me. I don't want to do it. I shouldn't have to do this."

"I know. Gotta go, I'll be in touch."

The call ended.

As he started to head back up the bank, he noticed something on a stack of rocks. It was a precarious little arrangement of flat stones, a tiny cairn on the shore. At the pinnacle, as though presented like a sigil, was a game piece. Paltro retrieved a glove and bag out of his pocket, plucking up the small thing and depositing it inside. Another calling card - so it *was* him, and he wanted them to know it.

He drove to the morgue with the dead girl in tow, looking at the black bag in his rear view. He heard a wet squelch every time he took a turn a little too fast. Every time he braked a little too hard, the damp body sloshed.

"I'm sorry," he said to her. "I get a little desensitized to this sort of thing. Part of the job, I guess. I just end up dealing with things my own way."

Like this, he thought to himself, *talking to dead people.*

"But it's always harder when it's someone so young. I imagine what you'd go on to do, who you might've been, what might've been different for everyone if you'd still been here. You know, the butterfly effect. You might've thought you were nobody, but you'll keep me up at night for years and years."

He pulled into the morgue parking lot beside the little silver sedan that belonged to Tresa. She exited the building like she'd been waiting for him at the door. She smiled, leaning over the rail to wave at him. He raised a hand to her, returning the smile softly. She was still wearing her black EMT uniform, and she had sunken pits around her eyes. He should be flattered, really. She didn't have to come help him here, especially working around her other job. Neither of them ever admitted the mutual attraction, and sometimes Deen would talk himself through the scenario just to rebuff her requests for a date again. *Life is short, Deen*. He told himself as he shut the van off.

"She on a gurney?" Tresa asked as he stepped out of the van.

"Nah, she was down in the water, got her on a stretcher. Want to give me a hand?"

She nodded, propping the door to the morgue open before she skipped down the ramp and helped him pull the body out.

"Is this the girl then? The one that's been missing?"

"Yeah, I guess you heard she's friends with Polanski's daughter."

"*Was* friends with Polanski's daughter."

"Nah," Deen said, kicking the doorstop away as he walked by. "Even if she's dead, they're still friends. Death don't kill love."

She smiled at him. "You're such a romantic."

They hoisted the girl onto the cold tabletop together, unzipping the bag and slowly transferring her out of it and off of the stretcher. Deen retrieved a pair of scissors and slowly began cutting away her clothes, which were intact. Some of the other victims had been missing articles or shown signs of real struggle, but other than the bruise on her cheek and ligature around her neck, there were no signs on the surface. Sequins flew through the air with each slice of the twin blades, clattering to the floor.

"So about dinner..." she started.

"What about it?"

"Invitation still stand?"

He laughed as he started gowning up and putting on his gloves. As she came over to tie the back for him he parroted her response from when he had last asked her, "I'll have to check my schedule."

She ignored the slight dig, snapping a glove around her wrist, "I'll be around seven tomorrow? I know a good Thai place if you're up for a little drive."

He nodded as though he would consider it, and they started working together on the girl.

They had hardly finished their organ assessment when there was a knock on the door. Deen looked up at the security camera feed on the corner of the counter, but the screen was so fuzzy it was hard for him to tell who was there. He could only see that someone was.

"Will you check and see who that is?"

Tresa peeked her head around the corner to investigate before calling back to him, "Robichaud and Torres."

Deen nodded, pulling off his gloves, "Thought it might be. You go ahead and take off. I gotta talk to them about a few details."

"Don't want me to hang around and help after they leave?"

"It'll be a long night, you need some sleep."

She seemed disappointed, jerking the glove off of her hand and tossing it into the waste.

"Seven tomorrow," he repeated to her, and she reluctantly smiled before she left.

As she went out, the two detectives came in. Deen noticed their frustrated demeanors and he placed a sheet over top of Ji-su. He knew that they didn't know the girl like Polanski did, but it was still a young girl. Torres seemed to relax some when she was no longer visible, but Robichaud was ever tense.

"So he signed the computer out under your name?" Deen asked, starting the conversation out there.

"Yes. So he knows who I am, who we are. That we're after him. He's toying with us."

Deen hummed in his throat, "I wonder why he is targeting you?"

He could tell by the look on Robichaud's face that he didn't know. Deen suspected that maybe it was because Robichaud was the most active in the community, the senior officer. Polanski had too much baggage, prior issues, and he never talked to the media. There wasn't as much *glory* there, maybe.

Robichaud didn't answer, but instead asked, "Is it the same guy then?"

Deen nodded, "I think so."

"Was she raped?"

"There aren't any signs of rape so far."

"So it isn't sexual..."

"It's always sexual... The girls were all strangled, suffocated. There's a climax to asphyxiation." Deen insisted. "Just because there isn't always penetration doesn't..."

Robichaud snapped, "Jesus Christ, Paltro. I don't need to know. I'm just trying to figure out this guy's motive. What's making him tick."

Deen would have argued that if he really wanted to know, he had to try and think like the killer. He knew Robichaud though, and patience was never his forte. They never came here to hear Deen's side, his opinions. They just wanted the information he had gathered: cold and cut. Clinical. tldr. *Bland*. He was just here to answer questions with short responses and, admittedly, sometimes it pissed him off.

"Was there a game piece with her?" Torres asked.

Deen nodded again, "Yes, placed where we would be sure to find it... on a stack of stones by the body. I initially thought her body had washed ashore, but I think she was placed down the embankment, maybe even rolled down. He wanted her to be found, and he wanted the piece to be found. He took some time there, this wasn't a murder-and-run. He's pretty brave."

"He's stupid. He keeps sticking around a murder scene that long, and someone will be able to ID him."

"Already have a rough description of the car," Deen agreed. "Wood paneled station wagon. Good condition. Newer model."

Robichaud scoffed, "How many of those can there possibly be in Delton County."

"Twenty-seven," Deen responded dryly, much to Robichaud's dismay.

"Can I see it?" Torres piped.

Deen paused, looking up at him with piqued interest, "See what?"

"The piece."

He studied the young detective for several moments. Deen saw the value in the way that Torres analyzed things, perhaps because Polanski was right: he really did think a little more creatively than everyone else. Maybe Torres *was* onto something.

"Yeah... why?"

Torres shifted, eyes moving over to Robichaud nervously, "I don't know."

Robichaud also shifted, speaking as Deen turned to retrieve the bag, "He left the matching game piece on my vehicle. With a drawing of an acorn."

"An acorn?" Deen asked curiously, handing the bag to Torres.

"Yeah. The worst part is he left it on my car when we were at the Cat's house. Interviewing the parents. He did it *while we were inside.*"

"Ballsy... and, you're right, stupid," Deen said quietly, but then he noticed Torres' expression. He seemed somehow frightened, perturbed. Deen looked down at the piece in his hand, but he saw nothing extraordinary about it. He walked forward, putting his hand up on Torres' shoulder.

"You all right, Torres?"

Torres didn't answer immediately, but instead showed Robichaud the piece. Deen noted that Robichaud didn't immediately react to what Torres was holding. Then, all at once, he jumped in his skin. He dug through his pockets, rabbit-earing them inside-out, dropping his cigarettes and folded receipts to the floor until he found it. He withdrew the piece in a shaky hand, holding it up to the one in the bag. Paltro moved alongside them to examine the two side by side.

"They're... different." he noted.

"A peony and a lotus..." Torres said.

"What does that mean?"

Torres' voice was hardly above a whisper, "There's another girl out there."

"Fuck," Robichaud snapped, throwing the piece across the room. Paltro watched it clatter to the opposite wall, making a note of where it landed. He'd add it to evidence, even if Robichaud didn't want to. Paltro liked things to be neat and organized at work, available for reference purposes when needed.

"I thought that was Ji-su's piece. I thought it was her matching piece. He's trying to tell us where this girl is."

"Not a very good hint..." Torres said.

Robichaud pulled out the drawing, a simple shaded acorn on top of a half circle. Deen shrugged his shoulders, seemed simple enough to him: "Oak Hill."

"Oak Hill... Where is that?"

"Outside of town, Oak Hill Road. Oak Hill Community, little unincorporated area. There's maybe ten families that live out that way." Deen responded. "Pretty poor area. Even comparatively."

Robichaud nodded, running a hand through his hair, "Alright, then. Torres, we need to get on it. We'll call Polanski..."

"It's his day off..."

"I don't give a shit. You don't *get* a day off when shit like this is happening."

"Robichaud, I would be careful about engaging... playing this game," Deen warned. This was something that perhaps would have been best brought up in private, but he wanted Torres to hear him. He wanted him to know the danger. It didn't sit well with him, the fact that the killer seemed to know who he was. If he was brave enough to leave notes and trinkets, and he was clearly stalking the detective... this wasn't safe. Deen knew that Robichaud wouldn't take him seriously, and he knew better than to suggest they let someone else handle this case. The FBI, the TBI... anyone. This was too close to home. Deen wasn't married, Tresa was the closest thing he had to a significant other. His family was all gone, save some distant cousins and this-and-that twice-removed... and he *still* didn't like this. Robichaud had a wife, Polanski had a kid.

"Oh, I'm going to play his fucking game."

Deen nodded, not an ounce of surprise on his face. "Of course you are."

17
Quentin

Despite acting as eager and fired up as he had to Paltro's face, Quentin had never been more nervous in his life. It wasn't even that he felt threatened by this psycho. It wasn't that there was suddenly some element of personal danger. He was worried about not catching him fast enough. He was worried about *losing* the game. That was what this was, right? A competition, a challenge. This was something that he had no choice but to win, and with serious stakes. If he didn't catch this bastard, and beat him at this game that he had *challenged him to* then it would be his fault that more women died.

These thoughts, of course, were what brought him here outside of Dr. Norrington's office, although it was not one of his regular days. He needed to talk to someone about all of this. About these emotions he had. He needed her to somehow convince him that it wasn't his fault, that it wouldn't be his fault. He sent Torres alone to drive down Oak Hill to look for anything suspicious. He didn't expect him to find much, but he couldn't help but think that Paltro's guess at the clue was likely correct.

His phone rang, but it was not his work phone. He fumbled around in his pocket for the personal phone that usually remained silent. No one called it but telemarketers and his wife, and sure enough... it was Emily. He was frustrated even at the prospect of talking to her right now, something else to compound on his stress, but he hadn't talked to her in... How long had it been? A couple of days? Even though he had slept at home most nights, in the same bed, brushed his teeth in same sink, he didn't know if they'd really spoken.

He answered reluctantly, "Hey."

"Hey," she responded. "Where are you?"

"Work stuff... a lot going on. We found a dead girl today, murdered. Just a kid."

"Did you sleep at the office last night?"

"I didn't sleep anywhere, I had a lot to look over."

"So you're at the station now? I could meet you outside and we can do lunch."

"I'm not at the office right at this very moment..."

There was a long pause, and Quentin picked at a string on his pant leg. She finally spoke again, voice cracking before she recovered, "Quentin, are you seeing someone else?"

Why did he feel guilty? He had never cheated on Emily in his life. He had plenty of opportunities, even maybe some chances that he had been tempted to take, but he had never betrayed her in that way. Why did it feel like he was hiding something? Was it because she didn't know he was seeing a therapist? Was it because he felt like he couldn't talk to her about his job? Because it stressed him out to just be in the same room as her? He wasn't cheating on her... but he wished it was as simple as infidelity.

"Quentin?"

He realized he hadn't said anything, and wasn't any closer to figuring out how he was going to respond. He took a deep breath, watching as Dr. Norrington pulled into her parking space and started towards the building. She paused on the sidewalk in front of his vehicle, seeming surprised that he was there. She looked down at her watch, sighed, and tapped the face with her finger. He nodded.

"Listen, we'll talk tonight. I promise."

She didn't say goodbye, or hang up the phone. He wanted her to hang up first, but instead he found himself cancelling the call to rush into the therapist's office.

Dr. Norrington was sitting in her chair with a notebook ready, legs crossed. She watched him expectantly, motioning to the chair across from her.

"Quentin," she said in greeting. "I'm surprised to see you here today. Is everything okay?"

"You got a minute?" he asked quietly, sitting down so heavily that the chair scooted backwards.

"Of course," she responded. "It is unusual for you to walk in."

Quentin wished she wouldn't bring it up, the fact that he might be acting out of some sort of desperation. He wanted her to just listen, although he knew it wasn't that simple and that wasn't her job.

"So, tell me what's going on," she insisted in the silence.

"This guy... he's messing with me."

"Who is?" she asked.

"*The guy.*"

"This perpetrator you've been after?"

"He does not know you. His actions are random. He does not know you exist separately from the department. He is not motivated by..."

"Oh, he knows me. He left a clue..." He paused, waving his hands in the air. 'Clue' sounded like such Scooby-Doo bullshit, "A note. He left a note on my car, he logged a computer out at the library under my name, he..."

"Quentin."

He stopped, looking up at her.

"I'm going to get him. I'm close. A woman saw him and his car leaving the scene of a crime."

"I think you're a fine detective, and I do think you will apprehend him. This type of criminal always gets too confident, and they slip up."

"When we catch him, it won't be because he slipped up... I don't need him to slip up."

"I wasn't suggesting you couldn't catch him. I just know this type..."

"You don't know this type. There's something different about this one."

"You seem to feel like you know a lot about him."

Quentin laughed, "His face. I can almost see him. I know his shoe size, hair color, build... I know what style of vehicle he drives."

"Are you making time for yourself? Outside of work, for hobbies?"

He scoffed, "Yeah. I don't have hobbies anymore... This whole thing is affecting my marriage."

Cecilia looked up from her notebook. It wasn't often that Quentin talked about anything other than work. It seemed to consume him and his every thought. She knew that he was married but had scarcely heard him mention his wife during their sessions. This was a promising new angle.

"This honesty is refreshing, Quentin. We have to remember that our actions have consequences, we have to consider that *before* the action. We have to think about other people and how they are affected by the things we decide to do."

"What do I do? At this point, I'm starting to think it's too late."

"Spend time with her. Just show her that her time and presence is valuable to you. Make her a priority again. You have to counteract this neglect."

"It isn't just neglect. She thinks I'm having an affair."

She looked over the top of her tortoiseshell glasses at him. She ventured to even think that if he was having an affair, it would at least mean he had some kind of interaction with people outside of his career.

"Are you?"

"No." He seemed surprised that she asked the question, and his stomach sank at the thought. The wound from the conversation earlier was still fresh. "No, of course not. I don't have time for an affair, even if I wanted to have one."

"So why does she think this? Have you tried talking about it?"

"She says I'm distant, thinks I'm thinking about someone else. Spending too much time away from home, late nights. It's all work though. All work. I'm never anywhere else. Work, or here. She doesn't even know I am still coming to therapy."

"It sounds to me like you are having an affair."

"You know better than that..."

She sat up in her seat, leaning towards him. "An affair isn't always physical, Quentin. You can have an emotional affair, where you're giving more of your time and dedication to someone else. It sounds to me like you are having an affair. You need to work on your marriage, step back, and reevaluate where you're spending your emotional support. Who you're spending it on. You might as well be having an affair... with him."

Quentin looked at her, chewing his lip nervously. This was perhaps the most therapist sounding shit she'd ever said to him, and he didn't like it.

He stood staring at his own front door like a nervous kid on a first date. Emily's car was parked out front, and he knew she'd seen him pull up. It was too late at this point to back the car back out and go sit somewhere, anywhere else. He dreaded the confrontation; he didn't want to fight with her. He would rather have no interaction at all than a negative interaction. But this was something he had to do.

He reached down and unlocked the door with his key, knowing the click of the deadbolt could be heard all through the inside of the house. No turning back now. He went inside, walking slowly through the foyer and into the living room, where he found her sitting on the couch watching a movie.

"Not at work today?" he asked.

She didn't respond immediately, so he made his way around, sitting next to her, reaching over to pause the film with the remote.

She looked over at him, "It's Tuesday. Do you know what day it is? It's *Tuesday*."

Tuesday was her day off during the week. Quentin didn't know if he'd forgotten, or if he just didn't know what day it was anymore.

"I'm sorry I've been so busy," he said quietly.

She nodded, but she didn't look at him.

"I am." He set the remote down. "I don't mean to take away from you, from us. It's just..."

"Your new case. I know. You've said."

"There's just so much going on, Em. Something that could be bigger."

She turned her full attention to him now, angling her body towards him as she folded her feet up underneath herself and reached over to clasp his hands in hers. He squeezed them back, looking into her soft brown eyes. She looked like she pitied him. He didn't want her to, but she did, he could see it.

"You can talk to me about it, Quentin. It may help."

"You don't want to know about all of this," he insisted.

"You're right. I don't want all the grisly details, I don't need all of the horror. I just need to help you, because I need you. I need you to stop isolating yourself so I can have my husband back."

He took a deep breath. "We aren't getting any closer to getting the guy. He's careful, he must wear gloves, and he cleans up. Sometimes he moves the bodies, sometimes leaves them. It doesn't look like he keeps any souvenirs. We have seen him on security footage once, have a witness that saw him leaving the scene of one murder... but nothing concerete. He's a fucking ghost."

"A ghost?" she looked at him dubiously.

"Well, that's what Polanski called him. He isn't wrong. We don't even know where to start. If it has Polanski rattled..."

She laughed, the warmth made his heart flutter, "You're talking about David Polanski. Do you remember why we had grocery store cake at our wedding?"

Quentin stifled laughter. He was surprised at how easily it came, how he felt relaxed all at once. Why had he dreaded this? The ease of conversation, the way he *loved* her even when they were just talking. Why had this become something he dreaded? How had this shadow crept in so silently?

"He fell through our three-tier wedding cake," She was giddy, suddenly flooded by memories that he could nearly see playing behind her eyes. "...and then, do you remember when the plumber came to his house *as scheduled* and he thought someone was breaking in?"

"Yeah, he stuffed a knife down the back of his pants to defend himself with and cut his asscrack. He showed me his stitches every day for a week."

"Honestly, he was lucky that the plumber was there to drive him to the ER."

"The plumber is lucky he didn't have his duty belt close by, he might've shot him."

"Or he would've stuffed it down the front of his pants and shot off his..."

Quentin snorted, "Okay, so maybe I shouldn't be consulting with Polanski as much."

It felt good, the stories and the laughter. He almost wished she would've left it at that. He had broken the ice by sharing, and now they were reminiscing about better times. Instead, Emily went on, bringing the conversation back to the case. He knew she did this because she knew it was important to him, but she didn't understand how sticky its fingers were. She didn't understand how he needed to escape it, although part of him refused to allow it.

"So, why does this killer do it then? What's his motive?"

"Why do any of these psychos do what they do? Get off on it, I guess. Power trip. I haven't thought about it much."

"Maybe... you need to think like him. To figure out why he does it. To get ahead. If you don't, you'll always be chasing him. A few steps behind."

He didn't want to try to think like him, that was the last thing on Quentin's mind. He didn't want to imagine what went through the mind of a man who did these horrific things.

"Listen, I don't want to talk about this anymore. I want to do something for us. What are you doing after work on Friday?"

She seemed surprised, even stammering over her words. "I... Nothing. I'm not doing anything."

"When I get off, I'll come home and we'll go to Sugar's. What do you think? We haven't been in forever."

"It really has been a long time. Is it even still open?"

"Oh, yeah."

"Do you still need a reservation?"

Quentin nodded. "I'll handle all of it. I'll text you when I get off and we'll go from there."

"Okay," she said, smiling. "Yeah. I'd like that."

His excitement did not last long. After the movie resumed and they sat together to finish, Quentin's work phone went off. When he didn't answer, it went off again and again.

18

Torres

He kept telling himself that he didn't mind being sent to do this kind of thing. He had gotten valuable information when he'd been sent to find Olivia Brown's car. He would like to think that he was being given some independence because he was trusted and valued. He knew that wasn't the case, however. He was sent to the place least likely to have anything substantial... to get him out of the way. They didn't want to hear about his theories, they didn't want him following them around, and they never wanted his damn coffee.

He pulled down Oak Hill Road, taking note of everything around him. The first road he came by had a little house on the left. It was tucked back and nearly hidden by a small grove of trees but otherwise surrounded by fields that appeared mostly unused now. The grass was chest high and the thickets had started creeping out of the wilds and across the pasture. He drove on down the winding road, which sloped to both the left and right, exposing a few little homes as it wound around the mountainside. Pastures faded into rocky craigs, and then there was hardly any roadside at all.

"We'd never find a body out here," Lucas said to himself, allowing his car to go around the mountain until he came to a rest stop. He pulled the car in and turned it around, trying to peer around the precarious curve to his right so he could drive back down the mountain. He started to pull out, but a car came around the corner so quickly that it nearly skidded into the guardrail. His heart leapt in his throat as their honk faded into the distance.

He put a hand to his chest before pulling out onto the road, committing fully and approaching a speed that would keep him from getting rear-ended by another speeding teenager. He drove by the pastures again, this time more slowly, scanning for anything suspicious at all. He halfway expected a giant sign that said PLEASE, LOOK HERE.

Ahead, he saw a woman crossing the road to check her mailbox. He came to a stop in the road, rolling the window down. The woman seemed hesitant, suspicious, and she looked both ways before approaching the driver's side.

"Yes?"

"Sorry to bother you, ma'am. I'm Detective Torres with the Whitebranch Police Department. Just wondering if you'd noticed any weird characters down here lately, or anyone snooping around where they shouldn't be."

She shrugged her shoulders, "Nothing more than usual."

"What's usual?"

"Druggies stealing stuff. I called about my husband's chainsaw. Do you not remember that?"

Lucas, of course, would have not known about a woman calling to report a stolen chainsaw. He opened his mouth to respond, caught off guard by her retort. She went on, waving her hand in the air, "I don't expect y'all to find it... Sometimes something sets off my motion lights in the back. We got some of those solar powered things, you know?"

Lucas nodded, glancing in his rearview to see if anyone was coming up the road behind him.

"Sometimes they go off at night, but it might be an animal or something, I guess. We keep everything locked up now. We should've before, but you don't worry about things like that out here. Not until you get burned."

"Very true. Hard to remember sometimes that our little corner of the world is still part of... well, the world."

"Nasty people. Nasty place," she muttered, stuffing her mail under her armpit.

He nodded again and then raised his hand. "Well, thank you. I'm sorry about your chainsaw. If you think of anything, or see anything, just call down and let us know."

"Have a good day," she said, passing in front of the vehicle and into her own driveway.

Lucas drove another little way down the road, still watching everything intently as it passed by. He pulled into a random driveway, coasting across the drive and stopping at the little house that sat in the middle of a slightly overgrown yard. Some small dogs, short and long with frizzy coats and bobbed tails, barked enthusiastically. He didn't get out but instead rolled his window down as the owner of the house wandered out onto the deck. He raised a hand as though to tell Lucas to just wait where he was.

"Good morning, officer," the man said in greeting. He was young, tall and slim with a red beard that mostly grew below his jaw, missing just a few teeth. He was friendly, not just cordial but also polite. Lucas leaned out of the car window enough to let his fingers dangle above the dogs, who came with their owner to greet him. They jumped up, mostly licking the air between them, but occasionally nibbling softly. Their tails patted dusty swirls up around the man's bare feet.

"I'm Detective Torres, just wanted to see if you'd noticed anyone down this road recently. Someone that you may not recognize, or someone behaving oddly."

The man pulled his lower lip in over his bottom teeth and put his hands on his hips. "How recently?"

Lucas squinted up at him through the sun. "Something come to mind?"

The man shifted and looked down the road across a few of the rolling fields. "Yeah, but it wasn't real recent. Might not be anything."

"I'd rather hear about it, Mister...."

"Marcum."

"Mr. Marcum."

He flung his hand in the air towards the fields that would eventually border the highway, "The other night my old lady was here and heard something as she was walking to her car. Scared her real bad."

"What was it?"

"I figured a fox, but it called a lot. More than they usually do, but it was that same noise you know. That blood-curdling scream. She called me later that night and said some guy almost hit her peeling out up the road when she was going to work."

"What night was that?"

"I don't know for sure. I mean, I could find out."

"An estimate is fine for now."

"Maybe a week ago? Two? Was on a Friday night for sure."

"Thank you for your time. Would you mind if I parked and walked the field there? Where you think you heard it?"

"Oh that don't belong to me. I only own the house here and the half acre it sits on. That all belongs to Glenda Harrison. She's kind of a sour old bitty, but she might let you go look."

"Thanks, Mr. Marcum. I'll go check with her."

The man reached down to pick up one of the dogs, brow furrowing with concern. "You ain't looking for a fox... are you?"

Lucas noticed the concern in the man's eyes. He knew that word was getting out that something sinister was afoot. Three dead girls, the last one just a kid. Lucas shook his head slowly, side to side. It was such a small movement that Mr. Marcum wasn't even sure it happened. Even as Lucas pulled out of the driveway, careful to avoid the barking dogs, he noticed the man standing in the yard watching him leave.

He went on down the road, pulling into the driveway adjacent to the mailbox that read 'Harrison' in faded letters. There were no cars parked out front, and he wondered if she was even home. He got out of the car slowly, a gentle breeze blowing a set of wooden windchimes on the porch.

He knocked on the door but gained no response, leaning to try and peek past the frilly curtain into the window.

"Mrs. Harrison?" he called.

There was still no response.

Lucas hesitantly walked around the side of the house by an overgrown garden. The only identifiable plant was pokeweed; it towered far overhead, and the ground beneath was littered with purple berries. He noticed the bathroom window was open, and he nervously peeked inside it as well. He expected the old woman to peek around the corner and accuse him of being a peeping tom. The inside of the house was still and quiet. There was an odor, but it was faint, and Lucas couldn't really place it. Maybe cat piss and mildew. He had a bad feeling about all of this.

He walked around the backside of the house to the small yard that had a utility line stretched between two metal poles, and beyond that lay the fields where the fox had screamed.

"Just start walking," he told himself. "If the old woman wants you to get out of the field, she'll come out and tell you. Waste of time if you don't start looking."

He headed out towards a tall tree that stood naked against the grey sky. He could see the Marcum house across a couple of hills, dogs still barking in the distance. He noted that about halfway across was a gate that led from Oak Hill Road into the field, and it was hanging rusted from the fence posts. That could have very well been where whoever nearly ran over Marcum's girlfriend. That or they were pulling out of Harrison's. Maybe Mrs. Harrison was a drag racer in her spare time. He amused himself with the thought of an old woman, barely able to see over the steering wheel anymore, burning rubber up and down the highway every night.

He tripped once, falling onto his knees and coating them with damp soil. He thought it had been a rock or branch at first, but on reevaluation he found it to be a rut in the ground, somewhere where a car had driven through and gotten a little too deep in the sod and kicked up some earth. He crawled on his knees for a moment to find the direction the car had been traveling, and he found himself pointed at that same ominous tree.

He stood there without the nerve to move for several moments. A trickle of sweat left his hairline and dripped down into the crevasse of his nose. He wiped it away so that he wouldn't snuff it up his nostril. He thought he could see something there, at the base of the tree. He had already decided that it was a body, somehow he just knew. He found himself walking towards it, the heaviness of dread making every step slower than the last. It was only when he stepped on a carpet of acorns that he brought himself to a halt again. He swallowed back thickness in his throat. The acorns, and the hill, and the little peony.

"You're a cop. You're a damn *detective*. Suck it up," he whispered harshly to himself, gritting his teeth. That same soft breeze blew from behind him, and he used its gentle pressure to start forward again.

It *was* a body. Maybe it had once been a girl. He couldn't tell anymore, and he didn't get close enough to identify it, just close enough to confirm it was human. She was propped up against the trunk, skull laying in her own lap. It still had a good layer of meat on it, but the eyeballs were gone. The birds in the branches above cawed at him. Her skin was mostly green and black, opening up to release pressure.

He started walking away much faster than he had approached, fumbling with the lock on his cell phone with his shaky fingers. He clicked

Robichaud's number, and the screen flashed No Service. He clicked Polanski's, hoping somehow it would go through for him, but got the same indicator.

"Piece of crap. There's a freaking cellular tower right freaking there." He motioned at the metal monolith blinking in the distance.

He skipped up the steps to the back door, knocking on it quickly.

"Glenda Harrison, please open up. This is the police." He panted into the door crack. He banged on it with his fists again, and he found that the door popped open. He shoved it open, finding it didn't have enough clearance on the bottom and dragged on the swollen kitchen floor.

"Mrs. Harrison," he called loudly into the house. "My name is Detective Lucas Torres. I need to use your phone."

The house was eerily quiet, except for a consistent tapping somewhere past the kitchen to his left.

"Mrs. Harrison?"

He walked through the room, looking for a phone to use. He found the laundry room and discovered that it was the source of the rattle. The lid on a large freezer was not closed completely, slightly ajar, and the element was working hard to keep everything inside cold. A small puddle of water had formed around the base, suggesting that it had been leaking for some time now. He entered slowly, pushing down on the lid to try to get it to suction close. It bounced back against him. He looked behind him, for a moment having forgotten about the peony-girl under the tree.

He lifted the icebox open to help adjust the lid, and that's when he realized that it wasn't a misaligned seal or a too-large box of hamburger patties. It was a body that had been folded neatly beside an equally dead Mrs. Harrison. As rigor mortis had set in, she had pushed upwards and popped the lid open, a last call for help.

Lucas couldn't remember walking out of the house and up to the highway. He was enveloped in a drunk-like delirium, stumbling and sick and out of his head. He didn't know why he didn't get on his radio or why he didn't drive somewhere to get service. All he knew was that before he realized it, he was standing in the middle of the highway, and the tears started when he couldn't get Robichaud to answer.

19
Rion

What made the spider's silk so strong? Was it structural? Compositional? Was it some sort of modern, scientific "magic" that just couldn't be explained yet? Rion wondered these things as he stared at the spider web attached to the head of one of the plant sprinklers. Even as it was beaten by the force of the water, it stayed mostly intact. Even after the spider had been drowned and blown away, it remained. He was immensely curious, and sometimes he dwelled on the answers to questions like this one. In the grand scheme of things, what did it matter? But right now, that's what he wanted to know.

He laid his badge under the front desk and went to punch out, meeting Evan at the clock. He was standing there, doing absolutely nothing, right in front of the clock. He turned around after he noticed Rion standing there and smiled, "O-Rion. Hey, buddy. How's it going?"

Rion tried to move around Evan, who cut him off and tapped the time on the clock. Two minutes until close. He was really going to stand there and milk the clock, wasn't he? He could feel a violent anger rising up behind his own eyes as he looked at Evan, although his face betrayed not a smidge of that emotion. He imagined slamming his head into that perfectly poised corner of the time clock, how he could pierce right into his temple with the screwdriver he had left lying in aisle six, or how Evan had a self-proclaimed peanut allergy and he would take great pleasure in force-feeding him cashews in the break room.

One more minute.

"Was your mama like a hippie or something? Orion is a weird name to saddle a kid with. I did go to school with a girl named Stardust or something though." Evan mused. "Now she's *on the stardust,* if you know what I mean. But Orion isn't even your name is it? Why don't we call you Teddy?"

Orion was the name of the great hunter in Greek mythology. He sometimes thought his mother had a moment of enlightenment when she had chosen his middle name. First name Theodore, less enlightened, but he had never gone by the given name anyway. It was always Rion, which on the tongue sounded just like the more common Ryan... and usually elicited little attention. Evan, of course, was going to make a scene about anything. Rion wondered where he had snooped to discover his full name, and he didn't like it.

"It's time," Rion said, motioning at the clock as it now sat upon an even time.

Evan quickly punched in his number and then patted Rion's back as he walked by. Rion flinched, nearly sick at the contact. He reached up to rub the spot he'd touched, like he could smudge the filth away. He clocked out quickly, and exited the building without loitering.

Once he was outside, he found himself walking down the street instead of directly to his parked vehicle. He was headed to Page One. It was a little bookstore nestled between two defunct stores: one an apothecary and natural remedies shop, and the other, once a boutique clothing spot. The town was full of these abandoned buildings. There was plenty of space for expansion and new businesses, but so many old owners would rather let their buildings rot than see them turn into another vape shop or sell them to some young entrepreneur wanting to open a new age shop full of crystals and smudge sticks... and so they did: they crumbled.

Page One had swapped hands a few times over the years, and now the owners were two pleasant men that frequently popped in and talked with customers. They kept candy or fresh cookies on the counter, and there was a little table in the corner with sweet tea or coffee. Rion didn't care much for them, although everyone else in the town thought they were the greatest people. If he wanted to go buy a book, he didn't want to have to talk to anyone. Today he slipped through the door, the abrasive bell jingling overhead as he did. A girl behind the counter, dressed head-to-toe in black, looked up at him from a book. She didn't greet him initially, and he moved on to the Nature and Animals aisle.

He scanned over the titles slowly. They ranged from the playful story about a dog's ridiculous adventures to analyzing the complex societal structure of the Hyaenidae family. He continued moving down the rows until he came to the section about insects. Spiders were not insects, but...

"Can I help you find something?"

He turned around to see the girl from the counter standing behind him now. He didn't initially respond, distracted by the graphic on the front of her t-shirt. It was a flat, basic representation of Ed Gein. He found it incredibly fascinating that people were so obsessed with killers. Not some character in a book, but *real* killers. Like him. Actually, now that he thought about it, Ed was more of a collector. He had only killed a couple of people. Rion was going to be far more prolific... He already was. Would people be wearing his face on their shirts years from now? Nah, he reminded himself that would require him to be caught... and he had no intentions of that happening.

The girl crossed her arms over her chest. "Eyes up here."

Rion was a little annoyed that the girl seemed to think that he was looking at her breasts, although they were quite large. He didn't *have* to look down to see them. He motioned to her, "I was admiring your shirt."

"Oh," she said, looking down and pulling the shirt as though to make the graphic on the front more clear. "Are you a fan of true crime?"

Rion smiled at the irony, shrugging his shoulders. "You could say that."

"We have a huge section of true crime over on the back wall. All kinds of serial killers, unsolved mysteries, macabre conspiracies..."

"Not really what I'm here for..."

She looked disappointed. "So what are you looking for?"

Rion looked back at the titles on the shelf and said quietly, "Spiders. Wondering about web composition."

"You're 'wondering about web composition'... You realize that makes you sound like a psychopath, right?" She laughed as she leaned over and pulled a book out that said *Spider Silk*.

"You have no idea," he muttered back.

"Well, lucky for you there are other psychos out there that wonder about spiderwebs. This book is popular among five-year-old boys and seventy-year-old widowers who want to read about how the military is using spider silk and other modern day applications."

"Thank you."

"You're welcome. Come see me when you're ready to check out... or if you need anything else."

He nodded, turning over the book she had supplied in his hand. He skipped through the pages, finding his answer now instead of purchasing the book.

Structural, compositional, *and* a little bit of magic.

Fair enough. He slid the book back into its place on the shelf, and put his hands in his pockets as he started walking to the exit. He noticed the girl was watching him and he grew a little uncomfortable. Before he got to the door she called out to him.

"You know that's basically stealing right?"

He stopped, turning to look at her.

She hopped off of the stool she was sitting on, "I take the time to find you the perfect book and you don't even buy it? Stand there and read a few pages and put it back. I mean..."

Rion slowly walked over to the counter, reaching down to pick up a discount book on the rack there. He laid the yellow-covered paperback in front of her, looking down at the whimsical font that was nearly unreadable.

She didn't break eye contact with him, but took the book and scanned it before giving him his total. He handed her a ten and she popped the drawer out and started counting out coins. He couldn't stand the sound of the metal scraping across the sloped sides of the plastic drawer. It made his mouth dry, and made this situation even more uncomfortable. He didn't like feeling like he wasn't in control here. She was dictating this entire encounter. It was not how things should be. He should have walked on out of the store, but she made him buy this book. He let her make him buy this book.

"Here's your change, your new book," she said, handing him the money and bagging up the yellow novel before grabbing a pen and writing on the receipt. "Here's a link you can follow where you can participate in a brief survey and get ten percent off your next order, and... this is my number."

Rion looked down at the numbers and the girl's name 'Summer' written above it. He didn't say anything immediately, and she sat back down and opened her own book back up, "Have a great day."

Now *she* was going to wish he'd just walked on out the door.

20
Polanski

David sat in the car quietly, licking his finger so that he could thumb through a page in the novel in his hands. Most people wouldn't peg him as a reader, but he couldn't often find a better way to pass the time. He peered through his reading glasses with the seat reclined, waiting for the clock to change to seven. He had been asked to come to the Delton Church of the Fellowship to interview the pastor Rudy Hodge. Brother Hodge was a well-known member of society, but some would laugh about how he'd been wild as a teenager, with the nickname Rocket. He had been a football player in a small town, where high-school sports were second only to God. He'd gotten on drugs, gotten clean, gotten in church, and become one of the most revered pastors in the county. He'd spoken at the high school and elementary schools at least once a year, and he was a familiar speaker at graduations and football games.

As people started coming out of the doors, lingering on the sidewalk outside to talk, David dog-eared the page he was on and set the book in the passenger seat. He popped a piece, or three, of nicotine gum and then began his slow walk to the front door.

Churches had this distinct smell... a little musty, perhaps floral (the dead, funeral-type floral, though). New carpet, maybe. That lingering adhesive odor, and the smell of the plastic it had been wrapped in. It wasn't at all the scent of incense, aromatic smoke ascending like the souls of the worshippers throughout his boyhood synagogue. It wasn't the sweet bouquet of wine sloshed onto velvet during kiddush, or the subtle smell of old scrolls and books and spice that clung to the curtains and pews.

He caught sight of Rudy Hodge through the remaining crowd, standing out from everyone else in his dark jacket and slacks. He was a tall man, broad shouldered, and these days a little portly. He had a head full of still-black hair and eyes that were just as dark. David passed through the people, several patting him on the arm or back like he was just another one of them. He just nodded, giving a, "Hey, how you doing?" when necessary.

"Brother Hodge."

David slunk up beside the pastor with a nod. The man seemed to be expecting him somehow, and reached out to clasp their hands together. David awkwardly nodded.

"Detective."

"I've got a few questions for you, Brother, if you have the time to speak with me today. If not, we can always arrange something later."

David almost hoped he would opt for the latter, but instead Brother Hodge spoke to him without looking at him.. He kept his eyes on the crowd, smiling and waving as people looked in his direction. He certainly did not do or say anything that suggested he was speaking to a detective about anything.

"She's dead isn't she?"

"Brother?"

The pastor turned towards a small room, putting his hand on David's elbow as though to lead him there. It was just a small offshoot of the larger chamber they were in. It was dark, mostly maroon, with velvety curtains and flooring. The walls even looked soft, and the musty aroma of mildew was even stronger there. It was dark, and until Brother Hodge flipped the switch on a small lamp, David had not even noticed the details of the room itself.

"Mary, she's gone? I can feel it. She was always such a light, really. The world seems a little dimmer..."

"Listen, I'm not at liberty to give you any details about the case yet."

"I know everything, Detective."

He found it ironic that the pastor would claim any omniscience, and he wanted to snark at him. He wanted to ask him who killed the girl? Who took her? But he also knew he needed cooperation.

"All I can tell you is that we don't have any good news. If you have any idea who might have wanted to hurt Mary, or someone she may have trusted enough to go somewhere with..."

"Oh, Mary trusted everyone. More than she should have," Brother Hodge said quietly. "She saw something good in the world; even in the darkest corners she saw something worth saving. She was going to do big things, good things."

"Someone said she was last seen here the night of your big revival. Do you remember her that night?"

"I remember her being here, but other than a face in the crowd... I don't know anything else. She was sitting with some well-known members of the church, no one suspicious. No one who could not be accounted for after she disappeared."

"Had she been hanging out with any odd characters?"

"Oh, many of them." Brother Hodge even laughed a little. "There was no one Mary didn't try to make friends with. Although, she had a particular man on the prayer list recently... Bennie Moss. It's my understanding that Mr. Moss has a serious problem with drugs. I know the last time she took a care package to Mr. Moss, she was pretty shaken up. She didn't want to talk about why."

"We'll pay Mr. Moss a visit."

David actually recognized the name. Robichaud had picked Bennie up multiple times for drug related charges, violating probation, driving without a license... You name it, Bennie had been picked up for it. He figured he'd pass this one off to Robichaud, so that he didn't have to go hunt the man down. Bennie and Robichaud had a more intimate relationship anyway.

A boy with red-rimmed eyes was suddenly standing behind Brother Hodge, having approached nearly silently. His shoulders were gaunt and jutted up so far that they nearly held a higher elevation than his head. He looked sick, not sickly, but rather like at any moment he might vomit on the floor between them. Brother Hodge went to his side, putting a hand on his shoulder.

"Elyas," he said quietly. "Please, have a seat in the sanctuary if you need to speak with me."

"I want to help," Elyas insisted. "I saw her talking to someone, the night of the revival. Mary."

Polanski shifted his weight to face Elyas more directly, nodding at him. "Who was he?"

Elyas crossed his arms, shivering, "I didn't recognize him..."

David noted Elyas' eyes shift to and from Brother Hodge. The detective turned to the preacher and said, "Brother Hodge, could you give me a few minutes to talk with this young gentleman, please?"

Brother Hodge was not happy with this request and even seemed flustered. He shot Elyas a look, as though blaming him for this silent request of privacy. He obliged, however, and walked into the hall.

"Alright, kid," David said, voice firm. "You need to tell me everything you know."

Elyas stammered, "I mean I don't know that much. I just like Mary a lot, and I didn't want Brother Hodge to know. I was watching her during the revival... That doesn't make me weird does it? I just like her."

"Nah, just makes you normal. You ever been normal, Elyas?" David smacked his gum loudly. "So you were watching her..."

"Yeah, and she kept looking at this guy a few rows back. Older than us, black or brown hair? Wearing a suit."

"How much older?"

"I don't know for sure..."

"Was he an old man? Are we talking grandpa or..."

"He wasn't as old as you, I don't think."

"Are you calling me old?" David quipped.

"No, no... I mean, I don't know how old you are. He was probably in his 30's... 40's..."

David was, in reality, a little disappointed that this kid thought he was at minimum in his 50's... but that wasn't important right now. He *was* in his 50's now, after all.

"Do you have anything else for me to go on? I can't really start building a report around you being jealous your girl was making bedroom eyes at some handsome devil in the back pew."

"She left with him. She packed up a care kit and left with him. He was really shady, I'm not just saying that. He didn't look right, you know? He looked at her like she was a piece of meat. I should've went up to her, I should've done somethi-"

Before Polanski could react, Elyas had vomited on top of his shoes. Smelled a little like spaghetti and he knew he'd never get the stain out of his socks, or the odor out of his soles. The shoes were just going to have to go.

21
Paltro

Deen sat on the bloody ceramic flooring of the small morgue with his legs spreadeagle in front of him. Sweat beaded down his forehead, despite the coolness of the room. He didn't normally make a mess like this. He kept his workspace very clean considering the nature of his work. He always took his time and was clean and precise.

This night had been quite different, however. First, he had to allow both Mary Allen and Glenda Harrison time to thaw. Their bodies were frost-bitten and contorted, displaying post-mortem injuries from being crammed into the too small space together. Glenda's body was hardly held together anymore, more of a mass of sopping wet tissue and discolored bodily fluids. He suspected that she had been dead for some time *before* being frozen. He could not determine any cause of death at this point, but nothing suggested that she was murdered... granted, he barely had enough left to work with to determine she was *not* murdered either. It just didn't match the killer's motive or selection. Although everyone seemed to feel like his choice of women were predictable, and Deen did feel as though he likely chose girls who displayed some sort of vulnerability, he thought it was likely that Glenda Harrison had not exhibited the type of vulnerability that this man was into.

Mary Allen had a sort of peace about her, Paltro thought. Her face, although damaged from both her trauma and the freezer's conditions, seemed to be at rest. Her eyes, instead of being open at their widest, were half-closed, almost as though they would flutter shut at any time. Frost on her eyelashes melted into her eyes, forming a trail of artificial tears that spilled down the sides of her face. He found himself growing more and more shaky as he worked on her body, taking note of her injuries and all of the little clues the decomposition process left him. It wasn't just all of the clues about death that were getting to him, it was all of those hints about life. The ways they dressed, the personal effects that he sometimes bagged up and labeled. He never did separate them from having been someone, as he thought so many people in his line of work may have done. He didn't think he would do them justice if he pretended they were less than human, less than who they had been just days before, sometimes just hours before. The day that he lost his empathy was the day he would throw in the towel.

He didn't have the mental or emotional energy to finish with Lisa York. She was also in an advanced state of decomposition and serious disrepair, mostly thanks to what he supposed was the handiwork of scavenging animals. She had little lines and marks on her bones that were not the work of man, and her head had come completely detached by the time she got to the morgue. No one had reported her missing. The young woman had sat beneath the oak tree on Oak Hill as a feast for crows and other animals, and no one had been the wiser. He had not delved into the reasons her absence had been overlooked, although his mind made up all sorts of excuses as to why no one had noticed she had been gone. Was she from out of town? Did she have no family or friends? Maybe it wasn't unlike her to go radio silent for a few days, a few weeks... Someone somewhere always cared, and in the end, Deen cared.

The last time he had felt this overwhelmed had been four or five years ago. A family had taken their children out on a boat on Soggy Bottom Lake, and the father had gotten a little too cocky with the way he was driving the boat. It had overturned, and all three of their children had drowned. Two little girls, and one little boy. Deen had been haunted by their faces, and the imagined sounds of their laughter on the boat before they'd suffered their fate. The way the water must have burned and been heavy in their lungs. He had woken up many nights feeling like he had been drowning himself. Just when he had started to heal, months later, their father had rolled through with a self-inflicted gunshot to the face.

Thankfully, he only had to handle those bodies until the funeral homes had come for them. He did not have to open them up, investigate their deaths.

He pulled his gloves off, tossing them onto the floor between his feet. He tried to pull his knees up to his chest so that he could hug his own legs, but the motion made him feel even more trapped and breathless. How many more women would come through here before they caught this man? How many more girls were there out there like Lisa York? Waiting to be found, with no one to know they were missing.

Deen had never closed up shop without finishing an autopsy before. He always finished what he started, every time. He had a serious dedication to any task he took on, and he loved his job. None of their stories were happy, death was a little melancholy on its own. It was a somber job, but something that he found fascinating and fulfilling.

Not today.

He let himself sob, chin against his chest. It was easier that way. It didn't hold much sorrow, and he thought of the tears as more therapeutic than anything. It was a good release of stress, allowing his body to soothe itself. He didn't have time to compose himself when he heard the door open on the other side of the room.

Tresa stood there, still halfway through the door's opening. She had a box of donuts in her hand and was dressed in plain clothes. She seemed surprised, even startled, by him sitting on the floor like he was. Although he had dried up his tears fairly quickly, it was clear by the look on his face that he was not in good spirits.

"Deen?"

She moved inside quickly, squatting down beside him as she went into a problem-solving mode. She set the box of donuts down, reaching over to put one hand on his shoulder and the other under his chin.

"Are you alright? Did something happen?"

Deen shook his head. "Just a little overwhelmed."

Tresa looked up, really noticing all three corpses for the first time. She took a slow inhale and exhale and settled herself on the floor beside him, sitting as close as she could get to him. She set the white box on her lap and opened it up to reveal the shining glazed rings.

"Donut? It'll make you feel better."

He wanted to argue that the sweetness would probably just contribute to a state of nausea, but instead he smiled and reached over to grab one of the sticky pastries. She took one too, and they ate quietly side by side. It was this reason he really liked Tresa, although he'd never been able to tell her that. She was a frightfully strong presence, comforting and supportive, and she knew it. It was exactly what he needed.

22
Quentin

The room was chilly, cold and grey, in both aesthetic and temperature. A green slime covered most of the walls, and the same color oozed from the man's nose as he stood at the door like a sleepy-eyed bouncer. Quentin walked past him without much more than a nod, he was not there for him... His beanie and sweatpants were both moth eaten, and he was too high to care that the two men approaching him were obviously cops.

Quentin slipped him a fifty dollar bill and walked on inside. He was sure that to Torres he seemed unphased by the passed-out bodies propped up against the walls and pinkish powder on the out-of-place plastic table. It looked like one you'd see at a yardsale, if people sold coke at yard sales.

He wouldn't admit that the unpredictability of some of these addicts really put him on edge, and looking at him you certainly couldn't tell. Torres was not hiding his discomfort, he walked so close to Quentin that their hands brushed. The fact that he was so obviously uncomfortable made Quentin want to make him even *more* uneasy. This wasn't some exclusive building for druggies or anything, but Bennie and his groupies did tend to travel together to a few of the 'historical' buildings in town. Everyone knew they were here.

The entire building smelled like burning plastic with a mildly floral sweetness. It seemed fitting that a killer who left flowers would be in a place like this, smelling like this. Torres hung back with uncertainty as Quentin approached a man that sat on a stack of cinder blocks beside the table.

"What the hell, Bennie?" Quentin asked, putting his hands on his hips as he squared up on the opposite side of the table.

Torres came up, nodding awkwardly. "Bennie."

Bennie looked up at Quentin as though he'd known him his entire life. He had a wrinkled piece of foil, cupped and holding a black and tarry semi-liquid. The smell of vinegar flooded Torres' nostrils, masking the somehow less offensive odor of the cocaine with its own putrid scent profile. They'd had enough run-ins for Bennie to know that Quentin wasn't going to waste his time with him for something as petty as drug use anymore.

"What? What about it? What the hell about what?" Bennie stammered aggressively, holding the foil over a small candle as he rolled the blackness around until it was mostly fluid. He started snaking his head around to catch the tendrils of smoke that rose up through a thin black straw.

"Cheap shit, Bennie. This is cheap shit. You're better than this. You're Whitebranch's *premier drug lord*, smoking ink out of... what the fuck is this? Is this a coffee stirrer?"

He smacked the straw out of Bennie's chapped lips, successfully also dislodging a scab that started oozing blood onto his stubbled chin. Bennie's jaw dropped and as he looked up in surprise the liquid became a clumpy solid, sticking to both itself as it solidified and the shining foil. That happened when you stayed in one place too long, Quentin figured.

"Knock it off, Bennie. I'm trying to talk to you."

"What do you want, Robe-chow?" Bennie asked.

"Need to ask you about a girl that might've been down here."

"Lots of girls come around here. Everybody wants a piece of this." He smacked himself in the chest.

Quentin thought he heard Torres gag quietly. He stifled a smile.

"Alright, Casanova. This girl wasn't your type."

"How you know my type, huh? I'm an equal opportunity lover."

Quentin interrupted, "Nice girl, young. Might have been here on behalf of her church. Name was Mary Allen."

"That does sound familiar," Bennie said, looking around to make sure no one could hear him. "What's in it for me?"

"You tell me what you know and I won't bust you for possession of your shit heroin. You're probably looking at a pretty hefty fine and some time at this point, aren't you? I heard they got you violating probation when you drove down to see your mama."

"She *died,* you dickwad," Bennie snapped. "I drove less than five miles. Less than five miles."

"On a suspended license, high as a fucking kite. Bet she'd be proud."

Bennie seemed to be angry all at once. Quentin knew that he wouldn't lash out, but he did have concerns that the vein in his head might explode before he gathered enough control to tell him what he knew about the dead girl.

"So, the girl."

Bennie sighed. "Brought some bibles. The little ones with tiny writing, like any of us could fucking read that. Real nice and soft paper. We used some of it for rolls."

"Pretty sure you're going to hell for that, Bennie."

"Jesus loves everyone, *including me*, the girl said."

"I think she may have embellished a little... but tell me more about her. Did anyone take special interest in her?"

Bennie scoffed, "Everybody took a little interest in her. She came in here dressed up, wearing jewelry, driving a nice car. She looked like she might have some money."

"Did anyone follow her? Threaten or harass her?"

"I mean, Stu followed her to her car. She had to keep telling him she would visit again. He was a little heartbroken when she drove off."

"Where's Stu now?"

Bennie's eyes narrowed. "Stu didn't do nothing to that girl."

"Did I say anything had been done to the girl?"

"You aren't here on a social call. Something happened to that girl. Was she robbed? Nobody like... you know... SVU'd her did they?"

Quentin pulled a cigarette out of his pocket, hands shaking. He didn't think Bennie would hurt anyone intentionally, and by extension he was pretty sure Stu was probably harmless too. It didn't help, however, that they had very little information on their killer, and it was getting a little tense. They were expecting someone to come up with some kind of lead, and at this point Quentin was desperately praying that this murder was unrelated to the last. He didn't want to hope that she had been the victim of an accidental killing, one where someone she had tried to help inadvertently killed her... but it would be better than being just another girl left in the trail of the murderer.

"She's dead, Bennie."

What color had been in Bennie's face suddenly disappeared, replaced by a pallor.

23
Rion

He had never wanted to keep anyone more than he wanted to keep Summer Glass. At first her disposition had been off-putting. She was too confident of herself, too sure of her control over him. He was exhibiting the same weaknesses that he sought out, but experiencing that would make him better. He would be more efficient, more confident. Now that he had her here, he almost couldn't bring himself to kill her. He knew that time was of the essence, because the police were really crawling all over the countryside right now. Her empty car would be found soon, and she would miss a day of work... He wouldn't be able to cherish his time with her any longer. He had taken her to an old rock quarry, a location much like the old dam: abandoned, spacious and somewhat secluded. While his favorite places would always be the fields, having somewhere like this with a little more guaranteed privacy was also nice.

Summer was lying in a crumpled heap at his feet, although still very much alive. She made a small noise as she slowly came to consciousness, hands tied behind her back with zip ties. He had met her by her car behind Page One after she got off of work last night. She had been startled to see him there, maybe even suspicious. He told her he'd lost her number, but he'd love to take her out. She agreed and he pressed, suggesting they go out then and there. He handed her a bouquet of flowers and insisted she set them on the front desk inside so they didn't wilt in the car. He said there was a horror movie double feature playing at the drive-in theater outside of town. He'd drive, he'd bring her back to her car. Good, classic horror he insisted. She enthusiastically agreed, if he was paying, and she grabbed her bag.

"Hello," he said quietly, nudging her with his shoe.

She rolled over, squinting up at him. He noted how she did not look particularly surprised, although she nearly gagged on the strip of cloth he had wrapped around her head and through her teeth. The only real signal that she was panicking was that her nostrils flared so slightly. He reached down to brush her dark hair out of her face.

"What do you think?" he asked in the same low tone. "Haven't you always wanted this. Kind of? A little? Haven't you fantasized about this moment, at the hands of a killer?"

It was then that a gentle quiver started taking over her features. She started breathing faster, eyes welling with tears. He much preferred her like this. Now she looked like what it was that he desired. That vulnerability, the refusal to accept the inevitable. *He* was inevitable, *he* was in control. Things were as they should be.

"You knew that something was wrong, didn't you?"

She shook her head from side to side.

"You seemed more instinctual than the others. I thought you might actually be too much for me. I admit it," he laughed. "I was intimidated. Especially when I found this."

He reached at his side to retrieve her bag, covered with buttons and patches. Band names, obscure horror movies, the macabre. He unzipped it and pulled out the handgun tucked inside.

"It's interesting. You were prepared... but for what? If not for me, then what?"

He reached down to hook his finger in the fabric across her cheek, pulling it out of her mouth. For several moments he waited for her to respond, to answer his question, to say something. He wondered why she would have a weapon on hand but choose not to use it. What good did it do to have one? A false sense of power and safety?

"Did you like the flowers?"

She was trembling and nodded. "Yes."

"Do you know what kind they are?"

"No."

He feigned surprised. "No?"

"I... don't like flowers," she admitted, voice wavering little. She seemed so calm. He couldn't tell, for sure, if it was sheer bravery and courage... or if she just didn't know what was going to happen.

"They were dahlias. I thought that was fitting. I'm glad you didn't fuss about leaving them inside. It's kind of important to me that they are found. I think it was fate that I found you, because... what flower would better fit you? I always considered it to be a strange flower to include in the line up..."

He pulled the dahlia flower game piece out of his pocket, and then she started screaming and kicking her legs against the rocks.

He laughed, "So now you know. Shhh..."

He dropped onto the ground beside her, wiping away her tears with his hands. "Think about it. Would you have it any other way? Do you want to get old and ugly and die in some nursing home in a puddle of your own piss? Is that really how you want to go? This is so much more beautiful, poetic. You don't have to worry about it... I'll take good care of you. I promise."

"You're insane. This is insane."

"Someone once said that the only real difference between genius and insanity is the length one is willing to go."

He put his hands around her throat.

24
Polanski

David sat quietly, staring across the parking lot as a group of girls left the school and walked to their cars. He knew that Anna would die of embarrassment if she saw him there. He was chewing such a large wad of gum that the hinges of his jaws were cracking with every bite. He had developed a nervousness about his daughter's wellbeing that kept him awake at night. How easy would it be for her to become the next victim? He had talked to her, her entire life, about how to protect herself in situations like this. Leah was always telling him that he just had to trust her. Why did he find it so hard to let go?

He averted his eyes as he noticed Anna and her two best friends walk out the door. He wondered if they felt the absence of Ji-su like he felt like he did. It was probably just because this hit so close to home, because he kept thinking about what it must be like... even though he didn't want to even try to imagine that. Ji-su had sometimes accompanied them to an afterschool adventure when they were young. He could still see their bright faces in his rearview mirror as they giggled and whispered about boys, they had to have been twelve, maybe thirteen. Anna and her friends walked past their parked cars and onto the football field, climbing up on the aluminum bleachers as a herd of boys trotted onto the grass.

He huffed, slumping back into his seat. He was really hoping she was going straight home, or that he could at least see her to one of her friends' houses.

David had also been checking his phone obsessively all day, waiting to hear something from Paltro or Robichaud, or even Torres. He knew that there was some weird son-of-a-bitch out there killing all of these people, but he couldn't shake the feeling that Brother Hodge was a real creep. The fact that Elyas seemed intimidated by him just made him seem more suspicious. It could have been, of course, just a young man embarrassed about a crush inside the church but... he couldn't help but feel like it was something more sinister.

The unofficial description Elyas had given him did seem to match the partial descriptions they'd received from others. This guy kept just barely getting away... just barely escaping being pinned down at the scene. Why couldn't they get just one step ahead of him?

The parking lot was clearing out around him as students and teachers went home. The only cars left were those at the football field and a handful that must have belonged to janitors and other employees. David paid special attention to all of the cars, looking for anyone out of the ordinary, anyone who might not belong.

He forced himself to turn the car on and pull out of the parking lot, driving down the road to the diner where he usually ate with a coworker. If there was anything that helped him feel better, aside from alcohol and cigarettes, it would be food.

He parked his car outside of Retta's Cafe and went to his usual seat, which was in a corner near the bar where he could sit with his back to the wall but still read the daily dessert menu. A young waitress came to him, bypassing some empty glasses on tables on her way. She was probably in her mid-twenties and had worked at the cafe her entire working life. She always waited on David like he was the only patron in the entire building, probably because she felt like she owed him something. He had walked her to her car one night and then, at her request, followed her home when she'd had an abusive boyfriend. Luckily, said boyfriend had reportedly overdosed a few years ago after he'd gotten out of jail. Pills, they'd said, although David knew better. All the same, the girl was safe and better off with him dead.

"What's it going to be today?" she asked with a smile, setting down a glass of diet soda in front of him.

"Tell Retta I just want the hamburger steak, onions and all that. You guys know how I like it. Fries today."

"Extra toast?"

"You got it. Go ahead and bring me some of that blackberry cobbler too."

As she walked away, he leaned over to steal a worn county paper off of the neighboring table, opening it up in front of him and putting on his reading glasses. Of course, the report on the front page nearly made him sick: *Delton Ripper? Bodies Piling Up in Whitebranch.*

He tried to resist the urge to look back at the article, trying to busy himself with the ads for used cars and free kittens, but found himself closing the paper to read the front page anyway. He wondered how much everyone knew now, and how much shit the Department was in. It looked like they were including the old woman in the kill count, although Paltro had expressed his doubts that she was a victim, that it was probably just an unfortunate coincidence. How had the guy found that house, and how did he know the woman was dead? David figured they might never know.

They knew about the game pieces, which was another shitshow on its own. People love a good gimmick, and that's all this was. A gimmick from an attention seeking bastard.

He could hear the radio on the bar playing the local station where the host, Wesley Williams, was talking about the murders as well. He wasn't saying much but was asking if anyone wanted to call in and give their opinion. The waitress returned to his table, delivering his plate of food with grease and melted butter pooling at the edges. He smiled up at her and said, "Can you turn that radio up just a little bit?"

"Yeah, sure. No problem."

As she turned the dial, he could hear a caller introducing himself, "Yeah, I want to talk about these murders. I own a business in town and let me tell you... The fact that this has been happening under our noses and we're just now hearing about it... Well it's terrifying."

The host responded: "Oh, definitely. I agree. The authorities have been really quiet about this whole thing."

The cohost: "Apparently the first murder was Lola Simmons, that's been what... Seven months ago?"

"Yeah, either he took a break or we will keep finding bodies."

"Don't be so morbid, Wes... back to our caller. What do *you* think about all of this?"

The man scoffed, "Listen, I'm not saying anyone deserves to be raped or murdered or anything. But I mean how stupid do you have to be? Why are these women running off with some guy they don't know?"

The host already seemed uncomfortable, vocalizing quietly as he tried to speak calmly, "There's a lot of variables we don't know. Maybe they *did* know him. Maybe they were abducted. These guys are usually smart, they're also professionals at grooming victims."

"I'm just saying, maybe if people started thinking a little bit this wouldn't happen and for god's sake, get a gun! You better believe someone comes after me, and I'm going to be armed."

"Alright, we really appreciate getting your unique pers..."

"Like I heard one of the girls was a teenager. Where are the parents? Why are teenage girls riding around with grown men? Don't tell me this isn't a grown ass man doing this. You know it is. At some point, I know no one wants to say this because it's not politically correct... But at some point aren't you *asking for it*?"

"Thanks for calling in."

The host laughed as the call was disconnected, "I think it goes without saying that the opinions of our callers do *not* reflect the views of our staff. We are mourning with our town, these girls are our friends, sisters, daughters. There is no situation where anyone deserves to be subjected to violence..."

The cohost dryly interjected, "Except maybe that guy who just called in, am I right?"

They laughed together.

David found himself standing beside the radio, he wasn't sure at what point he'd stood up, but now he was aware that people were watching him. He could feel that his face was red, his fists were clenched. The waitress leaned over the counter and flipped the radio off, jerking her hand back like she was afraid of him.

"Are you alright, detective?" she whispered.

David shook his head, plunging his hand into his pocket to retrieve a twenty and laid it on the counter.

"Let me grab your change."

David noticed through the order window that the owner was standing there, drying her hands slowly as she watched him.

"No, keep the change today."

"Do you at least want a box?" she asked, cheeks flushing.

"No, I'm good."

The owner came out of the kitchen, leaning on the bar as she slid a plastic fork and his dessert in a to-go box towards him.

"Don't pay any attention to that idiot on the radio. That's Danny White. Business owner my ass... He runs the hardware store for his daddy.

He's a dumbass. I know this whole thing is just as hard on you guys as it is us. Don't let him get under your skin."

"Thanks. I'm just going to head out... It's just been a long day, I'm going to head home."

"Take care," she said.

David went out the door and got into his car, tossing the to-go box into his passenger seat to remain uneaten. He wasn't going home.

It was dark now, and David had taken the gun off of his belt and tucked it inside the glovebox before leaving his car parked in an empty parking lot several blocks down from the hardware store. He stood on the opposite side of the street, waiting for the light inside to flip off. Two men exited, standing for ten or fifteen minutes to smoke a cigarette together. When they were done, smashing their butts into the pavement together, David heard one call the other Dan, before they split ways.

He was relieved that Danny was alone, crossing the street to follow him as he walked down, presumably to the same parking lot where David's own car was parked. He looked behind him, making sure the other man was out of sight and earshot. With perfect timing, Danny stopped to squat down and tie his shoe. David skipped forward to catch up, using his hands to shove the man over and into a small, incomplete space between two storefronts.

Danny was much smaller, he could feel his bony shoulders on his palms. The man hurt himself falling to the ground more than David expected. His hands were bleeding against the loose pavement, trousers torn.

David snarled at him, kicking loose rocks towards him. "Where's your fucking gun, you prick? Not so big now are you? You know what, I think you were fucking asking for it. Walking alone at night like that."

The man rolled onto his backside, still pushing himself backwards as he started begging David to just leave him alone. He still hadn't figured it out, he still didn't know what he had done. Before he realized it, he'd jumped on top of the man, punching him in the mouth and nose, and then the sides of his face when the softness of the man's skin started to make him feel nauseous. He could feel pain breaking through in his own hand, his wrist, his shoulder.

He had to stop himself, as the man gurgled and spat blood, face blackening before his very eyes. *You're going to fucking kill him.* He started to panic, feeling cold all over. He released the man's shirt, watching him fall to the ground and roll onto his gut to try and crawl away. David rubbed his face and his hand through his hair, leaving a wet streak of blood, before he took off running down the sidewalk.

25
Torres

Lucas was sitting in the cruiser doing absolutely nothing when the dispatcher mentioned a man had called in, just a few blocks down from Red's Hardware. He had claimed someone attacked him from behind, beating him to the point that he needed an ambulance. The suspect was at large, and could be in the vicinity. Man probably in his 40s/50s, red hair, white shirt and dark pants.

"I'm over here," Lucas radioed back. "I'll check it out."

The ambulance passed him as the police car rolled down the road, and he followed it several yards behind, cutting down a side road to watch a less travelled area that adjoined where the crime had taken place. The streets were totally empty, as was normal for this town after dark. So few people roamed around at night, unless they were walking from a bar or up to no good (or both). So when he saw a man tripping over his own feet, stumbling down the side of the road, and wearing a bloody white shirt... Well, he knew that was his guy.

"Eyes on him," Lucas announced to the radio.

"Need me to send Sams to back you up?"

"Actually..." Lucas said, throat constricting. He had to cough to clear his throat, "Mistaken, this isn't our guy. Some lady."

"Lady?"

"Sorry, she was burly."

"Alright..."

The real reason was because he suddenly realized the man was Polanski. David Polanski turned to face the car, blue and red lights illuminating his entire body. Lucas parked his car in the middle of the road, exiting quickly.

"Polanski?" Lucas breathed, rushing to his side. "What the... what happened? Get in the car, we've got to get you to a hospital... I mean a doctor."

"No," he protested, but allowed Lucas to guide him to the passenger side seat all the same.

He got in the car quickly, turning the lights off as he turned the vehicle around and headed to the nearest after-hours clinic. With no hospital, it was the only option unless they left the county.

They rode quietly for a few minutes, Polanski breathing heavily against the window. It was fogged up and rolling with condensation. His left hand was swollen, especially the third and fourth digit. He would be surprised if they could pull his wedding band off. It was bloody and swollen, even at the wrist, but Polanski was holding his shoulder like it was the main source of his pain.

"Was it you?" Lucas asked, stealing another glance over at him. "The assailant? Did you beat some guy up?"

Polanski did not speak, but nodded his head.

Lucas nodded in return.

"You don't have to tell me anything. Nobody's going to know. Let's get you patched up and make up a badass story, alright?"

Polanski scoffed, but took his hand to pat Lucas on the shoulder, "You're alright, kid."

"I'm sure he deserved it… the guy."

"I'm no saint. Maybe he didn't."

Lucas wouldn't pry. He didn't need to know. Polanski had beaten him, he must have deserved it. He didn't want to know if he didn't.

26
Quentin

It had taken pulling a few strings to get the reservation at Sugar's secured, but Quentin had not relented until he knew they would have a table available. He was still wearing his work clothes, but he had removed his tie and ruffled up his hair some. He took off his duty belt and swapped his shoes for sneakers. He thought it made him look just a little more casual.

Quentin pulled her chair out for her, something he wasn't sure he'd done in years. It didn't matter that she was perfectly capable of pulling out her own chair, which was the excuse he'd been using for not doing it the last several years. She didn't even protest with him. In fact, he thought he detected the slightest tint of blush on her cheeks, and he spent the rest of the night trying to replicate it. They laughed, and talked, the low sounds of orchestra music playing over a speaker.

"I never imagined this place would still be open," Quentin admitted, taking a sip of his crisp, dry wine delicately.

Emily nodded, eyes sparkling as she looked around, "I remember the first date we went on. You brought me here. Do you remember?"

"I think so."

He did remember. He remembered everything about that night. They both ordered a shrimp carbonara, and he ordered a soda until he heard her order some colored boozy drink, then he also swapped his beverage to something a little more stout. He remembered how her hair, maybe just a little darker then than it was now, gleamed under the low lights, how she kept having to push it behind her ears to keep it out of her face, and how every time she did her brown eyes were exposed to catch the light just enough to have him hypnotized. She was wearing this yellow, flowered dress that was playful and youthful, just like her. She wore heels that didn't last the night; she ended up carrying them out to the car with her when they were done.

"The real Sugar wouldn't know what to make of all of this. I bet she's rolling over in her grave."

Quentin snorted, "Grave? That old witch is probably propped up in a corner back there still giving orders."

Of course the real Sugar had indeed died, leaving the restaurant to be auctioned off - rumor had it because she knew her sons were no good and would ruin the place (not that it had been much when she had been alive). Some out-of-towner had purchased the property when it went up on said auction, turned it into this snazzy eatery that people travelled out here to eat at. It wasn't something most of the locals frequented, simply because it was now so expensive. Sugar would have fed anyone who came through the door, even if it was off of someone else's discarded plate with the nibbled edges cut off. Not that any of the patrons in the joint would know anything about Sugar. She was one of those old women that could cook like none other, but you could hear her hacking up a lung in the kitchen while she struggled to keep a cigarette between her teeth and the ash out of the pan. Her place had never been up to code, and they'd threatened to close her down more than once. What had become an upscale dining establishment in the small town had once been a place where the cook rarely wore close-toed shoes.

"Listen, I want you to invite your trainee to dinner," Emily said, leaning her face onto one of her hands.

Quentin squinted over his wine glass, "You mean like, right now?"

"No, silly. Like to the house. I just want to meet him. I think it could be good to spend more time with David and Leah again too. Like we used to."

"David's ah... David's in a bad place right now."

"Oh?"

The conversation was on hold as their identical plates were delivered and placed in front of them. They were perfectly arranged and garnished, each plate seeming to have the exact arrangement of noodles and shrimp, tiny red peppers adorning the sauce. Emily smiled and thanked the waiter. Quentin dove straight into his plate.

"Oh?" Emily repeated, twirling her fork around a mass of noodles.

"Yeah, we all are, I guess. Paltro, too."

She didn't respond.

"He'll be alright. We all just have to see this thing through. Finish it."

"Well, the trainee then."

"Torres."

"Yeah, Torres. Invite him over, no excuses."

"No excuses," he confirmed. "We'll have the little asswipe over for dinner."

She kicked him underneath the table.

Emily was a little tipsy by the time they got home. Quentin felt a little buzz too, and knew that he probably shouldn't have been driving. He'd been to plenty of terrible drunk driving accidents, and even when they claimed they were competent to drive, people still died. He'd pushed through the fuzzy feeling between his ears, however, turned the air on high and the radio down like that somehow helped. He was relieved when they pulled into the driveway.

When Emily got out of the car before him, he could hear her laughing as she walked up to try and unlock the door. Then suddenly it was quiet, he got out of the car, door making a jarring sound as he shut it in the night. It was then that she called his name, voice unsure. She suddenly sounded sober, scared. Quentin moved around to the front of the house, heart skipping a beat as he saw the front window that was beside their couch busted.

"Stand by the car, Em." he said, going to unlock the door. He didn't have his gun on him, what kind of cop didn't have a gun? He had decided against taking it to dinner, and had settled with leaving it on the counter with his work phone. He crept quietly through the house, finding the gun thankfully where he'd left it. With it in hand, he cleared each and every room, going into the living room last.

He found a large rock lying against the leg of the coffee table, wrapped in a white cloth with fine, burlap twine holding it together.

He opened it quietly, even when he heard Emily say his name again to ask him if he was okay. Inside was a game piece with an orange pompom dahlia on it, and a piece of paper.

Detective, you seem to be between a rock and a hard place... not unlike our beautiful little dahlia. Will you find her before she wilts?

27
Rion

The Whitebranch City Park was several acres, most of that home to a sprawling expanse of jogging trails. Maintenance of the trails was shabby during this this time of year, as the trees had started dropping copious amounts of leaves and it was impossible to keep them clear. Until the springtime, only the most dedicated joggers and cross-country enthusiasts visited the trails. Historically, the park had been part of a privately owned property. The city offered the owner enough to secure a good dozen or so acres and then placed signs to signal when and where the park's property ended and the private property began.

Elisa McBride had been coming to this park since she was in highschool, and she knew the trails like the back of her hand. She had recently gone through a very sour breakup with a long-term boyfriend and had found herself quite lonely. She tried to drive her sorrows away with hobbies: she was always doing a dance class or yoga, or trying a new coffee shop in town. She liked to curl up with a good murder mystery... but she was still lonely. That's where Dahlia came in.

Dahlia was a big scruffy white dog with pale amber eyes. Elisa had adopted her about six months ago from the local animal shelter. She was a matted ball of wirehaired fluff, no identifiable breed or combination thereof. Dahlia filled that hole in her life and gave her a reason to get up in the mornings again. The dog probably had a single brain cell in her adorable little head: pingponging around like the logo on an old screensaver, but she was loyal and friendly.

They had yet to perfect jogging together, even after those six months. Elisa was always tripping over the massive puppy, or kicking her in the heels. Dahlia would bounce along beside her, and then crisscross in front of her, bounding excitedly at the sign of any wildlife or other joggers. Elisa always laughed, trying to pull the dog into a more appropriate position but refusing to use any real force.

Today was more crisp and cool than Elisa had expected. She pulled a hoodie out of her closet and used it to cover her torso, popping in her earphones and turning on something upbeat before she headed out. They ran down the familiar, leaf-covered trails, breath materializing in the air in front of them in the cool autumn air. Elisa was not aware that she was being watched. As far as she knew… she was completely alone, just her and Dahlia.

Rion stood, silently, off of the trail next to a felled tree. He wasn't making any effort to hide himself, but he knew that in the silent stillness of the forest he wouldn't draw much attention to himself anyway. He had come here several times to watch the joggers on the trails, choosing the days when he knew the traffic would be less.

Sometimes, most times, all he did was watch. He had been satisfied for a long time with just the thought that he was a successful voyeur, but with his recent 'hands-on' experiences he found himself just a little antsy as he watched the girl jog down the path towards him. The trail curved around in a big circle that eventually led back up to one of the parking lots a mile back, so Rion slowly began walking the diameter between where the girl was approaching and where the trail doubled back so that he could watch her as she returned to her car. With the dog at her side, he hesitated to approach her or try anything. Dogs caused all sorts of problems for people who had intentions like he did. As dumb as the animals were, he thought sometimes that they could 'sense' what he was thinking.

He heard a thump behind him as he walked, and he turned to see the girl in the distance now lying chest down on the leaf-covered pathway. The white dog was bouncing feet off the ground as she galloped down the trail away from her fallen owner.

"Dahlia!" she screamed. "Dahlia, wait!"

The shrill panic in her voice made the hair on the back of his neck stand on end, but instead of going to the woman's aid, he quickened his step and headed the dog off on the other end of the trail. The dog saw him and briefly paused, tongue hanging out of her mouth as she smelled the air.

He clicked his tongue for the friendly dog, crouching down as the creature diverted its path directly into his chest. He nearly toppled over, standing quickly with the leash in his hand, jerking the pink leather upwards, pulling the dog several inches off of the ground with a yelp. The dog suddenly slunk into submission, urinating on the ground at his feet and licking its lips nervously. It was the only real redeemable thing about the disgusting creatures; they did seem to respond well to corrective cues.

He could hear the girl screaming for the dog, voice desperate and full of concern. If she screamed this way for the lost dog, he could not wait to hear her when she realized she was going to die. He walked down the trail with the dog, putting on a smile like it was the most genuine and natural thing in the world. He never could master the eyes, he had noticed. He stood in front of the mirror for hours some nights, smiling and talking to himself. The smile, he had that down. It was warm, inviting, comforting. His eyes, however, never held that spark that he saw in the eyes of his victims. That flicker of something warm and animated. Instead they were always dim, with an absorbent quality. You could see yourself, trapped in the sticky black of the pupil like it was a pit of tar. There was no light there. No matter how he laughed, moved his brows, nothing made them shine.

The girl appeared on the trail in front of him, still dusting her bare knees off with her hands. Each swipe left a dirty, bloody smear on her right shin.

"It's okay, I've got her," Rion called to her.

The girl looked up in surprise, and then she smiled. "Oh, thank God. I thought she was gone."

He motioned to the oozing wound on her leg, "Looks like you hurt yourself, are you okay? That was quite the fall."

Elisa didn't think about the fact that he could not possibly have seen her fall from where he had caught her dog. Rion sometimes liked to see how many hints he could drop, how uneasy he could make someone... how stupid some people could be, how unaware of their surroundings.

"Oh... yes, I'm fine thank you. Just a scratch. Thank you again for getting my dog. She's just a baby."

"Oh, it's no problem. I love dogs."

"Well, she seems to like you, too. Otherwise she'd be gone. I can't thank you enough. I'm Elisa."

"Rion." he smiled again, wrapping the leash around his hand until he heard it squeak. "Dogs are a good judge of character. They know the good guys."

"Yeah... I think they do too. I should probably..." she reached for the leash, awkwardly pausing when Rion did not immediately hand it to her.

"Dahlia, huh? What a... coincidence," he smiled again, more broadly.

"Oh? How so?"

He just shrugged, continuing to smile at her. She awkwardly pulled the leash.

Elisa laughed nervously, tucking a strand of blonde hair behind her ear, "Yeah... I'll take her now. Thank you, though. Thank you *so* much. I was lucky you were here."

"Yeah, good thing we ran into each other. I'd hate for something to have happened to this sweet girl."

He hesitated another moment before handing her the leash. She smiled once, and he watched as she walked briskly past him, following her with his eyes until she was several yards away. Elisa was breathing slowly through her lips, hands quivering as she tried to not look like she was walking away too eagerly. He was an attractive guy, nice, he liked dogs... but he was so *intense.*

"Hey," he called after her.

She stopped, heart pounding in her chest. *Just pretend you don't hear him...* She told herself, but she found herself stopped in the leaves, Dahlia looked up at her expectantly. Would it be too rude if she just started walking again? What if they had mutual friends? What if she ran into him at the store? She faked a smile, turning around.

"Yeah?"

"Would you want to grab something to eat later?"

"Oh, I don't know. I have a lot to do," she said, voice unsure.

"Come on." He insisted with a smile. "Ice cream, then? I have to be at work in..." He looked at the watch on his wrist, "Three hours. Just give me three hours. Free ice cream."

Elisa didn't respond at first, staring at him with nervous eyes.

Rion kept the smile on his face, body language relaxed. He knew she didn't want to, but she didn't want to offend him. Something was telling her that this wasn't a good idea, and that there was something "off" about him. But she was going to say yes. Stronger than gut instinct, stronger than survival, was politeness.

"Yeah," she finally said. "Okay. I'll have to drop Dahlia off at home. Where do you want me to meet you?"

He didn't want her to have her own vehicle, which always added an extra element of complication. He also wanted to know where she lived, what the house looked like, and to be sure she didn't stand him up.

"How about I follow you and we can ride together. It'll save you gas, and save us time. I'll be pressed to get to work in time anyway."

Elisa nodded quickly, starting to walk again, "Well... Okay then. If you're sure. I'm parked over on the south end."

Rion skipped to catch up with her, "You believe in fate?"

Elisa swallowed, mouth twisting nervously, "Yeah. Yeah, I do."

"Me too. We're going to have a great time."

"I *did* have a great time," Elisa announced as they returned to her house. He opened the car door for her and walked her up to the door.

"It was a pleasure,"

It had really been a chore. She had talked a lot, a *lot*. He had purchased her an ice cream and she had eaten it in the most obnoxious way possible too. He had not even been able to force down his own sugary, frozen confection.

He stopped just outside the door, like a vampire waiting to be invited in. She unlocked it and slipped inside, pushing the dog back with her thigh.

"Well, you're going to be late for work. Thanks again!"

"I hope we get to do it again."

"Yeah, maybe. Thanks." She watched him like she was waiting for him to leave. When he continued to stand there, she closed the door. He could see her through the frosted glass, still standing just on the other side to watch and make sure he walked to the car. He did take a few steps away, just to make sure no one was outside in their yard, or coming down the street. When the coast was clear, he went back and knocked on the door.

She answered almost immediately, "Listen, I had a really great time but..."

He forced his way inside, using his body to shove both the door and her backwards. The door caught her forehead, leaving a red welt as she put her palm over it and stumbled back. She reached for a knife on the counter, but instead he jumped ahead of her and grabbed it, nearly cutting himself on the blade. The dog barked incessantly but skittered across the linoleum, nails clicking and sliding as it fought for traction to get away from the turmoil.

During the struggle, he found himself with the blade to her throat, much like he normally would have used his hands. He sliced it from one ear to another, watching as the dark blood gurgled and bubbled. Her windpipe cut with a crunch like a fresh piece of fruit, and it made a muffled whistle as she struggled to keep breathing. He could hear the dog panting wildly. He'd nearly forgotten it existed until it came barrelling towards him around the island in a burst of pale fur and teeth.

He stabbed the dog as it lunged at him, but when he swung the knife the dog tried to skid away across the floor from fear of the movement alone. It did not totally avoid his blade, but the tip sank into its shoulder deeply enough that Rion felt it strike bone. The dog squealed and cowered, and Rion trapped it between himself and the dishwasher. It didn't really fight back, slinging its head around with its mouth gaping open full of useless teeth as it screamed but still allowed itself to be so easily killed. He stabbed it until it quit paddling against the floor, and then he let it relax, tail still quivering behind it. He took the knife to the sink and washed it clean, setting it on the counter top as he searched the doors underneath the sink for cleaner. Nothing there satisfied him, but he was able to locate a big blue jug of bleach above the washer and dryer. He cleaned the sink and the bloody pawprints on the floor from his scuffle with the dog. He draped a white towel from the bathroom over the dead dog, watching as red polka dots slowly bled through the fabric.

He would have to wait a little while for it to get dark, but while he waited he laid her on garbage bags and cleaned around her. The floor was bleached, the door handles. He stood now, in nothing but his underwear, in front of the washing machine with his arms full of his own clothes, stained with the blood of the dog, and the towels he had used to clean. Rion mimicked the jingle of the washing machine in a monotone rumble as he tossed the bloody towels and clothes into the drum and pressed start. While it washed, he sat on the couch in the living room and watched the television on mute.

28
Polanski

David sauntered through the kitchen to replace the ice pack he had tucked inside his sling. His hand was casted, enclosing two broken knuckles and a fractured middle finger. He had probably torn his rotator cuff, but for now they were just limiting mobility and seeing how he did. Surgery was not an option, he had said. This was not the time for him to be taking short-term disability... This was not the time for him to take a weekend.

Leah was still mad. He could tell by the way she carried herself. Even when she talked to him like nothing was wrong, he could see it behind her eyes. A little flame that suggested she could burn him alive if he pushed her the wrong way. She entered the kitchen, nudging past him to get a bottle of water out of the refrigerator. She said excuse me, and called him honey, but he didn't think she meant it.

"You alright?" he asked.

"I'm fine. You?"

"Sore... Swapping out my ice."

She shrugged. "Did it to yourself."

"I mean... do you blame me, though?"

She looked up at him as she was twisting the top of the bottle off. She cracked the lid in the same way her eyes threatened she would also do to his neck. He knew she did not want to condone his behavior, but deep down... she had to understand didn't she?

"People can have opinions that are different than yours."

"This isn't about opinions," David snapped, feeling himself getting angry. "Why isn't anyone taking this seriously?"

"Taking what seriously? Some idiot on the radio shit talking?"

"No, all this that's happening..."

"People can't put their lives on hold."

"I'm just saying... You'd think with a fucking serial killer on the loose, girls would put dating on hold. You'd think people could just say inside and... Leah, I'm saying it again. *Lock their fucking doors.* I said it. The door. The fucking door."

He pointed a finger aggressively in the direction of the front door.

"David, calm down..."

"Where is Anna, anyway? I haven't seen her all day."

Leah's cheeks were flushed and she was picking at the grout on the countertop. David waited for a response but gained none. He hated to press her, he really did. He felt guilty over the way he was acting, and the way he had acted before. He didn't want to fight with her; she would always win.

"Where's she at, Leah?"

Leah looked up at him, brow threatening and jaw set, "On a date with Bryant."

"You have got to be fucking kidding me."

Leah came around the island to stand toe-to-toe with him. Despite the fact that he was an entire foot taller, he took a step back. He knew better than to fight her. She was vicious.

"You sound just like him, the guy on the radio," she snapped. He could see that even through her anger, she kind of regretted what she had just said. It stung, but only because he knew she was right.

"That guy was a dick."

"You're a dick. Get out."

29
Torres

He was jotting notes down furiously in the notebook as he sat at Robichaud's desk at the station. Robichaud hadn't been in yet, and Lucas didn't have his own desk, so he figured that he wouldn't mind him using it for just a little bit. He wasn't even supposed to be here today, but he couldn't focus while at his apartment anymore. Every sound had him on edge, and all he could think about was his trauma at Glenda Harrison's.

His collection of notes was mostly on flowers, and their respective meanings, from the companion guide to *Love in Bloom*. He was startled when someone slammed their hands down on the desk in front of him. He jumped, knees bumping against the underside of the wooden desk as he tried to stand straight up.

It was Robichaud. He looked tired, more so than usual. He smiled at Lucas, as though his initial action was just in good fun.

"Gotcha," he said.

Lucas exhaled, shutting his notebook shyly. "Sorry. Just needed somewhere to think."

"Hey, it's no big deal."

"It isn't?" he tried not to look so surprised, but he couldn't help but be suspicious at Robichuaud's amicable tone.

"Yeah, so... my wife wants me to invite you to dinner."

Lucas opened his mouth to say something but he couldn't do anything but stammer. The way that Robichaud was looking at him like he was an idiot, per usual, didn't help. Why would he want him to come to dinner? He almost wanted to decline because that would salvage having his feelings hurt, or being embarrassed.

"Well?" Robichaud insisted. "Are you coming?"

"I don't know. I have a lot going on."

"Tomorrow night, show up about seven. Just sit and eat, talk a little. It'll really mean a lot to my wife that you show up."

He shifted uncomfortably in the chair, watching as Robichaud's jaw clenched. He suddenly looked less friendly and less patient.

"Please."

Lucas nodded, swallowing a nervous lump in his throat. "Okay. Yeah. Seven o'clock tomorrow. I'm just going to head out now."

"Yeah, sure thing. Thanks. Listen, has anything weird happened to you? Outside of work? Threats or anything? More clues or notes?"

"No," Lucas said, gathering his things up in his arms as he pushed the chair in with his hip. He studied Robichaud for a few moments. "Why? Did something happen?"

He could tell that Robichaud didn't want to answer. A minute change in the expression on his face told Lucas that something *had* happened, but he wasn't going to tell him what it was.

"Nah, just wondering. Listen will you do a call back for Polanski?"

"Call back? I'm technically..." He wasn't even working today. He paused, fumbling with the spiral on his notebook. He didn't want to cause any issues, and he supposed any work looked good on him. He wondered where Polanski was today, and he wondered if Robichaud knew what had happened the other night. He didn't dare ask.

"Yeah, I'll do a call back. Who is it?"

"Some kid named Elyas at Fellowship. He was apparently a friend of Mary Allen's, and Polanski gave him his card. He was supposed to call if he remembered anything else that would help, and he called this morning. He gave Polanski a decent description of the guy that matches prior descriptions. Give him a call."

He extended a piece of paper with a phone number to Torres, who took it and eagerly headed out the door.

He sat down in his car, not bothering to turn it on because it had no air conditioning. It was a warm fall, warmer than previous years. He felt like the cause might be the heat of hatred, the way some sickness shaped like a man had wiggled its way into the flesh of the town, somehow affecting everything down to the weather.

Lucas called Elyas from his personal cell phone, caught off guard when the kid answered on the first ring.

"Hello?"

"Ah, yeah, this is Detective Torres with the Whitebranch Police Department. I'm just returning your call."

"Oh, I was trying to get in touch with another detective... David Polanski?"

"Detective Polanski is out of the office due to some... unexpected health issues so I'm covering his calls right now. I hope that's okay."

"Oh, yeah... is he alright? I'll pray for him."

"Yeah, I think he's going to be okay."

Were any of them going to be okay? Other than Robichaud, who seemed totally unaffected to Lucas. He didn't seem concerned, laden with guilt and discontentment. He didn't seem like he laid awake at night wondering about the monster roaming the streets.

"I was cleaning the church, Brother Hodge pays me a little to vacuum and stuff... Anyway I was cleaning and there were some old flowers in the foyer. I get nosy so I was reading all of the cards on the flowers and there was a bouquet in a vase that said: 'Mary, I know you'll never see these. I hope they serve your memory well.'"

Lucas didn't want to be paranoid. "It sounds like a heartfelt memoriam. Someone just donated some flowers in her honor."

"Well, that's the thing... the flowers were delivered the day of the revival. The night she disappeared."

Lucas felt like his chest was tightening with every exhalation, so that he was able to bring in less and less air. His head felt light. Somehow he was shaken, even though he knew that Mary Allen was another victim. This new evidence made her death more concrete, more real.

"Are you sure?"

"I am."

"Does anyone know who delivered the flowers? Who signed for the delivery?"

"Nobody. There wasn't an invoice. They were just left there. There are cameras in the front and I have already talked to Brother Hodge, when I got his blessing to call Detective Polanski. He said he has a screenshot of the guy and he's going to bring it to the station."

"Where were the flowers ordered from?"

"I don't know for sure, but the card was from Roots 'n Shoots."

"Thanks, Elyas. I'm sorry about your loss. I know how difficult this is for you and your church."

There was a silence and then a shuddering breath on the other side, "Thank you. Thank you. Brother Hodge should be in sometime with the screenshot."

"Does he have the card?"

"What?"

"The card. The one in the bouquet."

"No... I threw it away. The trash is still out back. I will get it for you."

"That would be great."

"It'll be sitting inside the church on the entry table..."

"It's appreciated."

"Goodbye, Detective."

Lucas hung up the phone and headed to the church.

He was a little nervous to go inside Roots and Shoots, and so he sat in the parking lot for several minutes as he rehearsed what he would say. It was mostly because he was feeling a little deviant, because he had not been told to go to the store, and because he was off duty. The purpose of this venture was solely to satisfy his own curiosity, to see if he was right.

The store was quiet, other than the gentle hiss of sprinklers. He walked straight to the front desk, leaning onto the counter as he dinged the bell. A man emerged from an aisleway, wiping his hands on a forest green rag. He walked to the desk hesitantly, setting off more anxiety in Lucas as he worried that his presence was not welcome. It didn't help that even on his off days he wore a badge around his waist.

The man rounded the backside of the counter, depositing the rag somewhere out of sight. He wasn't wearing a name tag, but today neither was Lucas. He was tall, with dark hair and dull blue eyes. They were so flat and lightless that he thought they might have been black as well.

"Good evening, I'm Detective Torres. I just have a couple of questions for you, if you're able to answer them."

The man studied his face – a fraction longer and it would have been awkward. Lucas almost said something else to fill in the silence, but then the other man spoke.

"Yes, I think I can spare a few minutes. What can I do for you, Detective?"

"I was wondering if you could pull up some sales and delivery records for me."

The man nodded and moved to a small mounted tablet at the register. "Of course. What can I look for?"

"Did someone deliver flowers to Delton Church of the Fellowship or place an order for the church any time this past week?"

"I'll take a look... issue is we have the anonymous order form online and also the dropbox."

Of course. No man in his right mind would order the flowers for his victims without using the dropbox or online form. But there was something else... the handwriting on all of the cards was the same, even the flowers that Lucas witnessed the man delivering into the hands of Olivia Brown on the post office surveillance.

"If someone uses an anonymous service, can they customize a card?"

"I'm sorry?"

"Can they write their own card?"

"If they have their own blanks at home." The man shrugged. "Sure. They just drop it in the box with their payment and order form. It looks like there have been quite a few orders for the church recently."

"I'm looking for one Friday."

"I delivered that one. It was an anonymous order. Dropbox. Paid in cash."

"Dammit."

Now what? A dead end?

"I could always keep an eye out," the man suggested quietly.

"What's that?"

"I could keep an eye out for suspicious orders. Pay better attention to the customized cards. Give you a call if I see anything... If this has something to do with cards and orders of course. What should I be looking for?"

"Ah, yeah. That would be great, if it isn't too much trouble. Just any 'secret admirer' type notes, anything malicious... anything suspicious."

"I can do that."

"You can reach me at the department. My name is Detective Torres."

"Anthony Torres?"

"No, Lucas Torres."

The man waved his hand. "Oh, I'm sorry. My mistake."

30
Rion

Rion didn't know anyone named Anthony Torres, but teasing out Detective Torres' first name would be vital in trying to garner information about his personal life online. Being one of the younger men on the force, he expected that he would find a plethora of information on social media. He discovered the assumption to be correct, unearthing plenty of public posts and information about Lucas and his life. He was proud to be a police officer. He liked animals and taking random pictures of nature. He seemed to be fond of coffee and ice cream, and his mother.

More importantly, Rion noticed that Torres lived alone. He had pictures of himself outside of an apartment complex that Rion found fairly easily after driving through Whitebranch. He didn't know the apartment number, but some further snooping confirmed it had to be one of the upper levels. A drive through the parking lot to find where his personal car (a piece of shit) was parked gave Rion a pretty good idea of which building was his. It was on the end, facing away from the others near a dumpster.

Another thing he knew about Lucas Torres was that he idolized Robichaud. This was understandable. Something he did not understand was why Torres had ventured out on his own to the garden center. Was he trying to show up Robichaud? This would be his eventual downfall. Insult to Robichaud would not be tolerated. He could figure this out without Torres' help. Rion would not let Torres get in the way of his relationship with Robichaud, their intimate game. Did Torres have some kind of idea? What did they know? This element of mystery and suspense was not pleasant for Rion. Torres wasn't stupid, Rion would give him that. It took a little bit of brain to figure out some of the clues that had been left behind. He knew that he had a copy of *Love in Bloom*, and he was catching on.

He had always thought of a gun as such an impersonal way to kill someone. From the selection to the execution, every victim was something personal to him. Guns were loud and messy and incriminating all on their own. He wanted to be close enough to touch them, feel their warmth, and smell their fear. He wanted to feel the way their heart fluttered, in its last frantic moments, like a bird against the walls of a cage. Then everything was quiet, frozen in a moment of stimulation: there was something perfect about those moments right after death. He *cherished* those moments.

Still, he stood there in his kitchen holding the dead girl's revolver, turning it over and over in his hands. He wondered why she hadn't gone for the gun when she noticed something wasn't quite right with Rion. He had noted her discomfort early in the night, and he had thought she would have been a fighter. Instead, he had wrapped his hands around her throat like it was a thick piece of fabric, twisting and crushing until she had suffocated. Her lips had turned just the lightest shade of blue, purple veins creeping across her pale skin. The whites of her eyes had erupted with pink, causing the dark irises to nearly glow. Another pretty thing. He remembered them all, and she would be one of his favorite creations.

Rion stuffed the revolver back into a drawer. He didn't like to keep things, because things had a way of finding their way to the surface. He thought he might need that gun, if he did not come close enough to touch Robichaud like he did the girls. To feel him like he did the girls. He didn't want to have to stoop to that level. The cold and quick death of the gun was not for Robichaud. He deserved more than that, but if it came down to it he would use it.

He might be a romantic, but he knew when you had to call it.

31
Quentin

Quentin stood next to Paltro as they stared down at the dead woman in the grass. It was too familiar, it was feeling too normal. He didn't want to get used to it, but he could feel it. Paltro even looked tired, and this kind of thing never did bother him. He was kind of *at home* with the dead, but he seemed to look more and more drawn as the days went on. They all did, he supposed.

"Her name is Elisa McBride. She had her ID and purse with her, still had debit cards, credit cards, cash... no obvious robbery. This was obviously not where the murder took place, so we found her place of residence and went there. Door was locked, lights were off other than a lamp on the table. When we got in, there were no signs of struggle, no visible blood on first walkthrough. Laundry was still going, but everything smelled strongly of bleach. Dead dog in the kitchen with a white towel laid over it. Stabbed to death."

"Stabbed the fucking dog," Quentin muttered.

"Seems like he may have stuck around after she was dead, for a little while. He cleaned up. Maybe he waited until dark so he could move her body outside. No one in the neighborhood noted anything suspicious, though they said the dog was barking at one point but apparently they've called animal control multiple times on the dog being loud or escaping the yard."

"You've really done your legwork on this one," Quentin noted quietly, looking over at Paltro out of the corner of his eye. "You alright?"

"Yeah, just trying to get ahead of this thing. Trying to find anything I can to give us that step up that we need."

The sound of keys made both men look over to see Torres trying to step over the crime scene tape, only to trip when it caught up between his legs. He recovered well, holding his coffees up in the air triumphantly.

Torres paused several feet away, looking down at the girl. "Man. She's..."

Quentin interjected, "Dead?"

"Well, I mean... yeah."

"Certainly looks that way. Did you come all the way out here to give us that intuitive assessment? That's why we have this guy."

He jabbed his thumb in Paltro's direction.

Paltro didn't smile, but contributed, "To be fair, I'm only here when they're dead. Because they're dead."

Torres tried to be chipper, handing Robichaud one of the cups of coffee with a smile. "Got you a coffee, Robichaud. Just the way you like it."

Quentin jerked the cup away abruptly, "Go do something useful. Keep the media back, they're like vultures. Before you know it they'll be all over us."

Torres nodded, muttering, "You're welcome..."

Then he left. Quentin let out a long exhale. He felt a little guilty about it, but Torres was virtually useless in these situations. He saw Paltro now looking at him, quietly. He filled in the silence quickly.

"Alright, Paltro. I want to know what you know, when you know it. Keep me updated. We'll get this guy."

"You got it, but... Hey, look. You should take it easy on Torres. He's just... enthusiastic. It's actually kind of refreshing to see somebody who is still excited about their career when we're surrounded by all these burned out, bitter old men."

Quentin laughed, "Oh? Like who?"

Paltro raised his eyebrows. "Like you. You had gotten better about it... Not so harsh. I had noticed, he had noticed. He just wants to do his job, and he needs to be recognized for his effort."

Quentin sipped his coffee. He knew Paltro was right. Torres was young, still excited about his career. It was all he had, Quentin supposed. At his age, Quentin had been engaged already and planning to start a family. He had a house and a car payment. Torres lived and breathed the department, other than visiting his mother in No Business. Maybe that's why Quentin was so hard on him, he wished he had a chance at life before this job ripped it all away.

He cleared his throat. "Do we think this was him? The same killer as the last five?"

Paltro shrugged, looking down at the girl again. "Hard to say. She certainly seemed like his type."

"Does he have a type? No consistent age, hair color, socioeconomic status... Nothing."

Paltro was quiet for a few moments, slowly moving into a crouching position beside Elisa's body. "He does. It's in the eyes. Even when they're dead, you can kind of see it. You know?"

Quentin made an uncomfortable noise, watching as a fly landed on her face and crawled across her unblinking eye. He reached up to scratch his cheek. "Where's Polanski?"

Paltro motioned over his shoulder. "He's not right today. Couldn't stomach it."

Quentin saw him now for the first time, standing next to Quentin's parked cruiser. He was smoking a cigarette, picking a piece of rust on the hood of the car until it was growing like a festering sore. He also wore a sling and a cast, and his hand looked fucked. Quentin left Paltro, walking over to the cruiser where his partner stood.

"You alright? Get in for a second."

Polanski threw his cigarette into the grass and got into the passenger side of the vehicle. He exhaled heavily, filling the car with the smell of smoke.

"Smoking? That bad?"

Polanski put his face in his hands. "I did something bad, Quentin."

Quentin fidgeted in his seat, reaching up to pick at the steering wheel. "What's up, man? What's going on?'

"I beat this guy up... this guy that called into the radio. He was talking about the girls, about Ji-su, saying they brought it on themselves. I went and found the guy. Beat the shit out of him. Hurt him bad I think."

Quentin was surprised, to say the least. Usually if someone was going to lose his cool, it was going to be him and not Polanski. Of course, Polanski had done plenty of his own dirty deeds but something like this... Well, it meant he was having some real issues.

"Sounds like he deserved it..." Quentin whispered, trying to be supportive.

"It still ain't right."

The way Polanski's voice cracked made Quentin have a pang in his gut. He didn't want him to feel guilty, even if there was a better way to handle the situation.

"I know... but everything is fucked up right now. You're under a lot of stress... You have a daughter."

"Most detectives never have to deal with something like this. Not in a town like this one. I mean... Damn, it really is a serial murderer isn't it? A spree?"

He didn't want to admit it, even now. Even when the facts were obvious and undeniable. He felt as though speaking that truth bore it into existence.

"It has to be one guy... has to be," Polanski continued.

"Do you think we can catch him? Before he goes after another girl?"

"We have to."

"Lot of pressure..."

"Right?"

"Scary to think he's gotten away with this much." Even this was hard for Quentin to say. He still felt like it was his fault; somehow because he had been unable to apprehend the suspect, he had been allowed to continue killing.

"He's so clean... too precise. He's taking his time, not frenzied.... not yet. He has a head on him. This is like a big game to him, see how long he can keep evading us. He likes to leave clues and always moves the body. Unpredictable. Most of these guys have patterns, a clear MO. A style. You know, like a normal human being. They have a playlist, and if you listen enough you can eventually guess the next song. Not this guy. Easy to feel like he's a ghost or something... But he's still a guy. He'll mess up."

Quentin laughed, quietly noting, "It's funny. I was just telling Emily you called him a ghost."

Polanski seemed to relax suddenly, melting back into the seat, "How is Em? Haven't seen her in months."

"Feels like it to me too."

"You guys alright?"

"Yeah, I'm working on it. Seeing a shrink."

"A shrink?" he laughed.

Quentin awkwardly rubbed the space between his eyes. "Yeah, you should try it. Her name's Cecilia Norrington. She's down off Rhode Avenue, the blue building. Under construction right now, but she's going to have a really nice set of offices there when they get it all cleaned up."

"Ah yeah. I know the place. I don't think I need somebody in my headspace though."

"If one of us needed it, it was you."

Polanski snorted, "Shut up."

Quentin sighed, back to business. He started the car, turning the air on low, "You know Paltro said something about him having a type... something about their eyes? What do you think?"

Polanski shrugged, "I think Paltro's a quack... I don't think the guy has a type, I think he's opportunist. Just gets them when the getting's good."

"Yeah... makes sense." He wanted to agree with Polanski on this one, since they often did see eye to eye on this sort of thing. There was something about what Paltro said though, and the way that he seemed to look at the girls, that made him think that maybe, just maybe, there *was* something subliminal in the eyes of these girls. Something that this psycho was drawn to. Was it a vulnerability? Something he knew that he could grab onto and twist and manipulate to get the girls alone, into his car, or off guard enough to attack?

"Might be good to suggest a countywide curfew until we get somewhere on the investigation. Glory of a small town. Never know what sewer he'll crawl out of next," Polanski suggested sheepishly.

It wasn't a bad idea, Quentin mused, "Yeah, you know... I think I'll see if Chief can swing by the diner and I'll suggest it to her. Won't be able to enforce it completely, but maybe it'll help put a strain on his hunting habits."

"She'll make you do the interview, wonder boy. Just don't give the creep a big head, alright? He probably already thinks he has us chasing our own tails. Yeah, maybe need to hit him where it hurts. In the ego."

This type of guy was usually narcissistic, weren't they? Maybe Polanski was right, maybe going straight for the old ego was exactly what they needed to push him into making a hasty mistake.

Quentin and Pat Welch sat across from each other at Retta's Cafe. She liked to eat there almost as much as Polanski, but she argued that she tried to watch her weight so she didn't frequent it nearly as often. She also sat by the door, as was usual for her, she always liked to have sight of and direct access to an exit no matter where she was. Quentin was uncomfortable, both because he didn't want to be having this conversation and because he wasn't close enough with Pat to consider lunch something to look forward to. But Polanski was right, this had to be done. Quentin had ordered a loaded burger and onion rings, Pat had opted for breakfast.

"So you'll do the interview, then," Pat said, tucking a napkin onto her lap. It wasn't a question, it was a statement.

Quentin shrugged, "Yeah, if you want. Although I think someone with a little more charisma might be better off doing it though. "

"We don't need charisma, don't need someone to sugar coat this."

"I'm glad you said that because... I think we need to do just the opposite of that. Me and Polanski were talking..."

"Well... 'Me and Polanski were talking' is never a good start to an idea, but I'm listening."

Quentin waited to respond as a perky red-headed waitress walked over and set their plates in front of them. An onion ring on the haphazard stack fell to the table and Quentin snatched it up and started eating it immediately.

"Do you all need anything else?"

Quentin shook his head no, but Pat responded: "Hot sauce."

Somehow she did seem like the type to throw some hot sauce on everything.

The waitress returned to the kitchen with no signs of coming back, so Pat started cutting into an over-easy egg. "Go on."

"I think we need to be brutal. I think he's gotten too comfortable, he's taunting us."

"You mean like a smear campaign? Drag him on the radio?"

"Yeah, something like that."

"That's ballsy, Robichaud. Could bring too much attention to you, if he knows who you are. Not exactly something I can give you permission to do... but I've turned my head more than once. You know that. I can turn my head again."

"I'll ask them to leave my name out. Do it anonymously."

"I think that's best. We don't know what this creep is capable of. All I know is if we don't get this handled soon we're going to have to call in the feds. We're getting in over our heads here."

"I've got to get him, it's all that matters to me right now."

"I know it feels that way. Sometimes we don't get them though. There was a string of murders over in Heresy County a few years back... You remember that?"

"Yeah, yeah I do. I always thought someone probably did get him though. You know, put him down nice and quiet away from the reporters. Hopefully the way he deserved. He just... stopped killing."

"Stopped, put down, or moved on. If our guy moves on, he won't be our problem anymore." She paused, brow furrowed while she looked up at one of the fluorescent light bulbs like it was a physical idea beacon. "You know what, I like this plan. Scare him. Put the heat on him."

"Yeah, I will. I'll get it organized."

What neither Quentin nor Pat noticed was the man sitting in Polanski's regular seat just a few booths away, drinking a black coffee and pretending to flirt with the waitress as he eavesdropped on the conversation.

32
Paltro

Elisa McBride's house had been unsettling. Deen had dreamed about it after the initial investigation: nightmares of its infinite quietness. It wasn't Elisa's pale face, surrounded by the nearly blinding veridian of the field, or the way the hum of insects seemed to become deafening as they approached her. It was something about a home that was suddenly abandoned: the way that everything in that home was Elisa, how pieces of that woman were hidden in every nook and cranny, the way the house begged to tell her story. Life there had been so suddenly snuffed out that it still glowed with some kind of animation, as though the universe hoped for some sort of viability.

Deen had combed every inch of the house quietly, finding pieces of the puzzle as he went. He had noticed no obvious blood other than what had seeped out of the dead dog. Luminol caused the entire room to glow, but he suspected the use of bleach, judging by the odor and empty bottle in the garbage. He did find a strand of dark hair, and plenty of partial fingermarks. The man had apparently gone through and wiped surfaces he had touched as he went. The dryer had beeped to remind someone that there were clothes inside. He went up to find some towels folded on top but otherwise it was empty.

He sat on the edge of his bed with his elbows propped up on his knees, staring at the green light on his refrigerator's ice maker down the hall. It created a fuzzy halo in the darkness. Behind him, a small shuffle against the sheets broke his dazed concentration. He flopped back onto the bed, crawling over to the opposite side.

"Did I wake you, baby? I'm sorry," he whispered, kissing the fat-headed dog on the snout. Her tail thumped against the sheets loudly. He scratched behind her ears before getting up out of the bed and slipping on house-sandals. The dog yawned, crawling across the bed on her belly before sliding lazily off and onto the floor to follow him.

He sat down at the kitchen table after retrieving a glass of milk, turning on his laptop and allowing it to wash him and the room in a blue glow. The desktop image was innocent enough: the too-close up face of the same dog that now lay on top of his feet on the floor. He right clicked and made the icons on the desktop visible. Rows and rows of folders appeared suddenly, hiding the canine's face.

Deen knew that if anyone ever found what he had on his personal laptop, he would likely lose his job, if not face jail time. Folders of dead people, wounds... little things that fascinated him, and sometimes he just felt the desire to look at them. A morbid lust, not unlike the one he was sure the killer felt. Not one unlike an author of horror seemed to crave, or people who slowed down to look at a car accident, movie goers or collected taboo torture films. It wasn't unusual, he told himself.

A folder titled "Wildflowers" was the one he chose today, taking another sip of the cool, smooth milk. He had heard someone on the radio refer to the situation as the Wildflower Murders, both due to the girls being found in fields and the little flower tokens left behind. The folder popped open, but instead of photos of gruesome injuries and macro shots of wounds, the images showed only their eyes.

All of their eyes, illuminated by the overhead lights at the morgue. Windows to the soul, a peek at something that he had sought out.

A vantage point that he had enveloped himself in as the curtains slowly pulled closed.

33
Quentin

The Spigot was a bar just outside of Whitebranch, on the southern end of the city limits, down a dusty little backroad that ended in a gravel parking lot. Quentin had spent a lot of nights after work at the bar, sitting on the very end to avoid socializing as much as possible. Someone always slid in to try and chat, but he found that short and simple responses drove the majority of the people away. Some of them still hung around, sitting beside him awkwardly as he downed another glass of whatever the bartender recommended that was on tap.

What he didn't do very often was bring someone with him to The Spigot. Tonight he entered the familiar doors of the old building with Torres in tow.

They sat down at the end of the bar, where the bartender came over. He was a tall, awkward kind of guy but had a charming personality. The way he leaned on the bar, just teetering on the edge of too-close, was more relaxing and nonthreatening than it was intrusive. Quentin was never much of a tipper, but he always tipped the bartender at The Spigot... just in case not doing so could somehow make the beer less palatable.

"Been wanting to talk to you," Quentin admitted quietly, waiting until the bartender was out of earshot.

"Am I still invited to dinner?"

Quentin was surprised by the question and he scoffed, "Of course. My wife would never let me *uninvite* you, even if I did want to."

He noted that Torres did not seem comforted by this, staring at the light lager that sat in front of him. Quentin wasn't surprised that the younger man had chosen the beer that most resembled watered down piss, both in appearance and taste. People who didn't like beer always chose those pale drinks.

"I know you're wanting to talk. I know you were upset by what you found at the old woman's house. I understand that it must be tough to have seen that... all of that."

"I don't think you do understand. You don't seem bothered by any of this. You aren't... I mean..." Torres rubbed his thumb over the condensation on his mug nervously, but he didn't say anything else.

Quentin took another long drink of the amber beer, waiting for the younger man to continue. In the silence he cleared his throat, "You can say it. Whatever it is. It's fine."

"I just feel like this is a little out of our league."

Quentin sighed, rolling his eyes and leaning back on the bar stool so heavily that he nearly toppled over.

Torres quickly went on, "I'm not saying we don't have great detectives... You know that I think you and Polanski are great detectives..."

"We've dealt with homicides before. This isn't new."

"It isn't just a homicide, though. Not a drug deal gone wrong or domestic shit that we usually see. Doesn't it... unsettle you? Like make you feel uneasy?"

It did. It really fucking did. He didn't know why he didn't want to tell Torres this, he told himself it was maybe because he didn't trust him.

Deep down he knew it was really because he wanted to protect him. He wanted him to enjoy his job, he wanted him to feel like he knew what he was doing. Even though he liked giving him hell and liked putting him down and watching him stumble around stuttering and flustered. He didn't want him to really fail, not at this point. Not after what they were going through. He wanted him to tell people how he helped solve this huge case when he was older, he wanted him to help bring this guy down.

He instead insisted, "Nope. Not new. Somebody killed somebody else. Murder is murder, and a killer is just a man... and man makes mistakes."

"It's just that this is like Jack the Ripper loose in Mayberry. None of this is coming out the way I wanted it to. I don't mean to insult you or the department or anyone."

"I get it."

"Do you?" He seemed to work up enough courage to confront Quentin now, sitting up a little straighter in his seat. A wave of gold sloshed over the rim of his glass. "I feel like if you did, you'd have pushed the Chief to call in some outside help. State police or something. Every minute this guy is free he is dangerous. He's leaving a trail of dead women and we're just following along behind him. So *do you* get it? Or do you just not give a fuck, Robichaud?"

Quentin didn't want to tell him that he was actually the one who had pushed the Chief to hold off on calling in help, that he wanted to bag this guy himself. He had convinced himself it wasn't about pride, but in the end it was something just like that. This was the town he had grown up in and he had sworn to protect it as a police officer. The killer was just a man. A man in a small town. Someone knew him; Quentin might even know him. As long as he was just a man, he could be stopped. He had carried the death of Lola Simmons with him and it had eaten away at him, that looming mystery.

"I do," Quentin finally said, dropping the volume of his voice as the bartender walked by. "I do. We're going to get him, though. He's just a guy. Like you and me."

"No, not like you and me. I can't eat a sandwich without leaving crumbs everywhere. This guy is choking girls out in their own homes and our forensics guys walk in and can't tell anything has happened until they start doing their... whatever magicky stuff forensics does."

"Someone will figure it out," Quentin assured him.

"I think... I think it's about the flowers."

"Torres, *please*. Stop with the flowers."

"The guy knows flowers. He has the game or the book. They don't sell it anymore, you know."

"You know it isn't that simple. It's never simple."

Torres looked him in the eye. "You're right. It's never simple."

34
Torres

Lucas sat outside of the Robichaud home for several minutes before he decided to finally go inside. He had arrived ten minutes early and now walked up to the door five minutes late. He held a bouquet of flowers in his hands, something discounted at Roots and Shoots. He wondered if it was in bad taste, but he thought it might be a good gesture all the same... especially if Robichaud truly believed the flowers meant nothing.

He knocked on the door, waiting nervously. His heart was pounding, and he felt a little bit nauseous. They had a nice house. It was cute: not too small, but not gaudy. The yard was just a little overgrown and he noted two newspapers on the stoop, but otherwise it was well maintained. He thought about his own apartment with a week's worth of laundry piled in the basket and the same spoon and bowl he washed and used for everything.

A woman answered the door, smiling broadly at him. She was dressed like she was ready for a nice dinner but still very casual, and Lucas suddenly wished he'd worn a better outfit. He was in a t-shirt that ran just a little small and a pair of faded jeans that would make girls blush. He clutched the flowers to his chest and returned her smile.

"Mrs. Robichaud, thank you for having me over for dinner tonight."

"Oh, it's a pleasure. Please, call me Emily."

"I'm Lucas."

"Lucas, come on in."

He walked in, kicking his shoes off at the door, which seemed to delight Mrs. Robichaud. When he had told his mother he was coming to the Robichauds for dinner, the first thing she had said was *you better take off your damn shoes at the door.* He followed her to the kitchen where the scent of spaghetti sauce, Italian spices, and garlic flooded his senses. He hadn't eaten a *good* meal in a while, and he was already salivating.

Robichaud was plating the spaghetti, sloppily throwing massive spoonfuls of pasta onto three plates.

"Torres."

He felt immediately relaxed by seeing Robichaud. He was consistent - even though it was his day off, he was wearing a white button up and slacks. It made Lucas feel a little less silly for wearing his badge *everywhere*. There wasn't an off-duty and on-duty Robichaud, there was just Robichaud.

"Sir."

Robichaud snorted and motioned to the wilting flowers in Torres' hands, "Those for me?"

He had admittedly forgotten about them and looked down to see the trail of petals he'd left from the door to where he stood now. "Oh, no... No, these are for you, Mrs. Robichaud."

She took them from his hands, lifting them up to her nose with a smile, "Oh, thank you!"

"They've seen better days..." he admitted with a little blush on his cheeks. "I don't have AC in the car so they got a little wind beat. Sorry."

"Don't be silly. They're beautiful. Just a little water and they'll be as good as new. Come sit at the table."

Robichaud sat at the head of the table and Lucas sat across from Emily. He tried to appear controlled while he ate the spaghetti, and not like he had been living in a cardboard box his entire life. He wondered how Robichaud avoided dripping sauce on his white shirt. He could already feel some above his own eyebrow from an enthusiastically slurped noodle.

"So, Lucas. Tell me about yourself. Where are you from? Do your parents live here?" Emily asked, pinching off a piece of garlic bread.

Quentin interrupted, mouth full of food, "Lucas?"

Lucas looked at him, blinking in confusion. He didn't know his first name. Robichaud didn't know his first name. He had worked with him for how long now? Under him, directly involved with him, basically working *for him...* and he didn't know his name. Torres knew Robichaud's *middle* name, his birthday, how he liked his coffee, what size shoe he wore, and what his desert island band was (Creedence, by a longshot). Robichaud didn't know his name. It made him feel even less valuable than he usually did in the presence of the older detective.

"I'm... I'm Lucas." he patted his chest gently.

Robichaud stared at him for a moment, chewing the tough crust of the five-minute garlic bread, "You don't look like a Lucas."

Emily cleared her throat, jaw tightening as she looked in the direction of her husband.

Lucas went on, steadying his voice, "I'm from over in Heresy County. No Business."

Emily engaged immediately, demeanor pleasant and comforting, "Never heard of No Business. Is it near Wright's Post?"

Robichaud, who seemed oblivious to any hurt feelings, responded as he chewed, "South of Foster's Hollow. Little shit stain on the map."

Emily gave him another unnoticed side-eye, but Lucas shrugged. "He's not wrong. Mom still lives there. Never knew my dad. Well. I kind of knew him, but he left when I was young."

"I'm sorry to hear that. It must've been hard."

"Nah. Was harder when he was there. We were better off without him. Mom's lonely without me because it was always the two of us, but the commute was hard on me. She's really proud that I'm doing this line of work. I wanted to be a cop my entire life, that's all I've ever wanted to do."

He regretted saying it immediately, worried that he sounded like a kid at show-and-tell day at school. Emily's smile was still warm, eyes glistening with kindness. He liked her. He wondered how she put up with a dick like Robichaud day in and day out, and still remained soft like this. He picked at a chipped edge of his plate, a little sharp edge underneath the lip.

"Well, I hear you're an excellent officer so far. Quentin has nothing but nice things to say about you."

Lucas faked a smile, trying to sound more chipper. "That means a lot. Gruff old man, it's hard to tell sometimes."

Emily winked at Quentin. "I know."

As down as he felt, he tried to brighten the situation, "Mom loves him. I think she has a crush. No offense, Mrs. Robichaud. She's always asking me how he is, and when she might get to meet him."

Quentin actually smiled, burying his face in his hands.

35
Rion

Today was incredibly special. He had not been able to overhear the entire conversation at the cafe, but he had confirmed that Robichaud was in fact doing an interview on the radio about *him*, about the case, about their budding relationship. He was finally going to tell the world about them. It was something that Rion did not want to do alone, he wanted to share the moment with someone. He needed someone to revel in the excitement and thrill with him.

That was where Sharon Cook came in.

Sharon had been talking to Rion on a singles app for weeks. He had avoided meeting up with her earlier because she was not as 'safe' as some of the girls he sought out. Divorcee with an ex-husband that she was proudly civil with. Two kids. A sister that visited regularly. These were all things that Rion didn't want to have to deal with. But then there was her enthusiasm to meet with him, the desperation, the desire. Now was her time.

He had parked his car a good distance off of the highway, down a trail that had once been popular for picnicking. It was overrun now with poison sumac, so it had fallen out of favor, and Rion found this to be ideal. The car blocked most of the view, and it was difficult to see where he was located from the road (but it was easy to see the highway from where he was parked).

He had bound and gagged Sharon, propped against his rear wheel. She was dazed and disoriented, her short blonde hairs matted in a black wad of blood on the left side of her head. She'd come to at least an hour ago but still didn't seem to quite have a grasp of where she was or what was going on. Judging by the tears, Rion knew she had decided it wasn't good.

Rion had left his door open with the radio playing. A catchy tune emitted from the speaker, and he found himself dancing. He wasn't the type to dance like this, not really. He just didn't dance. He got no pleasure out of things like that. He thought, maybe, it was just because he had never been this excited for something. The anticipation was *killing* him.

The song ended and the radio host came over the speaker. "Alright, folks. I have a really special guest here tonight. This is one of Whitebranch's own. He's asked to remain anonymous and you're going to see why... Let me tell you, this is really, really exciting, guys."

Rion dove onto the ground with Sharon, jerking her back into a sitting position beside him. She screamed against the bright yellow handkerchief between her teeth, turning her face away from him as though he were something too hideous to look upon. He kept his arm around her shoulders, squeezing her against him.

"Shhhhh... Listen, listen. He's on!"

"He's here to talk to us about the serial killer we have on the loose in Delton county. That is what's going on isn't it? There's been a lot of speculation but no definitive confirmation by authorities."

Robichaud's voice next. Calm, cool, collected, confident. Rion got chills, his entire body wracked with them, goosebumps making his hair stand on end. His heart leapt in his throat, and he put his free hand to his lips.

"Yes, we do believe all of the recent murders of local women have been by a single perpetrator."

"Terrifying. Absolutely terrifying. We've been calling him the Delton Ripper, although his spree has been called the Wildflower Murders. What is with the little game pieces? The police seem to be wanting to keep that hush-hush, but that seems to be something my viewers are fascinated with."

"All I can say is that the pieces seem to be a calling card. We have a few leads we are following, and I can't tell you more than that. "

"Do you have any suspects? Is he someone local? Or her... Could be a 'her;' this is the twenty first century, after all."

Quentin chuckled, "Oh, it's a man."

"Oh? How do you know?"

"I can't say much..."

"Uh-huh, go on."

"Let's just say he isn't going to be a problem much longer. We have him boxed in. It's all coming to a head."

Rion suddenly dropped his arm from Sharon, brow furrowing.

"Wow! Listeners, we really are getting the absolute prime in details here. I can't believe this. What closed the case? Nail in the legal coffin for him, so to speak? Can you tell us that?"

"Well, it's never easy to find these guys at first, especially when you aren't sure the crimes are related. This guy, though... he is predictable, stale as old bread. It was clear once forensics got involved, we have a stellar forensics crew by the way, that it was the same dumbass... Can I say 'dumbass' on the radio?"

"Well, you just did. Twice. But let's keep it clean."

"Okay. Look, I'm just saying he's not the smartest criminal we've ever tracked. The hardest part about catching him has been wading through the mountain of evidence he leaves behind when he thinks he's cleaning up."

"I thought he would be like a sociopath, I think that's what they call them in the crime shows. You know, really smart. The Ted Bundy type: good looking, charming, manipulative."

"Nah, not this guy. He's living out the fantasy that he's untouchable, that he's some genius and criminal mastermind. But time's up."

Rion's face had drained of any joy. The excitement, the exhilaration, was replaced by fury. Robichaud and the host continued to talk about the case but he couldn't hear them anymore.

"Why would he... He doesn't believe any of that. He's trying to upset me. They have no idea." He stood up so abruptly that Sharon toppled over, falling to her side. She was trying to wiggle her hands free of the zipties, blood oozing from the tight edges. Rion barked at her, "They have no idea what I am capable of."

He shrugged his shoulders, holding his hands up and taking a deep breath. He smiled with his eyes closed, "He's bored. I just need to spice things up. This is the only way he could... He could communicate with me. Through the radio. Like the guy in the movie with the stereo, you remember that movie?"

Sharon shook her head from side to side, clear snot pouring from her nose as she cried on the ground.

"It was romantic," Rion insisted, crouching down beside her. He reached out, running the backside of his fingers across her face.

Sharon must have seen an opportunity, because she took it. She pushed herself away with her feet and then kicked up as hard as she could, both feet hitting Rion right in the forehead. He was initially pleased to reach up and feel that his nose was intact and had not been struck, but then his ears began to ring fiercely. The world was suddenly blindingly bright, and he was dizzy.

"Fuck!" He stayed on his hands and knees at first, world spinning around him. The back of his head hurt, his forehead hurt, he'd bit the end of his tongue. Sharon was trying to get onto her feet, but her own knees were weak. She stumbled away and fell, lying on her back and scooting away from him again.

Rion went after her, grabbing her throat with his gloved hand and lifting her up onto her feet. He nearly had to drag her back over to the car, the tops of her shoes crackling against the gravel as she refused (or could not muster the energy to) walk.

"Shhhh, shhh, shhh. What's wrong? Don't you think our little date is romantic?" he asked, pushing her hair back as he combed his fingers through the tangled mess, leaning his chest against hers.

She blinked at him, confused and breathless under the pressure of his body.

"Don't you?" he asked again, shaking her once to be sure that he had her attention this time.

She was startled by the volume of his voice, it seemed, more even than his rough handling. She nodded yes.

"Let's dance. Do you like to dance?"

Despite her screaming protest, he pulled her against him, spinning in uncontrolled circles. She fell to her knees more than once, but he just pulled her back onto her feet, the flesh of her shins and knees collecting tiny fragments of rock.

He spun her again, into his car. She slammed against it so roughly that it rocked. A song was playing on the radio again now, something more upbeat. She tried to slide down onto the ground, but he came to hold her up, pulling a knife out of his pocket. He would make a show out of Sharon Cook. They would not forget her, and they would not forget him. He didn't like this idea, but he reminded himself that sometimes art got a little messy.

She did not notice the weapon, which was better, he thought. It wasn't until the first penetration of the blade into her abdomen that she looked down. Her eyes were wide, still confused. He continued to stab her again and again, like had Elisa's white dog. She collapsed backwards against the car, weak and ashen. Her entire body shook as she bled to death. He continued to stab her, having to hold her body upright with his own, spilling pieces of organ and fat and tissue onto his shoes.

He then let her fall to a heap. She left a bloody trail down the side of the car, which he tried to wash away with a bottle of water, and then he saw the scratches where some of the stabs had pierced through to scrape against the paint of the car above the gas cap.

He had no choice but to leave Sharon there by the roadside, but he was sure to drag her to where she could be more easily seen. There had been a risk that someone would notice him carrying her body, but he had been lucky enough not to be seen. Then, as day was fading into the twinkling twilight of evening, he returned to the quarry where he had left Summer Glass.

She was still there, body expanded some but mostly intact. Discoloration and decomposition had altered her state. This was not like he wanted her to be found, but Robichaud had not discovered her in time. Now he was going to gather her up, and put her somewhere she *would* be found. He had lined his backseat with trash bags, like that somehow protected them against this type of thing.

He dragged her body into the car, leaving a snail-trail of ooze and maggots. The carpet of fluid pulsated with their tiny bodies, wiggling with excitement. He didn't fault them for loving the dead.

As he was driving down a long stretch of highway that would eventually lead back into town, Rion heard the plastic rustle in the backseat. He glanced into his rearview, vision blurry. Was it because of the blow to the head? He still didn't feel right. He wondered if a trip to the chiropractor would be in order for his neck. His face was bruised, but not swollen. He could cover it with a little makeup and part his hair to cover it for a few days.

He heard the noise again, followed by a crackling sound. He looked into the rearview again, his hazy vision allowing him to see that Summer Glass was sitting upright.

And she was looking right at him with her own beautiful, bloody eyes.

A coldness overtook him, was it fear? Somehow though, his body didn't react like he thought it would to seeing a ghost, a zombie, a reanimated corpse. This wasn't real. It was just his head, his injury.

Summer spoke, "What exactly are you expecting to accomplish from all of this, Rion?"

This was new. He didn't shy away from talking to himself or inanimate objects, but dead girls usually don't start talking back. That's why he liked the dead girls... Quiet, pretty things. Everyone liked their own little trinkets, those were his.

"Who are you?"

"You don't remember me? I thought I was your favorite," she scoffed, rolling her eyes.

"She is dead."

"She is a revenant."

"What do you want?"

"They're going to find you. You know better than... all of this. Moving me around. Just adding more steps and more things you can mess up. You knew better than to kill the girl today in broad daylight, dragging her body by the road. You're being foolish, you're losing your mind."

Rion was exasperated, "I'm not going to mess up. I know what I'm doing."

She leaned forward, "You literally killed a woman in broad daylight. You dragged a ripe, dead body and put it into your backseat. What if you get pulled over? Is your taillight out? Are you swerving? Is there a roadblock?"

"He couldn't figure out the clue. You just laid there in the dirt."

"Oh, hello, officer. No, that's not my corpse, I don't know how that got there."

He ignored her, talking over her and continuing on: "They were never going to find you. Not until you were just bones and teeth."

"That's usually the goal."

"He said I'm obvious, that I'm predictable. Then why didn't they find you? Idiots."

"Well, you won't think they're idiots when someone identifies you. People have already seen your face. It's just a matter of time."

He muttered, "No one saw me."

"Yeah, you keep thinking that. What is that smell? Is that me? Can we crack a freaking window?"

Rion didn't want to listen to the girl, who was most certainly *not* really sitting up and talking to him in the backseat...

He rolled the window down an inch and a half.

36
Polanski

David took a long drag of the cigarette, pulling so forcefully that air whistled around the moist paper. The smoke filled his lungs, making his entire body feel like it was swirling. His heart fluttered; his head felt fuzzy. He held it in as long as he could and then exhaled, engulfed in the white cloud. The guilt of being back on cigarettes and off of that god-awful gum was gone. He knew that Leah thought he was falling back down into a dark place, where he would go back to cigarettes and then to alcohol... This was different, he had insisted. He had failed here, but he was forced to find a way to feel in control, to cope. He had started to realize that it was never about the nicotine.

He flicked the spent butt onto the ground as he reached down and patted Torres on the back as the younger man vomited onto the ground beside him, tie flung up on his shoulder to avoid the stream of pungent void. Paltro was already at work behind them. The girl was being bagged up, and he was taking photos and making notes. How was he always so well put together? David had rarely thought about quitting his job, even on the hard days. He thought about how hard they were, sure, he thought about how he hated the events, the system, sometimes his coworkers, sometimes the media, sometimes himself... but he never thought about throwing in the towel.

Not until this.

"Get up, kid," David whispered, patting him again. "Pull yourself together."

Torres was shaking, David imagined to his very core. The younger man's skin quivered and crawled underneath his palm, body shaking like he was cold. He didn't deserve to go through all this shit. Maybe the rest of them deserved it, somehow. For their sins and transgressions, they were now enduring this personal hell.

"Shit," Torres managed to say, voice vibrating between his chattering teeth.

Paltro sauntered over, clipboard tucked away in its waterproof enclosure under his arm. He pulled a piece of hard candy from his pocket, crouching down to hand it to him. "Ginger, I think it'll help," he said quietly and then came to stand beside David. At first he didn't say anything, and David knew he was waiting on him to initiate.

"It isn't him, is it?" David said, looking out to the patch of grass still stained with blood, a purple puddle teeming with insects. "Body mutilated..."

"It's him." Paltro confirmed, cutting him off. "And so is the girl on the highway."

"The older body?"

"Yes, game pieces on both."

"It doesn't make sense. Why would he tote around a dead body like that? Why would he cut this girl open? Up until now he's..."

"Respected them," Paltro interjected.

"I don't think this guy knows the first thing about respect."

"Agree to disagree, we can both agree that something has changed. A tide has turned. Something has become more important to him than his desires, his methodology."

"It's reckless," Torres said, loudly sucking on the ginger candy as he righted himself to face them. "He's getting reckless."

David shook his head, "That only means he's going to start screwing up. This is it, this is his downward spiral."

He could tell Torres disagreed, looking even more sick than he had before.

"Any new clues? Anything that helps?"

Paltro nodded, much to David's relief. "Tire tracks, shoe print. The girl from the road had rocks in her hair and embedded in her skin, they should give us a clue as to where she was murdered or where she was moved from. I'm going to look for anything and everything. There's this, too."

He retrieved a plastic bag from his pocket, holding it in his dark palm. David initially thought this was a weird place to put a piece of evidence, but when he saw what was there, he understood. It was a note, handwritten, on a napkin.

Detective, here is the real number six. You think I'm stale, predictable... Here's to excitement with seven, eight, nine...

"Who is that to?" Torres asked shrilly.

"Who do you think?" David said, voice quiet. "It's Robichaud."

Paltro nodded. "The interview."

"I knew it was a bad idea," Torres breathed. "Oh, God. Does he mean he's already killed three more? Does he mean he's looking now? Jesus Christ, we've got to do something."

David tried to not bark at Torres when he asked him to calm (the fuck) down. He knew he was just worked up, but David was doing his best not to fall apart right now. Paltro thankfully told Torres there was nothing more they could do.

"I've got to call Robichaud. He needs to be careful."

"Good plan," Paltro said, motioning to Torres. "You come with me. I'll grab you something to settle your stomach and drop you off at the station."

"No, no... I can't ride in there with them," he admitted quietly, embarrassed.

Paltro shrugged, turning to walk back to the van.

"You'll have to give me a minute to call him. Just go sit in the car." David said. "I'm trying not to be hateful, kid. I'm trying really hard."

"I'm sorry... I..."

"It isn't you. It isn't. It's just... just shit, you know?"

"I know. I'll be in the car."

He dialed Robichaud's number, surprised when he answered halfway through the first ring. He was supposed to be spending the day with Emily. David wondered how that was going for him. From the outside, it certainly seemed like their marriage was falling to pieces, but at least they were trying.

"Polanski? What you got?"

"You been following?"

"Yeah, some... just needed to know what was going on."

"I'm sure Emily liked that."

"She doesn't know. We're out for ice cream. I ducked into the men's room. I told her I was taking a piss, so I don't have all day. Another body?"

"Two."

There was silence. He knew that Robichaud needed time to process the information before David delivered worse news. The gutted girl, the old body, the note. This was getting out of hand, and he knew it. He knew that Robichaud knew it too, but he wasn't the type to give it up, and neither was Pat. If Robichaud insisted he had it under control, she was willing to buffer. Now was not the time to take things lightly. There was a monster on the loose preying on women, and he didn't know about Robichaud, but he personally had two women he needed to protect.

"Two bodies? Together?"

"One was eviscerated. I mean gutted completely. Tongue to rectum nearly intact together, lying separate from her body. Another body laying in the middle of the damn road, that one was old though. She's been dead awhile..."

"Did you say *gutted*?"

"Yeah. Not like him, I know. He's pissed off, Robichaud."

"Dammit... What the fuck have I done..."

"He's getting reckless. We'll get him. I got this under control."

Maybe he wouldn't tell him about the letter. Maybe he didn't need to know. What would it change? Would it inspire him to let someone else take over this shitshow? He didn't want Robichaud to feel guilty, not deep down. He always had David's back, and was always in his corner when he needed someone there. David needed to do that for him too.

"You sure you don't need me there?"

"Yeah, I got Torres. We'll get this all logged and see you tomorrow."

"Alright..."

This was his last chance. He closed his eyes, gritting his teeth, "Hold up."

"Yeah?"

"There ... there is one more thing. There was a note. It said the old body was the real number six, and he addressed the radio interview. You calling him boring, predictable... He's stepping up his game, and he wanted you to know. You need to be careful. You need to keep your eyes open."

There was nothing but static on the other end of the line.

37
Torres

Another day spent working off the clock... Robichaud would be proud of him. He'd call it a good work ethic. His mother would call this selling his soul. She always told him a job could be a career, but it should never be a lifestyle. This *was* his life, even though recently he had found that maybe he wasn't best suited for the job.

At least not in the current climate. He was fine with all of the usual work, but this particular case, all of these murders... it was too much, and it was taking a toll on him. He saw their bodies behind his eyelids when he closed them to sleep at night. Every woman he passed on the street was another possible victim. Today he was thinking about the flowers again, especially the set that had belonged to the girl on the road: Summer Glass.

Summer Glass had been missing, but it was still such a new disappearance that no one was even sure that she was truly gone. She had left work with a man; it was on the camera in the parking lot. None of these cameras were ever crisp enough to get a really good look at him. He looked like a generic white guy when he was just pixels. He could have been anyone in this small town. Lucas had watched the clip until his head hurt, trying to get a glimpse of the tall man's face.

The flowers that were on the counter were dahlias, little fluffy flowers that Lucas had maybe glimpsed growing out in the wild but never saw in stores. He thought that maybe they'd be a specialty item, something that had to be ordered. Maybe only certain stores or florists would carry them. He dreamed that he'd walk in and they'd confirm that the Flowers4U2 on the corner would be the only availability...

Roots and Shoots was comfortable. He'd already talked to the clerk once before. He walked in, not surprised to find the same employee pruning plants near the door. The employee greeted him with a small smile and a nod, but continued trimming away. Lucas wondered if he even remembered that he was a cop.

"Hey, you might not remember me..."

"Detective Torres, of course," the man said with a nod.

"Ah, good. I never did catch your name."

"Rion."

"Nice to meet you. I have a few questions again, about plants."

"I'll do my best to answer them for you." Rion assured him, walking behind the counter and laying his pruning scissors on the top.

"I'm wondering about the availability of certain flowers. Specifically dahlias."

The man seemed to be surprised at his question, and responded, "What species, in particular?"

"I don't know... Is there more than one type of dahlia?"

"Over forty species in the genus Dahlia, plus all the plants that people call a dahlia that are not a true dahlia."

Lucas stammered, "Do you sell *any* dahlias?"

"No."

"Is there a store here that does?"

"I'm not sure. I don't really shop at any other nurseries or garden centers."

"Have you recently sold any dahlias, maybe a special order?"

The man hesitated but shook his head, "You'd have to ask Mr. or Mrs. Rice, the owners. Sandy and Howard Rice."

Lucas motioned to some abandoned receipt paper in front of them, spinning it around and laying down a pen from his pocket.

"Yeah, if you could just write down their name and contact information for me that would be great."

The man across the counter scribbled down a name and number and handed it back to him. Lucas looked at the name on the paper longer than he should have, like he had forgotten suddenly how to read. It was the way that the S was shaped, the way it curled just a little too much on each tip, and the way the h dipped down lower on the left side, the precise way that the 'a' was formed. He traced his fingers across the letters slowly.

He had stared at these letters before, just in a different arrangement. He had seen them before on each of the handwritten notes to the dead girls. On the notes to Robichaud.

He looked up, sure that his face had become ashen, to find the man across the counter staring right back at him.

"T-thank you," Torres said, snatching the paper and shoving it into his pocket. "I appreciate your help... your cooperation is really appreciated. Just... thank you."

Rion reached over to grab the pruning scissors on the countertop, which caused Lucas to take a step back, to make sure he was out of arm's reach. Rion smiled, a warmer smile than he had seen from the man so far. There was something deceptive about it, something terrible. It made Lucas sick, staring into the man's dull eyes.

"Dahlias are really something special, Detective. I hope you find what you're looking for."

38
Paltro

Deen leaned down to stare at the spinning bag of popped corn, watching for the perfect moment to open the door. Tresa stirred around in the kitchen behind him, dancing with the dog. He removed the bag and dumped the contents into the same red bowl that he used every time he popped popcorn. Tresa moved over to him and slid a bottle of popcorn butter across the counter.

"Butter," she said.

"Check."

"Dill."

He pulled a jar of dill weed out of the cabinet and shook it in the air. "Check."

They seasoned the popcorn together and took their sodas over to the couch. The dog hopped onto the cushion beside Tresa, laying her head in her lap as her nose twitched aggressively at the sour scent of the dill popcorn.

Deen mouthed the word 'traitor' at her as Tresa stuck a piece of popcorn between the dog's front teeth. She chewed and smacked loudly, tail thumping against the arm rest.

Tresa scooted closer to him, folding her feet up on the couch as she smashed his arm into his side. He hesitated to raise it up and put it around her, and maybe he would have gotten the guts to do it if his phone hadn't started ringing. He pulled it out of his pocket, surprised to see that it was Torres.

"Should probably answer it," she said.

"Yeah... he doesn't usually call," Deen admitted. He swiped the green phone icon and put it to his ear. "Torres?"

"Hey, Paltro. You busy?"

Deen looked over at Tresa, who had taken it upon herself to pause the movie and was chewing popcorn slowly and quietly.

"Just a little. What's up?"

"I figured something out and I... I just need someone I know will back me up on this. I know you will, won't you? I know I've said I had a hunch, but just trust me... this is big."

"Of course I will. Are you alright? Do you want me to meet you somewhere?"

He noticed Tresa sit up straighter, leaning forward intently. He raised a hand to let her know everything was okay, and she relaxed.

"No, I don't want to talk about it on the phone. I have something I need to show you too. Paltro, I think I know who he is."

"Can you prove it? That's important."

"I can't really... no, not legally. It isn't concrete... but it's enough for me. I think it's enough that we can look into him. I know it's him."

"Alright. Tomorrow?"

"I have to go see my mom, but when I get back."

"How about before you go?"

"Yeah, yeah that'll work."

"Okay, I'll see you then."

He disconnected the call in the middle of Torres saying goodbye, laying the phone over on the end table. Tresa settled back on the couch beside him, and pushed play. The movie resumed and Deen immediately motioned towards the screen. "Do you see the 'X'?"

"Yes."

"Everytime someone is about to die, there's an 'x' somewhere on the screen."

She smiled, sighing as she chewed a piece of popcorn, "I love easter eggs. You never miss them, either. You always know."

They sat in silence for a few more moments, but he could tell she wanted to ask him about the phone call. He was almost a little insulted that she didn't because it meant she didn't think she had that liberty. There was a boundary there for her, the politeness of a friend.

"Torres says that he thinks he knows who the killer is."

"Did he tell you who?" she ventured.

"No. He said he wanted to meet me tomorrow. He is afraid no one will believe him."

"Why wouldn't they?"

"Robichaud doesn't take him seriously. I think he feels threatened by him."

"Threatened? Robichaud?"

"Yeah. Torres is young, motivated, he really loves his job. He has no family to tie him down, no relationships. And he's a nice guy. Too good for all of us, all of this. Genuine good guy."

"Robichaud is a good guy too. He's a good cop. I think he's just gruff, you know?"

Paltro inhaled deeply, focusing on the screen of the television, but not the movie itself. He allowed himself to drift, unblinking as he admitted, "You know... I've encountered both the best of people and the worst of people... and if I'm being honest, sometimes I'm not sure there was a difference."

39
Torres

It was early enough in the morning that there were still dewdrops clinging to the gossamer that lay across the lawn. Pieces of damp grass stuck to Lucas' toes as he walked across the small patch of greenery in his sandals. Snails left messages of an ancient language in their own secretions on the sidewalk the night before. He had a bag of garbage, only half full, in one hand, and was using his shoulder to hold his phone up to his ear with the opposite shoulder.

"I'm going to be a little late. I've got something I have to do for work," he said into the phone, walking leisurely.

His mother was exasperated. "You're off today."

"I know, this is just something I've got to handle. It won't take long."

"Are you still coming? If you aren't, I'll go with Melanie to bingo."

"Yeah, Mom, I swear. I'll be there. How are you feeling? Has the doctor got back to you about your results yet?"

"Not yet... I called yesterday but they said they hadn't heard and would call me as soon as they knew something."

"Ridiculous... If you were a golden retriever they'd have called you by now."

"Dr. Guillen wouldn't delay on purpose..."

"I'm sure he's a nice man. I'm sure. I'm just saying. Healthcare, Mom. That's all I'm saying. Healthcare is ridiculous."

"You should be thankful we have always had such good health..."

"Yes, I am thankful. I am. Listen, I've got to go get ready."

"Okay, be careful."

"Yeah, uh-huh. I will."

"Love you."

"Love you too."

He tossed the bag of garbage into the dumpster and stuffed his phone into his shorts pocket. He hiked them higher up as the weight nearly dropped them off of his hips entirely. His badge being clipped to his waistband didn't help either. He felt a little naked without his badge, even on his days off, but, man, he loved to wear some comfortable shorts.

He headed across the parking lot to the back entrance of the apartment complex where his own car was parked. He was going to go straight to Paltro and then he'd go to his mom's. He knew she loved bingo, but he also knew she hated when he didn't come see her at least once a week. This was the only day he'd have the opportunity.

He heard the squealing of tires and looked up just in time to see a vehicle speeding towards him across the parking lot. Initially he was so puzzled that he stood on the spot, but that was when he realized it was coming straight for him. And it wasn't showing any sign of slowing down.

His heart jumped in his chest, and he thought it left his body as he breathlessly tried to dive out of the way of the car. Unfortunately, he was not fast enough. The right front bumper caught his shin as he jumped, and then he rolled over the hood of the car, slamming into the windshield. Instead of cracking, he just bounced up off of the glass and across the top of the car, ribs slamming painfully into the roof rack before he finally rolled down the back of the car and hit the pavement.

The moment of motion seemed to last forever, and he saw it all happening seconds at a time. When his body came to rest, he was flooded with pain. It washed over him in waves, one started from his head and the other started from his toes. He could hear screaming, but he couldn't focus on anything more than the pain. It took him several moments to realize *he* was the one screaming.

He tried to yell something intelligible: help, somebody, please... but he found that his tongue was so swollen that he struggled to breathe. He thought he could feel two or three pieces moving independently, like a severed and multiplying head of Medusa. He gasped around it as blood poured out of his nose and down his throat, choking on both his own fluids and the exhaust of the car.

Lucas could hear a car door opening, and that was when he realized the man was coming around the back. He tried to roll over and reach for his phone, which had fallen out of his pocket and was ringing on the asphalt near him. The smallest motion sent shockwaves through his spine, however, and he gritted his teeth and resorted to lying still for now.

Although his head was spinning, he recognized the face of the man immediately. The guy from Roots and Shoots. He knew it. Despite it all, he felt a little satisfaction. He was right, *he was right.*

"Detective Torres. Nice to run into you..." Rion said, crouching down beside him. He pushed the phone away from him with a gloved hand and then pulled a piece of paper out of his pocket. "Can you deliver this to your friend Detective Robichaud for me? Hmm? Can you do that?"

Lucas knew that this was it. There was no getting out of this. He was going to die right here on the parking lot. His mom was going to wonder where he was, she was going to call his phone and call it again. How would she find out? Would someone know to call her? Would she find a ride and discover his body on her own? God, he didn't want her to see him like this. His face was fucked up, a jagged bone was sticking out of his leg where the front of the vehicle had initially struck him. She would never be able to stop seeing him like this. The same way those dead girls lay in the dark when he closed his eyes at night, she would see her only son. It would break her heart, and he couldn't bear the thought of it. His chest ached as tears started pooling in the corners of his eyes.

"That's a good boy. Here... we'll trade."

He unclipped Lucas' badge from his waist. Lucas made a swing at him, grabbing a handful of his shirt and pulling him. Rion reached up and effortlessly unwound his fingers from the fabric. He tucked the note in his shorts' pocket, patting it then from the outside. He cried out in pain as he tried to roll away again, the firm pavement offering some kind of comfort through stability. Rion got back into the car.

The brake lights flipped from parked to reverse.

40
Quentin

Polanski threw a wad of paper across the room and hit Quentin in the side of the head. His elbow slipped and his face nearly slammed into the desk. He hadn't been sleeping well. He'd been trying to make sure not to fall asleep at his desk, because he knew Pat was really on a warpath right now, but he couldn't help slipping away whenever he felt like it. These were fleeting moments of rest that he did not want to waste. Of course, it didn't help that the Department was literally one massive room, with only two separate rooms offset. One was the breakroom, but they also used it for interrogations, and the other was Pat's own office. The cells were down a narrow hallway, past Pat's office. The walkway between them was so small that, if they wanted, the inmates could reach out and grab ahold of you.

All of the detectives who had their own desks were literally in the middle of the floor, like an old fashioned newspaper office. The ceiling towered overhead, with a defunct balcony roped off and gathering dust. It had once been an old theater, he'd been told. They'd banked for years on getting a new building: fundraiser after fundraiser gathering money that seemed to go absolutely nowhere. If it wasn't the mayor coming up with a different way to spend the money, it was the department head (Pat herself) insisting they need to put it away 'for a rainy day.' Days didn't get much 'rainier' than this.

Emily blamed him, in some way, for the two most recent victims. Quentin was probably bothered by that so much because he blamed himself too. His actions have consequences, that was what Dr. Norrington would remind him of. He needed to think before he acted, before he spoke, and realize that there would be effects.

"Let's go get something to eat," Polanski said loudly.

Simultaneously a kid, probably ten or eleven walked through the front door. He startled himself as it closed behind him, removing his backwards-facing ballcap like he had just walked into a holy place. He used his free hand and his wrist to hold a folded handkerchief up to his chest. His eyes were wide, staring up at the ceilings and across the desks at the detectives. Some deputies moved around aimlessly to look busy, but one in particular, a tall man with slicked-back black hair, approached the boy.

Quentin recognized it as Julius Brannon. It didn't surprise Quentin that he'd be the one to approach the boy that wandered in. He'd probably lost a baseball or his cat was up a tree, that would be something that Brannon would take on without a complaint. He was the stoic, almost a little creepy-type. There was just something about him, something that bordered on sinister, and it made Quentin sometimes wonder what he did in his time off. That austureness aside, Brannon was as smart as a whip and highly innovative. He had one of the best track records in the business as far as closing cases... Quentin's fierce competitiveness and jealousy prevented them from working together though, even in a situation like this where you needed all the good minds you could get. Brannon didn't have the benefit of being one of Pat's favorites like Quentin did.

Brannon crouched down by the kid, lengthy legs folding upwards at the knees like a cricket's, pants legs hiking up to reveal patterned socks. The boy seemed just as frightened and put-off by the pale, tall man as Quentin would have been if he'd come over to him at that age. He asked him what he could help him with, voice soft and comforting. That was when the boy unfolded what he had clutched against his chest. Quentin watched curiously, wondering if it would be a dead animal (a little girl had brought in a crushed bird in a napkin once, pleading for help) but whatever it was caught the light in the building and reflected onto Brannon's face.

Brannon stood up and turned around, long arms swinging around his body as he did so, "Torres?"

Quentin sat up more straight in his seat, chair squeaking. He exchanged a glance with Polanski who shrugged, "He's off today, what is it?"

Brannon reached down and took the entire handkerchief. "Where did you find this, buddy?"

"A man gave me twenty dollars to bring it down here, he says that it was lost and he didn't have time to bring it in."

Quentin had a bad feeling about this. It crept up his gut and into his chest: a burning and grittiness in his throat. He was standing now and said, "Polanski, call Torres now."

He watched as Polanski fumbled with his cell phone with his only good hand, already red-faced and sweating. It was the look on Quentin's face that seemed to propel him with such urgency. He was sure he had no color left there, no spirit. He was sure he looked like the dead.

Quentin walked over and pulled the handkerchief out of Brannon's hands, the weight of the badge seemed to increase exponentially the longer he held onto it. He found himself noting the blood in the crevasses. He wasn't looking for it, at least he hadn't thought he was, but his eyes moved to it first thing. He dropped it to the floor and bolted out the door. He could hear Brannon trying to talk to the boy, keying in on the panic, and Polanski yelling for him to slow down.

"Robichaud, hold up! Ah fuck..." he hissed as the door swung into his arm. "What's going on, where are we going?"

They both dove into the car, Polanski cranked the air on and struggled to buckle himself in as Quentin jerked the vehicle into reverse. He took his corner around Pat's car a little too sharply and hung his rear bumper on her's.

"Slow down! Jesus Christ." He struggled until Quentin heard a click of a successful buckle.

The radio between the seats came across with dispatcher Lisey Utz's sweet voice bubbling across, "Units in the area please be advised we have a hit and run with possible fatality at the Giraldi Place, back parking lot. Ambulance en route."

"Fuck!" Quentin screamed. He was sweating now too, his stomach was rumbling, and he thought he was going to end up with the shits.

Polanski was quiet. He knew now too. Quentin knew that he realized what was happening. He knew that Polanski was going through all of the scenarios in his head, all of the positive possible outcomes. Was there one? If not Torres, some other poor person. If Torres... Polanski had his arm propped up against the window, leaning his brow into his hand like he was lightheaded.

No matter how fast he drove or how many assholes he ran off the road, it felt like they were never going to arrive at Giraldi Place. As the building loomed ahead, Quentin thought he could see a greyness take over his vision. He felt heavy, and tired, and sick. He pulled into the parking lot and barely got the car into park before he sprinted over to the sobbing woman on the pavement. She kneeled over a body that was mangled beyond recognition.

She was trying to tell them what had happened, but Quentin dropped to his knees beside her, feeling the bloody mess for a pulse that he knew had stopped too long ago. Polanski dragged the woman away, asking her to step back into her apartment for a few minutes. Quentin could hear sirens in the distance: the hellish howl of the meatwagon as it came from the opposite end of the county. He had to do something until they got here, to preserve him until they could work their magic. This couldn't be it. This wasn't it.

Quentin started doing CPR, putting all of his weight behind his fists as he did compression after compression, and then a breath. He hesitated initially, leaning over the bloody face. He could see through the unblinking eyes something that he recognized. The gentle shimmer still of a friend who had just left this place. Like a shadow on the other side of a window as he passed by down the street. Like a seat still warm and compressed on the bus.

Torres' lips were cold as Quentin touched his own there against them, and they still tasted of cigarette smoke. Pieces of broken teeth transferred to Quentin's mouth and when he licked away the blood he could feet their grittiness on his tongue. He repeated again, and again. Ribs crunched underneath the force, popping and cracking like bubble wrap. Every press brought a wheeze from Torres' lips. He could hear Polanski crying as though he were trying to muffle the noise through his hand, pacing back and forth.

Polanski couldn't handle the sounds anymore: the crunch, crunch, rasp, the sound of Quentin panting, and the squeak of his belt and grind of gravel under his shoes.

"Stop, stop, stop, just fucking stop. He's dead. He's gone. He's fucking gone." Polanski found his voice, speaking with spittle, tears streaming down his face to mix with the saliva on his lips.

Quentin couldn't stop. As he passed beyond the point of hoping to try and revive Torres anymore, he started pounding his fists against his chest out of anger and frustration instead.

41
Paltro

How was it that the hardest was always yet to come? This was certainly a new experience, preparing a friend. No autopsy was needed for Lucas Torres, as it was clear how and when he had died. Brutally, and too young. Deen took the time to clean his body before he would store it for the embalmers to come and retrieve him. He knew that the casket would likely be closed. Torres' head was nearly crushed, swollen and bulging. Skin had been stripped from his cheeks and brow. Still, Deen washed his face with a soft sponge, beginning with clean water and turning it red like wine in the steel pan. It felt so final that Paltro rolled his chair over to clutch Torres' hand in his own, squeezing the stiff fingers with his head bowed.

"I'm sorry," he said quietly. "I should have taken you more seriously. You were asking that of me, weren't you? I didn't, and I'm sorry. I am realizing a little too late that I'm just as guilty as the rest of them. How arrogant of me to think that I was any better..."

He covered his bare body, preparing to slide him into the cooler. He first folded up the tattered shirt and shorts to bag and have ready for disposal. That was when he felt a crinkle in the shorts pocket. Paltro initially thought the slip of paper might have been a receipt of some sort, maybe an indicator to

Torres' last purchase or last meal. He almost left it a mystery, but curiosity got the best of him.

He retrieved the bloody, now urine soaked note and unfolded it slowly. It was something much more important than a receipt.

Detective, do I have your attention yet? This one was going to get in the way of our little game. I know you are hot on my trail, but he was getting too close and too comfortable... I know you understand my removal of this obstacle. I have never killed a man before but experienced today with your young detective that when faced with death, they hold a similar vulnerability that is to be desired. Perhaps it is the human condition to hold that beauty in the end, if it is offered. Perhaps he will not be my last, but for now I have more plans to paint this little town red in your honor. I know you did not mean those hateful and untrue words that you said on the radio. At first, I was angry. Then I realized you just wanted to see me grow. You just wanted to see something new. Don't worry, I am not done spicing up our lives yet. See you soon.

He didn't feel like he was emotionally ready to read these words out loud to anyone, but especially not Robichaud. Not yet. He couldn't help but feel a little bit of resentment towards Robichaud and the way that he had put them all into the line of fire. He knew, of course, that there had been no way to anticipate such an outcome. What were the odds that this killer, who seemed to be fairly level-headed and 'smart' about his deeds... would snap like this? Going after the young partner - when was it time to take out the rest of the team? Would he bomb the place? Drive through the school parking lot to kill Polanski's daughter?

He pushed the thoughts out of his head. He didn't want to think about that. He just wanted this hell to end. He would approach Robichaud about the note, about making sure they turned this case over to someone else. At this point, if they didn't, a witch hunt would be in order. This town had plenty of experience in those.

His phone buzzed, and he didn't even have to look to know the caller was Tresa. She had been calling and texting him since they
received the news of Torres' death. He knew that she was trying to be supportive, but he couldn't bear the pity, the shared sorrow. Somehow it made it feel heavier for him, although maybe Tresa felt the opposite. Maybe she needed him to help her shoulder the pain. She did not know Torres as well as he did, but she was mourning all the same. Isolating himself from her was selfish of him.

He quietly whispered his goodbyes to Torres while putting his body away. He would never look at the young man's face again. Not in the morgue, not at the funeral, not in photos hidden in forbidden folders. Only on those long nights when Deen was kept awake by ghosts, Torres would join them.

42
Rion

It had been a little while since Rion had visited his mother. He had lost some track of time, which was uncharacteristic of him. Recent events had him admittedly a little stressed, a little preoccupied. He did feel like he was experiencing a slight crisis, a downward spiral. He needed to reel it in, get back to his routine. Routines were safe, less room for error. So he went to see his mother.

He never felt like he had any sort of obligation to his mother, no real attachment, however that did not seem to keep him from travelling to see her once a week in the past. Today he sat in her room in the same chair he always did. It was stiff and uncomfortable, royal blue with an uneven silver houndstooth pattern. He sat with his fingers laced together, watching the nurses pass by in the hallway more than he watched his mother.

She was nearly vegetative at this point, forgetting who he was or why he was there. It was pathetic. She lingered here, why? What was the reason for a body to hold on after all of this time? Did it think that she still had some kind of purpose? He could not imagine what worth someone like this would have. The resources poured into these people, the time and money and manpower.

Rion had a strange feeling today that someone was watching him. The sensation piqued his paranoia, causing his stomach to turn and turn until it was in knots. He could not find anyone in the corners, peeking into the room (other than the little candy-stripers who seemed to think he was attractive and mysterious: he had more than once thought about going after one of them… but he visited the facility too much for that to be plausible. Maybe after Mother was dead).

His mom turned to look at him, eyes somewhat clear for the first time in a long time. She had those moments, but they were fleeting. More often than not she just lay in the bed without moving, breathing with her mouth open, staring somewhere that he was sure did not exist here in this world.

"Rion?" she gurgled.

"Yes,"

"I thought that was you. Did you get milk while you were out?"

"I did. I put it in the fridge."

"What took you so long?"

"I met a girl," Rion said.

His house seemed too quiet when he returned, shutting the door and locking both the lower lock and deadbolt. He went to the couch and turned on the television, muting it as he flipped through the channel. He could not stand to listen to the people on the television. All of the noise and talking and sound effects were too much. Too chaotic. Too unorganized.

He heard something, the sound of something scratching, and the hair on his neck stood on end. He turned slowly to the source of the sound, too close to him. On the cushion next to him sat the ghost of Summer Glass. She had reached up to pick loose a piece of flesh dangling from her face, flicking it onto the carpet.

"So what now?" the Revenant asked him, propping her blue feet up on his coffee table.

Rion turned away from her, forcing his eyes to stay on the tv screen. He could feel himself shaking. "Get your feet off of my table, please."

She scoffed, "Hell no," and rubbed her calloused heels on the surface. He thought he could see bloody flesh peeling off and sticking to the wood, but when he blinked enough it disappeared. He had some control over this. Whatever this was.

"You aren't really here," he insisted.

"Oh, I am. Just maybe not in a way you can understand."

"You are *not* here."

"Are *you* here? Are you dead somewhere? Gunned down by beloved Detective Robichaud? Is this just your purgatory?"

He sat quietly on the couch beside her, listening to the way that she wheezed in her chest and inhaling the scent of her decaying flesh. He had to prop a window open to get rid of the stench, which elicited a paranoia that perhaps his neighbors could also smell it. Which was asinine because, he reminded himself, *she wasn't really here.*

"So what's your plan, Rion?" she asked as he came to sit on the couch again, but farther away from her than before, he leaned against the arm rest.

"I'm not talking to you about my plans."

She folded her feet up underneath her on the couch, turning to face him. He wasn't sure he would ever sit on this couch again. Not after she had sat here. She spoke at him, with her lips near his ear. Her breath was cold, like a draft from the beyond that wafted under his hairline and around the other side. The coldness had fingertips that wound into his hair and around his throat. He found it difficult to breathe.

"You will talk to me about your plans because you have no choice. I'm here, and I'm in your head. I know everything you've done and everything you want to do. I know how bad you're falling apart and how you're going to fuck up everything. Your little reign of terror is almost over; the kingdom is crumbling. So tell me about your plans."

"I'm waiting for a few days... but I'm really going to surprise him."

"He will never expect it," she agreed, settling back onto the couch.

He looked over at her for the first time, into her dead eyes. She was horrific. Why had his mind brought such a thing to him? It wasn't guilt. He did not carry that burden. He had no regrets. He did not see these things as vile, or disgusting. *Regular* people loved this, they just didn't want to admit it. Watch someone flock to the scene of an accident to try and get a peek at the gruesome injuries, and you'd know. It suddenly struck him that these visions could stem from Sharon Cook kicking him in the head. Perhaps he had some trauma. Those types of injuries could cause hallucinations, and he *was* under a fair amount of stress.

"Where'd you come from?"

She looked at him, and for a moment he thought he could see through her. Maybe just a glimpse of the wall behind her through the thin veil of skin. He blinked, hoping she'd wisp away entirely, but instead she became more solid.

"Do you really want to know?"

"I don't believe in all of that. Afterlife, souls, something *else*."

"It's a funny thing, Rion. When a man jumps off a building, gravity could give two fucks whether he believes in her or not. He's still going to paint the ground."

She leaned towards him again, "How's it feel to see that ground rushing up at you, pretty boy?"

Rion got up off of the couch, and locked himself in the bathroom until he was sure she was gone.

43
Quentin

He wasn't right. He wasn't even sure what 'right' felt like anymore, not at this point. Everything had seemed to be going well in his life, and he had thought that maybe things were starting to look up for him. Torres' death had caused such a shock to ring through the force that none of them had spoken to each other since his body had been recovered. Quentin had followed the ambulance to the morgue, where Paltro, as stone-faced and somber as ever, had taken Torres' body inside. He'd asked Quentin not to come in, which was surprising. He knew that Paltro would need to mourn in his own way, and maybe Quentin *would* have just been in the way.

Polanski had stayed behind, dutifully, to speak to the woman who had seen the car drive away. Quentin didn't know where he'd gone from there, but he didn't come to work the next day. Pat had given Quentin permission to take a few days off as well, but he'd refused. Even today, when he wasn't scheduled, he wanted to be anywhere but here.

Emily never *said* she thought it was his fault. He didn't know why he imagined that she thought he was guilty. Maybe because she had thought it was a bad idea to shit on the killer on the radio in the first place. He could remember the way she'd looked at him when he told her the plan. The way she made that exaggerated blink, eyebrows bouncing upwards and lips becoming tight. And now, he knew that she'd been right. His therapist was right. Everyone had been right. This was all his fault.

He sat at the table in his underwear, staring into the black depths of a cooling cup of coffee, steam rising up to make the air aromatic with the bittersweet smell of the medium roast. Emily came around the corner in a salmon-colored top that flowed around black dress pants. She was fastening an earring onto her left lobe, one that matched the dark necklace around her throat.

She looked at him sympathetically, and for some reason this just pissed him off. He didn't want her to feel sorry for him right now. "Quent... Are you not coming to the funeral?"

"No. I can't."

She approached the table, putting her hand on his shoulder. "Sweetheart, I know it's hard. I'll be there for you. You've got to pay your respects. They'll expect you to be there."

He jerked his arm away from her, snapping, "I'm fucking tired of people expecting shit from me. I don't want to go. I can't go. I can't see the pictures of that kid on the table, and his fucking mother sobbing."

"Quentin..."

"I had to see him, you know. Lying in the parking lot. We didn't even know if it was him. You want details? His leg was broken, nearly every rib he had was fractured, his spine, his nose, his cheek bones. His head was basically crushed. He had the skin peeled off his face on the pavement like an eraser on a fucking piece of paper. I wasn't sure, I didn't want to believe it until they found his wallet. I called his phone while I followed the ambulance, hoping he'd answer and I could tell him about the mix up and how pissed I was that he'd scare me like that."

Emily's eyes had filled with tears, nostrils flaring as she attempted not to cry. He regretted everything he said. He didn't want to say any of that; he didn't want her to know it. He didn't want her to have to think of those things that he had seen and the things that he couldn't get out of his head.

She whispered, lips wet with tears, "They asked you to be a pallbearer, how am I going to explain..."

"Emily, I don't fucking care. Read my fucking lips: I'm not going. I don't give a fuck what you tell them."

She nodded at him, using the back of her hand to smear eyeliner off of her face as she walked too quickly out the door, slamming it behind her.

He buried his face in his hands as soon as she was gone, sobbing into his own palms. In some ways, he felt better releasing that anger and pent up frustration, but the guilt of her bearing the brunt of the attack was worse. His entire body hurt, everywhere. He cried until he had nothing left. His eyes felt ironically dry.

His phone buzzed across the table, and he picked it up to see 'Paltro' flashing across the screen. He almost didn't answer, assuming that he was going to ask him why he wasn't at the funeral. He was surprised Polanksi hadn't called him yet.

"Not a good time, Paltro," he said, voice cracking more than he wanted it to.

Paltro's deep voice came across the line calmly, softly, "Hey, I know... I know. But that's why I wanted to call you now, I wanted to wait and let everything settle for a few days because I know we all need it... but I think this needs to be out there now. Are you there? At the funeral? Can you step away somewhere?"

"No. I'm home. I can't... I can't go."

"I get it. I do. I'm not going either. I paid my respects to him on my own."

It made him feel better, somehow, that Paltro wasn't going either. The fact that he had called about work was also comforting. At least until Paltro actually told him why he was calling.

"So what do you have?"

"There was a note... with Torres' body."

Quentin sat up straighter in his seat, leaning heavily on the table, "A note? No one said anything about a note."

"Well, I haven't logged it yet. I don't think I'm going to... Robichaud, it was addressed to you specifically. Do you want me to read it to you?"

Quentin's heart skipped a beat. He opened his mouth to say something, but he was too damn scared to ask. That's what it came down to: he was afraid. He didn't want to hear the letter; he didn't want more confirmation that the killer had done this, murdered Torres, *for* him. His palms had become so sweaty that he nearly dropped the cell phone, so he pressed it more firmly against his face.

"You there?"

"Yeah... yeah I'm here. Go ahead. Read it."

As Paltro read the letter, Quentin just became more sick. He wasn't sure if he could fight through the nausea until the phone call was over. He kept his eyes closed, hand gripping handfuls of his own hair.

When he was done, Quentin managed to mutter, "That son of a bitch... Get rid of that. Burn it, trash it, whatever."

Paltro responded quickly, the sound of paper being torn up could be heard in the background, "Done. There's something else. The witness at the scene wrote down the license plate number of the car that was leaving the scene. The description of the car is spot on. When we ran the plates, the number didn't come up with the same vehicle."

"Stolen plates?"

"I don't think so, but I'm going to look into the owner of the car if I can get the go-ahead. What else they drive, who they know. It's also possible she wrote something down wrong in the moment. She was very upset."

“I understand that. Thank you, Paltro, for doing what you do. I don’t think anyone thanks you enough.”

“Yeah, I appreciate that.”

“Thank you, thank you, thank you. Let me know what you find out.”

“Be careful out there.”

“You too.”

44
Rion

He didn't like this.

He didn't make a habit of doing things he didn't like, unless they were an absolute necessity. He didn't like feeling uncomfortable or out of control, and there was too much here that he just couldn't plan for... but after three days of throwing the idea around, he decided to go for it. He could improvise.

The small house had an equally small yard with a little white fence that couldn't keep anything in or out. He supposed it served as some sort of symbol of American home life: the little white picket fence. The house was a pale blue and seemed freshly clean. He had watched her from across the street for a few hours. Her father had been here, or a man that he had presumed was her father. He had mowed the tiny yard, sweating as though he had mowed a football field and not the patch of grass out front. She had brought him a bottle of water, and they'd laughed together, then he had changed the oil in her car, leaving a little black patch on the driveway to the carport, where he'd sloshed the bowl of spent motor oil.

He had stayed longer than Rion had anticipated, but he was patient when needed. He had his sights set on this girl, and he was going to do something that Detective Robichaud would never expect. He thought Rion was just an opportunist, that he didn't have the balls to go *after* a girl. Well, he would show him now just how daring he could be. This was a pretty, young girl: tall, slim, athletic. She had friendly eyes and a genuine smile. She was probably the type that made friends easily, probably trusted too quickly. Sometimes Rion liked to imagine their lives, for whatever reason. It was also important that this girl lived in the same neighborhood that Elisa McBride had. The little houses were cookie cutter identical, other than the paint and yards. He knew the layout of this home before he ever stepped foot inside. That little detail was what made this safe enough for him to attempt to execute.

Rion could see the girl through her front window, sitting on the couch cross-legged as she watched something on her television and ate popcorn out of a bright pink bowl. She finally got up, setting the bowl down and moving to the window where she pulled the blinds. He watched her reappear in an upstairs window, where she grabbed a towel and clothes and shut those blinds as well. He exited his car, leaving the door unlocked. The house was at the end of a dead end road, which appeared as though it was originally intended to be a cul-de-sac, but instead the nearest neighbor was several hundred yards away. She had probably desired this place and its little bit of privacy... but now it was giving him the distance he needed to be discreet.

He went to the front door with a black shove knife in hand. He leaned against the door and turned the knob as he prepared to slip the smooth tool between the door and facing to force it open when it simply opened for him... Rion would never fail to be surprised by the stupidity and trust of people. Why would *anyone*, but especially a young girl who lives alone in an isolated home, leave her door unlocked?

To his left was a flight of stairs, and he ascended them slowly, shoes making the smallest staticky sound on the carpeted steps. He could hear the crackle of a shower running upstairs and he followed the sound diligently. He saw no sounds of life in the house otherwise. He knew that the girl lived alone and was alone... but there was always the chance of a dog.

He came around the corner and entered a bedroom, simple and quaint. It smelled lightly of lavender and verbena, a scent Rion found was popular among his victims, although he did love the irony of meeting a girl who smelled like patchouli. The light in the bathroom was on, and steam rolled underneath the nearly closed door. He walked more carefully, more slowly, and pushed the door open. He crossed the pink bath rugs and approached the curtain calmly. He would admit this setup was fairly exciting, something a little different. Maybe he would thank Robichaud for the adventure.

He jerked the curtain open, and to his surprise... the shower was empty. He stared for several moments, planning his backwards retreat down the stairs, remembering the floorplan. Where would he hide to wait for her? Perhaps the closet. Under the bed.

Then he heard a gasp behind him. He turned slowly to see the girl standing there in her lounging clothes, pajamas and towel stacked neatly in her hands. Color drained from her face, and her eyes widened. He could see the pupils expand, and her muscles tensed so subtly before she dropped the clothes and took off. Rion wasted no time and went after her.

She screamed as she sprinted down the hallway towards the stairs. When she reached them, she took every step in quick order while Rion used the handrail to allow him to sail down several at a time. She reached the end table where a phone sat, and he had just enough reach to smack it out of her hand. Then she was heading straight for the door. He experienced a small moment of... was it panic? Concern? If she got out the door, she would scream. If she screamed, her voice would certainly carry down the road and to the neighbors. Rion pushed himself forward, reaching out to grab her by her ponytail just as she got a foot out the back sliding door. He jerked her backwards, and she flew through the air before landing on the floor with a thud. He jumped over her, slamming the door shut so forcefully that he felt the floor shake beneath his feet.

He imagined she would be disoriented, but instead she was back on her feet and going back up the stairs. Rion followed suit, now more slowly. There was nowhere for her to go. She was screaming for help, but he knew the sound would be so muffled that no one would be alerted. She went back into the bedroom and then the bathroom, trying to shut him out. The door snagged on one of the pink rugs and Rion shoved his way inside hard enough that she stumbled backwards and fell into the running shower. The curtain popped off of the rail, sending the clips clattering to the floor as he jumped on top of her and began punching her in the face.

Rion had never beaten someone to death. It was messy and exhausting, and not at all practical. While asphyxiation was also time consuming and took *much longer* than one would imagine... it was satisfying for him and therefore worth the effort. The girl screamed far longer than he thought she was actually alive, the screams drowning out into a noise he associated with a young animal instead. High pitched whining wails that gurgled and sputtered between the moist squelch of his fist hitting the flesh of her face. Her teeth had split his knuckles open on his left hand, causing him to recoil and stop his assault briefly. Her face was hardly recognizable as human anymore. her left eye totally obscured by swelling and damaged tissue, lips bulging against her broken teeth, nose pushed far to the right. He thought he could see her entire skull swelling before his very eyes, blood oozing from her scalp and nose and from behind her eyes.

And she still fucking made noise.

"Shut up," he snarled quietly, grabbing her by the shoulders and slamming her body into the floor of the shower. "Shut up, shut up, shut up. You've ruined this, you've made me look *weak*. Look at this fucking mess you've made. Look at this fucking mess!"

She was finally quiet, and Rion put his hands against his own head, which was pounding with stress. He was covered in blood. The shower walls were covered in blood. There was the smallest spray of blood on the toilet and the rugs. That stain would be set in the rug if he didn't wash it immediately. He stood up, kicking off his shoes and stripping off his clothes. He left them lying in the bottom of the shower alongside the girl's body, letting the water continue rinsing excess blood down the drain. That would be less for him to have to deal with later. The water was getting chilled, so he washed hastily, selecting a mango scented body wash, and rinsing his hair but opting out of using her purple shampoo.

When he was done, he washed his clothes, the stained rug, and his towel on a thirty-six minute 'quick' cycle. While things were washing, he unscrewed the shower drain to clean it out and gathered up both his trash and the girl's personal garbage. His car still smelled faintly of Summer Glass, and he was sure the scent of trash wouldn't hurt. He swapped the clothes over to the dryer, and while he waited, he went downstairs and ate her popcorn. It was still warm, buttery. The grease was almost too much, and he preferred more salt.

He pulled on his still somewhat damp clothing, took the trash to his car and brought in a tarp and rope. He locked the door behind him. Even though sunset was approaching, he found that one never could be sure when a visitor would pop by to chat.

He rolled the girl up inside the tarp and then painstakingly cleaned the shower and bathroom floor with bleach. He put her into his car, stacking the garbage bags on top of her. She was tall enough that he had to wad her up against the opposite door. He went back inside with his gloves on long enough to vacuum up the debris from his shoes and to wipe down the door handles and washing machine and dryer.

Then he went home, stopping only at the levee to dump her body, sticking a pretty little blue columbine piece in her mouth.

45
Quentin

The new office of Dr. Norrington was worth the wait to most of her patients, but not Quentin. They had gone from what was basically a renovated closet, with desks crammed on every wall and two chairs in the center, to a full fledged office. It had mahogany shelves full of books no one in their right mind would read, a spacious single desk, and the original two chairs. He was thankful today that he could slump down into his same old chair with the cigarette burn on the arm. He needed some consistency right now.

"Quentin?"

He looked up at her, putting a hand to his chest as he realized that his heart was pounding. He had to breathe through his lips to keep from hyperventilating. He was cold all over, gritting his teeth to keep them from chattering.

"I just need a minute to breathe," he whispered.

"I think you're having a panic attack, Quentin. Take a deep breath. In through your nose, out through your mouth."

He followed her instructions, shaking.

"Do you want to go home? You do not have to do this today."

He shook his head. "No. Let's just talk."

"What's going on? What has you in this state today?"

"I just need to know if this is all my fault. My partner was murdered, two more girls were killed.... brutally. And Emily..."

Dr. Norrington interjected, "How are things going with your wife? I know that when last we talked, you'd been going to movies, lunch... That was good. You seemed happy. Today... you don't seem happy today."

"You don't understand, you can't understand," he insisted.

"Why do you come to these sessions?" she lay her notebook down, leaning back in her chair. She fixed him with a hard stare from behind her glasses. He was caught off guard by her suddenly aggressive demeanor.

"What?"

"Why do you come? You always seem to have your mind made up about what I'm going to say. So, why do you come?"

Quentin opened his mouth to respond, but he wasn't able to. He felt calmer now, maybe because of the confrontation.

"You take one step forward and two back. You have got to learn to let go. There are things that are not under your control. There are things you can't stop. People you can't catch."

"But do you think... my interview. Do you think he killed again because of my interview?"

"I don't know that, Quentin. I am not analyzing that man, I am not trying to understand that man."

"But do you think it is my fault? You tell me all the time I need to take responsibility for my actions, that there are consequences. Was this a fucking consequence? I'm not asking you to analyze him, I'm asking you to *tell me* I fucked up."

She sighed, exasperated. "Let's talk about something else."

Quentin stood up so suddenly that the heavy armchair scooted backwards. He saw Dr. Norrington flinch, reaching down for her pen like it was a weapon. He recoiled, stepping backwards a single step.

"He beat that girl to death. Her show on tv was still paused at twenty minutes, seventeen seconds. I keep thinking about that. She was probably on the edge of her seat. She had nine minutes, forty-three seconds to finish that episode. Now she's dead. He bagged her up, cleaned her house, probably ate the rest of her fucking popcorn, and dumped her at the levee. He ran over my trainee. Just a kid. Killed him."

"You aren't supposed to tell me these details. We've talked about this."

"You asked why I come to these sessions. I just need someone to fucking hear me."

Dr. Norrington removed her glasses, looking up at him before motioning at the chair to encourage him to sit back down. He hesitantly took a seat again, straightening his tie against his breast as he muttered an apology to her. He was out of control. He was an asshole, and everyone hated him, everyone was done with his bullshit, and he didn't blame them one bit.

"Quentin, we have talked about actions and consequences. You have always been the type to act a little recklessly, sometimes with no regard to others, and we have been addressing that. What you never seem to want to address is the fact that you constantly paint yourself as the villain. You have such an immense regret that you carry, but for what? These things that happen are out of your control. You have made poor decisions, who hasn't?"

Quentin wished he was comforted by what she was saying.

46
Polanski

David was not ready to come back to work yet. If not for Leah, he wasn't sure he would have made it through Torres' death. Being in law enforcement anywhere carried with it a certain element of danger, he supposed, but in a small county like Delton it was not exactly common to lose a coworker in such a traumatic way. Most of the officers that died did so at home in a recliner from clogged arteries or, if they were less fortunate, overdosing on prescription pills. Leah had really pulled him through everything, especially when he broke down again at the funeral because Robichaud didn't show up. He'd been pissed, threatening to go to his house and drag his sorry ass there himself. However, Leah had told him that she had talked to Emily and that this was how Robichuad was going to mourn on his own. He just wasn't strong enough to come. Her attempts to placate kept him from doing something rash.

He knew it was hard. Robichaud was arguably closer with Torres than he had been, although he thought that maybe Torres had thought better of him than Robichaud, but it did not excuse him from just *not showing up.* David still remembered the uneven weight of the casket as they carried it to the hearse, the sagging edge where Robichaud would have (and *should have*) stood.

David came around the long side of the three tables with a paper cup of coffee in his good hand. He sat down and slid it across to the young woman who sat at the head. She was distraught and clearly shaken up. Her body quivered underneath her heavy and oversized jacket, which he assumed belonged to a male friend. It still smelled like cheap cologne and had a faded letter on the sleeve. She cupped the coffee in two hands, as though she held it for comfort and not consumption.

He settled down in the chair, awkwardly holding a silver pen in his free hand. He should've been working his way out of this damn cast and splint by now. He wasn't healing well. His wife said stress was keeping his body from doing what it needed to. He figured it was just part of getting old, and it really sucked.

"So, tell me again, exactly, what happened."

The girl took a deep breath in and then released shakily.

"Take your time. I know this kind of thing can be hard to talk about."

"No, no. I'm fine. I'm just shook up," she insisted.

David sipped coffee from his own ceramic cup, by now cold. Preparing her a cup of the chocolatey coffee mix in the machine had taken him too long, leaving his own brew to become too cool. It was almost unbearable for him to even drink it.

"Can you start with telling me what he looked like?"

"Well, he was good looking."

Really helpful, thanks, he wanted to say.

"Okay... can you give me some more details? What race was he?"

"White guy, probably six foot, average build. Brown hair. Pretty eyes."

"Pretty eyes... What color were they?"

"I don't know. Maybe blue?"

"Do you remember what he was driving?"

"One of those four-door type cars, with the bigger trunk space? Open– like in the back. Not like an SUV but..."

"Like a station wagon?"

"Is that what they're called? That's not the word I'm thinking of."

"Just tell me what happened. Where did you run into him?"

"Well, he called me over to his car."

David was surprised. "Just like that? Just pulled up to you?"

"Yeah, he just pulled up, rolled down the window, and asked where I was headed. If I needed a ride. I said no thank you. He didn't really like that. It was like a switch flipped. He went from smiling and everything to just stone cold. Robotic."

"Then what?"

"Well, he drove off, but when I was a few blocks down I noticed his car again. I got a little nervous, because I knew it was him. Then there he was. He came out of nowhere, grabbed ahold of me from behind. He put one hand around my mouth and picked me up off the ground."

Color had drained from the woman's face, and she put a hand up to her mouth as she remembered the moment, touching a split on her lip.

"I know this is getting harder to talk about. Thank you for taking the time to tell me about this. It could really help with our case. How were you able to get away from this man?"

"I am *not* a victim, Detective. I whacked him in the head with my purse."

David tried to hide his surprise. He would have imagined it would be much harder to get away from this monster. This guy certainly fit the description, what little they knew of the man. The car also seemed to be the same.

"With your purse?"

She reached under her table to grab an oversized orange bag, dropping it onto the table with a thud. What did she carry around in that thing, bricks?

"Ah, I got you. Your *purse.*"

"I just kept hitting him and screaming for help. There was this group of girls coming up the opposite side of the street. He must have gotten spooked because he jumped into his car and sped off."

"Well, thank you so much for your time. I'm so sorry you had to experience this."

"Is there anything else I can do? Did I help?"

"Of course."

"Oh, I also have his plate number... if that's important."

David nearly choked on his coffee, he held the cup over his mouth to make sure all of it had finished dripping out of his nose before he belched.

She seemed a little disgusted, and held up her cell phone, "Would it help?"

"Yes, immensely."

"Okay," she said, scrolling through her phone photos. "I have a picture of the back of his car. I took it as he was driving away. It's blurry but..."

David jotted down the number quickly. "Can you email this to me?"

She nodded and he produced a card from the back of his notebook, circling the email address at the bottom. She took the card, and he escorted her back into the main lobby of the department.

He checked his phone and called Leah, just to check in. He wanted to call Robichaud to see how he was holding up, but he refrained. The other man would talk to David when he was ready. The phone rang and rang, and finally he heard her voice on the other end.

"Hey, how's it going?" she asked, bubbly.

"Good, just talked to a girl who thinks this guy tried to abduct her."

"*The* guy?"

"Yeah, I think so. He's really acting out. We're going to get him."

"I hope so. Was she okay?"

"Yeah, she's alright. I don't think she realizes how lucky she is."

"Anna wants to go to the game tonight, it's a big one for them. I told her I'd have to ask you first."

He didn't want to respond because he didn't want to be the bad guy in this situation. Teenage girls were hard anyway, and it only made parenting harder when you were the uptight and less 'fun' parent. He tried to stifle his concern about them being out all night, in a mass of strangers, with people milling around and so much noise that no one would ever hear her scream as she was dragged away.

"David?"

"Yeah."

"Yes?"

"Yeah."

"Yeah?" she sounded surprised, dubious about what he meant.

"Yeah. Tell her she can go if I can pick her up and you drop her off. No talking to anyone from the other school, no running around with douchebag Bryant afterwards. Game and done. Tell her I'll be in the parking lot at ten sharp waiting for her."

"I think those are acceptable terms."

He laughed, "Good."

David had spent hours preparing the girl's statement, making sure it was all squared away and logged and he could get all of the info to the right people (but especially Paltro, because he was the brains and if David wanted anything done, he knew Paltro would get it done). The station was mostly empty, other than Pat's office, where a dim light was muted blue by the frosted glass. He kind of worried about her and all that was going on. It was just in his nature, as much as he wished it wasn't, to worry about those people around him and how they were affected.

He reached over and picked up his phone, spinning his chair around to face Pat's office. He heard her landline ringing, and he knew she'd answer because no one ever called her on that phone. Her silhouette looked down, hesitating, and then seemed to look straight at him, right through the opaque glass. She reached over to answer, and he heard her on the other end of the phone.

"What's up, Chief?" Polanski drawled.

"What do you want, Polanski?"

"How are you holding up?"

"I'm okay. It's tough."

"Yeah. It is tough."

"I called the state police."

David hesitated, clearing his throat.

"I know we were all hoping we could do this on our own... but it was a bad call. It was reckless, and foolish of me. I take full responsibility for... for everything. For the murders, the media, for Torres."

"Pat, none of this is your fault."

"We should've called for help after Mary Allen... when we were sure they were all homicides and they were all related. We are sitting on ten bodies that we know of, and this guy is still out there and pissed off."

"I know, but don't act like the state or even the feds didn't already know about this. It's all over the news. They just don't give a shit about a podunk town like Whitebranch."

"That might be true..."

"It is."

"But it doesn't excuse anything. I should have never let this go on."

"It was all of us. We wanted to think we could... control this. Stop it."

"We handle our own, I know..."

"I'm resigning, too."

"Don't say that, Pat," David insisted, voice exasperated.

"I don't need to be doing this anymore."

"What else would you be doing?"

"I don't know... What did you want? I stayed here so I could be left alone... and here you are, pissing me off."

"Just checking on you, Pat. Burning the midnight oil isn't like you."

"Ain't quite midnight. Just about ten thirty."

"What?" Did she say ten thirty?

"Just making a joke, Polanski. Don't get your panties in such a wad."

He looked down at his watch, its arms actually reading ten thirty-seven. He was over a half hour late to pick up Anna. He stammered something about having to go and rushed out the front door, not even locking it up behind him.

His car hit the curb on the way out of the parking lot, lurching him upwards so roughly that his head struck the ceiling of the cab. He was always an avid safety-belt wearer, ever since his younger brother died in a car accident in high school, but he hadn't even fastened it before he pulled out this time.

He called Leah, struggling to hold the phone up to his ear with his shoulder and drive with one hand. He finally pushed the setting for speaker mode, accidentally dropping the phone down onto the floorboard.

"David?" He heard Leah's voice from near his feet.

"Leah? Is Anna home?" he yelled, turning down onto Main Street: a bee line to the school and football field.

"No, I thought you guys were running behind."

Cold sweat. His ears were hot and ringing. Was he fucking crying? He wiped underneath his eyes with the back of his hand, misaligned cruiser pulling consistently to the right. He needed to calm down. It was fine.

Everything was fine. Games always went on longer than they were supposed to. There were people everywhere. He was upset over nothing.

However, it didn't feel like nothing. Especially not when Leah's voice came across desperate and worried, "David?"

"I forgot," he breathed. "I forgot. I worked over and forgot."

"Did you try to call her?"

"Has she called you? No, I didn't try to call her. I'm pulling in. I'll call you back."

"David, no..."

He put the car into park, reaching down to find the phone and disconnect the call. He stumbled out of the vehicle into the mostly empty parking lot. He dialed Anna's number, struggling to find it for several moments. He so rarely called her, his own daughter. Why didn't they talk anymore? Why didn't they do things like they used to?

"Please pick up the damn phone," he pleaded, walking towards the empty arena. There were a handful of teenagers milling around still, mostly picking up trash from the bleachers. He knew that freshmen and sophomores often got extra credit for cleaning up after games. When Anna didn't answer, he put the phone into his pocket and looked for the nearest adult.

A corpulent woman sat on one of the lower seats with a notebook, scribbling away. Her full, blonde hair seemed to be styled for someone much younger. Her makeup was 'on point,' as the young people would say, and her clothes were casual yet sophisticated.

"Excuse me," David called, walking over to her just a little too briskly. The woman reached down around her waist, and for a moment he had concerns that she might be armed. He slowed his approach, holding up his hand to insist that he was not a weirdo. He was sure he looked strung out at this point, face puffy and wet, hair matted to his head with sweat.

"I'm sorry, I'm Anna's dad."

"Oh, Mr. Polanski." She put her hand to her chest. "I'm Mrs. Elvie, or... Or Coach Elvie, I guess. Depending on who you ask."

"Mrs. Elvie, have you seen Anna? Is she still here?"

Elvie laid her notebook down on the bleacher beside her, squinting out at the group of kids who were still working. She cupped her hands around her mouth and whistled. The kids looked up.

"Penny!"

A young girl jogged over with a trash bag in her hand, smiling in greeting.

"Penny, was Anna at the game tonight?"

"She was," David insisted.

Penny nodded. "Yeah, she was here."

Elvie looked at David expectantly, as though she was trying to figure out why he was here and why he was asking about his daughter. David didn't want to admit that he'd forgotten to pick her up, didn't want them to think that he was a bad father. *Did* that make him a bad father? Or was it enough to just be human?

"There was a miscommunication between her mother and me and I got off work late. I'm a cop. She was supposed to be here and she's not," David lied.

Penny looked at Elvie and then at him. "She got a ride home."

"From who?" David asked, turning his body away from Elvie and towards the teenage girl.

"I don't know... some guy on the other team."

"Who was he? Do you know his name?" David found himself approaching the girl, who backed away almost immediately.

Elvie stood up, putting herself between David and the girl, he retreated back a step.

"Mr. Polanski, I'm going to have to ask you to calm down. Is something wrong? Is Anna missing?"

David put his hand to his head to keep everything from spinning, "Fuck, fuck, fuck. I need to find her."

"He seemed like a nice guy, Mr. Polanski. I'm sure he's taking her home." Penny insisted, pulling her phone out of her pocket. By this time, two other girls had wandered over and stood a few feet away nervously.

"She isn't home," he managed to breathe, almost falling onto his backside as he seated himself on the bench.

Elvie came over, placing her hand on his shoulder. "Have you tried to call her phone?"

"She didn't answer me."

His chest and neck felt tight, and he leaned into himself. He was breathless, and indigestion and nausea flooded over him.

"I think I'm having a heart attack," he admitted, tilting forward in case he passed out. He could hear Elvie tell one of the girls to call 911.

His phone was ringing, but he couldn't get it out of his pocket because of the immense tightness in his shoulders and chest. His jaw seemed clenched against his will. One of the girls, who was just a blur of color at this point, squatted down beside him: "Mr. Polanski, Anna messaged me and said she's fine. Mr. Polanski?"

He could barely hear her over the roar of static in his ears.

47
Paltro

Tresa kicked him under the kitchen table, and he jolted back to awareness, clearing his throat. He looked up at her, smiling apologetically before adjusting his glasses on his nose. They were in her kitchen: bright, white, clean and fragrant, with the aroma of lemon. She had little ceramic and wooden foxes and owls on every surface. Deen didn't even have a real table in his kitchen, just the hightop with a single bar stool, packed with papers on top. Curtains always pulled tight, and the apartment was always dark. He wasn't much for decor. Tresa's place was a perfect reflection of her personality, and maybe Deen's was a counterpart of his too.

"Where you at today, Deen?" she asked.

He sighed, reaching down to pick at the plate in front of him. She'd taken time out of her day to make him dinner, even if it was a casserole... It was still his favorite, she made it *almost* as good as his grandmother.

"Just been thinking about Torres and this case. He seemed to think he knew who the guy was. I just wish I had taken it more seriously."

"There was no way to know that this guy had gone after him. It was a bad coincidence. Bad luck, bad timing."

"It's the way of the universe, like in the movies. You never take that chance."

Tresa shook her head as though she disagreed, but she didn't say anything.

"His mom didn't want his personal items," Deen said, looking up at her.

"Like what?"

"Like the clothes he died in."

"That's understandable. I wouldn't want them either."

"I mean... like his apartment key."

Tresa laid her fork down, the sound heavier than he felt it should have been. They stared at each other quietly for several moments, and Deen folded his hands up in front of his mouth.

"What are you suggesting?"

"Well, I was thinking we could go look through his notes on the case."

"*We*?"

"I was just... suggesting. They're going to throw out everything in his apartment."

Tresa pulled her lower lip between her teeth, leaning back in her chair and crossing her arms over her chest.

"You know you could get into a lot of trouble for this, Deen."

"So could you, if you go with me."

They were at a standoff.

"I don't know. What are you hoping to find?"

"He seemed to know who the guy was, or thought he did."

"Do you think he killed him because he was close?"

"I do. I really do. Torres was smart... Nobody would give him that credit, but he was."

She sighed, standing and taking her dirty plate to the sink. She returned to take Deen's plate, with food still on it, and set it on the island.

"The first sign of trouble and I'm throwing you under the bus," she said with a smile.

He shrugged. "I'll tuck and roll."

Torres' apartment at Giraldi Place was nothing spectacular. It was one of a couple of apartment complexes in the county, all of which looked very similar. This was the only one that was not income based that Deen knew of, but it didn't make them any nicer. The interior of the apartment was very plain: beige walls that were, in some areas, two tone from moisture build up, greyish tile floor throughout, and white appliances.

A basket of dirty laundry was packed and ready to go beside a neatly made bed. Books were lined up on shelves made of cinder blocks and planks, holding various titles that ranged from fantasy to self-help. All of the books were worn, probably second-hand, paperbacks with bent covers and dog-eared pages. The room smelled like those same books: a sweet and musky scent like almond and chocolate.

On Torres' bedside table was a picture of him and his mother and a golden crucifix necklace. The police had retrieved certain items for his mother, and he wondered why she had not taken the photo and the necklace. A folder lay at the foot of the bed, and Deen opened it with one finger. It was exactly what he was looking for. Torres must have had intentions of coming back inside for it, or he had forgotten it there.

"Tres," he called.

She entered the bedroom slowly, arms crossed over her chest as though that would keep her safe from any ill.

"This must be what he was going to show me. It has all of his notes on the flowers, the girls... and he took pictures of the notes, the handwriting and..."

He picked up a business card for Roots and Shoots, with a name and number written on the back of it. He held it down to the notes, speculating that they were written by the same person. Dammit, Torres really *had* made close contact with the killer. Tresa was standing beside him now, unnerved.

"So he was at the garden center?"

"I'm wondering if he's an employee there..."

"Surely not, Deen. I go in there and get potting soil all the time. Surely not. *Surely not.*"

"Torres seemed to have thought so. Let's get out of here. I'll look over all of this later."

All he had to do was put a few dots together. He already had information on this guy: rough descriptions, car type, shoe size... If he could get a look at the employees there, or even ask the owners of the store... they might be able to nail him down.

He grabbed the folder and, when Tresa was out of sight, he also took the crucifix from the bedside table and put it into his pocket.

48
Rion

It hadn't taken him long to find out where Emily worked. He had followed her for a couple of days, figuring her schedule out and waiting for his opportunity to get her alone. Today had been a particularly long day for her. As all of the cars left the little parking lot except hers, he found it time to act. He used a hammer and nail to puncture her front driver's side tire, retreating quickly to his parked car on the other side of the street, and then he waited.

Nearly an hour later, she came out to her vehicle.

Rion wanted to be fair when he was playing with Robichaud, so he gave him a chance. All Robichaud had to do was pick up the phone when Emily called. All he had to do was come and get her, and change her tire. They could have gone home together.

That's all he had to do.

Rion had a feeling that he wouldn't answer his wife's call. Not with the workload he was under. Rion had been watching the news, which had mentioned that the investigation was reaching a peak. Rion had, in some ways, really screwed up. They had his fingerprints, DNA... Luckily, Rion had never committed a crime. He'd never worked anywhere that required his fingerprints. For now he was invisible. This was it, he would need to lay low after this. Relax for a few months, a year. If he could stifle the urge now. The fire seemed to burn out of control when you let it get a little too hot, stoked it just a little too much.

The media had really started digging their heels in too, leading to protests around the small courthouse in town – people asking why the police hadn't apprehended the killer– and the public refused the curfew due to sports season. It was always the police's fault in their eyes. Why couldn't they catch him? Why *wouldn't* they catch him? He couldn't imagine, with the people starting to turn on the police like they were, that Quentin would have time to answer a midday call from his wife on his personal phone.

And he was glad that Quentin didn't let him down. She was *so* pretty.

Rion watched her as she held the phone up to her ear, squatting down to try to see why the tire was flat. Even though she wasn't aware that anyone was watching her, she modestly smoothed her short dress around her backside. He cruised around the circular drive to pull up beside her, rolling the window down as he smiled.

"Having some trouble, ma'am? Battery?"

She sighed, stuffing her phone inside her small purse before motioning to her car. "Tire. I have a flat."

"Do you have a spare? I have a tire iron, I could change it for you," he offered, unlocking his car and coming to stand beside her. He shoved his hands deep into his pockets to keep from immediately reaching out to touch her. It would be premature. He needed to be patient although he could hardly resist the urge.

"I don't have a spare," she admitted, cheeks flushing pink. "Thank you for the offer though, I'll be fine."

"Is someone coming to get you?"

"I'm going to call my husband... or a friend of his."

Rion nodded, moving back over to his own vehicle and putting one foot inside on the floorboard, hanging his arm over the top of the door casually, "Want a ride up the road to the gas station? You could get a tire there and wait for your husband. Looks like it might rain."

As though on perfect cue, thunder rumbled distantly, somewhere over the Rotten Fork river to the northeast. He was satisfied with this, even though he didn't believe in signs, as a *good* omen. This was going to be a good day. Blessed, as the soccer moms would put it.

"I really think I'll be alright," she said, looking over at the dark sky in the distance.

"They have a great pork tenderloin sandwich on Tuesdays. I know the Coopers, the owners that is. So I'll buy you lunch too, to make up for this... no good day you're having."

She smiled, seeming to be flattered by his kindness and generosity. He returned the smile, looking down to make sure his eyes didn't give it away.

"Would you mind?"

"Not at all. I'm heading that way anyway. Gotta get some spark plugs. Hop in, be sure to lock your doors. They may not be able to drive it away, but that doesn't mean some punks wouldn't steal anything they can out of it."

She laughed, pushing the lock button twice on her key fob. *Unnecessary,* and he clenched his jaw at the harsh double beep of the horn to confirm, *twice*, that the car had indeed obeyed the command.

She sat down in his front seat, tucking her purse between her ankles on the floorboard. She smiled again, face absolutely shining with goodness. She was truly a gem, truly a pure soul. This was his unicorn. It almost would have made him feel a little dirty, if he hadn't wanted her so bad.

"Thank you again. I have to tell my husband all the time that there's still good people in the world. He's so... down about people. Society."

"Oh, I hate to hear that. What does your husband do? Like for a living? Politician?" he laughed.

"Well, he's a police officer."

Rion smiled at her apologetically. "That's a stressful career. I know it's even harder for the spouse."

She looked over at him curiously, almost suspicious.

"My father was a police officer. There is no doubt that the real burdens fall on who is left at home."

Rion remembered his father in his last moments, the way he had gripped onto his shirt sleeve and asked him to call an ambulance. He had worked in construction all of his life. He had a bad back that arched out and pushed his chin to his chest, calloused hands that cracked and bled, knees that gave out on him. He was weaker than he had ever been, because he had given everything he had to that time clock. The fear of the pain turned into the fear that he'd been right about his son all along just before he had succumbed to death.

"It does make it hard for us to go anywhere together. He's always on edge."

"A little bit of caution can go a long way. Wouldn't you rather think every person is probably a monster, than to think they're all angels and get into a car with the boogeyman?"

She looked over at him nervously again, but smiled, this time her lips forming a crooked little line, "Well, when you put it that way..."

He turned down the dirt road, which had never been gravelled, that led to a foreclosed farm. He had scoped it out a few times, even venturing as far as to ask for an official tour by the real estate agent. It still wasn't under contract. He could see Emily sit up a little straighter in her seat as he turned, and he torqued his hand forward on the steering wheel.

"I've never been down this way before... to get to Cooper's Station?" she said hesitantly, hand moving down to pull her purse up into her lap.

"A shortcut I know of. There's some roadwork on the highway."

"What happened to your hand?"

A dramatic change in subject. He looked down at his swollen, bruised knuckles. He had covered it with foundation as much as he could, having matched his skin tone painstakingly in the aisle before he purchased it... but he supposed after a little while things came through. Things always came through.

"Lost control," he whispered, slowing the car as he came to a bend in the drive, just near the old farmhouse. "I have never done that before..."

"Why are we slowing down?"

"Have you ever lost control, Emily Robichaud?"

"What are we doing here?"

"I know your husband has."

"My husband? Who... What are you talking about?"

"I'm sorry. No matter how I split it, no matter what scenario I play out in my perfect vision of this... all roads lead to this one."

She unbuckled, jerking the door handle open in one fluid motion. She was nearly out, and he reached and grabbed her by her hair like had with Quinn Collins. She screamed, the sound filling the inside of the car. She reached into her purse and pulled out something that looked like a keyring of a cat's head, pressing her fingers into the eye sockets and swinging backwards at him. The cat's ears were rigid and punctured Rion's shoulder. He found himself howling in pain, especially as one of the ears broke off in his chest. He held onto her all the tighter, dragging her out through the driver's side of the car. She swung her fists at him, grappling and grabbing for a grip on any part of him she could. He slung her down onto the ground and she was on her feet in an instant.

Rion opened the back door, retrieving the tire iron from the backseat. Emily was running as hard as she could. He could hear her panting as she screamed for help. Expending precious energy that would wear her out, no one was accustomed to running like this. Literally running for their lives.

When you were in those scenarios, the last thing you wanted to do was scream at the top of your lungs.

Emily was tiring already, although she pushed on. Her screams grew more exasperated, but she had fixed her eyes on the horizon, somewhere across the golden field where she had seen a house, or something. Maybe a mailbox. Maybe a barn. She had her sights set, and she would not stop.

Rion was a little faster, he had paced himself. He still felt like he was approaching her in slow motion, wind blowing her hair and dress around behind her, by now having lost both shoes (which he had to skip over to avoid tripping on). He was almost an arm's length away, he could reach out, fingertips grazing her shoulder.

He took his other arm and swung the iron over his head.

49
Polanski

He had no intention of working that day. His doctor told him that he'd likely only had a panic attack the night of the ballgame, but recommended he avoid 'extreme stressors'. The nearest heart center was over an hour away, and they told him minutes counted when someone was having a real heart attack. They recommended he talk to someone, a therapist, and to watch his diet. That was perhaps the worst news of all: he did have some heart disease and so they recommended he avoid fried foods and go for healthy fats. What the fuck was a healthy fat? David lived for things dripping with grease.

David had struggled with the aftermath of Anna's (not) disappearance, and all of the could-haves and what-ifs. He had told her how much he loved her, nevermind that she had ridden home with a complete stranger that she had never met. The act was not malicious, and seeing her terror at the sight of him in the back of the ambulance, and the way she regretted not contacting him.... He could not hold it against her. She was just a kid. She was expected to act like a kid. She would make bad decisions *like a kid*. It was his job to make sure she was safe while she learned these hard lessons.

He was sitting at home with Leah on their front porch, enjoying an orange club soda and some saltines. Leah lived on club sodas, and he'd grown to like some of the citrus ones, even if they did give him heartburn later.

His personal phone rang and he looked down at it. Leah started to snatch it out of his hand and he playfully pulled it away. It was Paltro, which was unusual. He never called David, let alone like this.

"You should answer it," she responded. "He usually doesn't call unless he needs something."

"Maybe he has a lead from the info I got from the girl the other night."

She nodded.

He reluctantly answered the phone, "Paltro?"

"Polanski... this is bad, man."

Was he crying? David figured he wasn't, because Paltro showing any kind of real emotion seemed a little too mythological to be believed... but his voice had cracked, he sounded strained. Was it Tresa? What would have Paltro so upset?

"What's going on?"

"We got a call about a body found at the Lancaster Farm. It's Emily."

"Emily?" David breathed, mind disconnecting the name from the face. Leah must have noticed the color drain from his face, because she sat up and put her hands to her mouth.

"She's dead. Please get out here. I know you're not on but I don't want Brannon handling this."

"Are you sure it's her?"

"Yes. It's her."

"Are you sure she's... Are you..." he belched, wrapping his arm around his stomach.

"Yeah, Polanski. She's dead. I'll give you more details when you get here."

Paltro hung up the phone, leaving David with nothing except a flat ringing tone in his ear. It sounded like the note that his daughter played on a steel tongue drum she bought at a yardsale when she was six. A droning, bell-like whir. His head was spinning.

"David?"

He turned to look at Leah as though he'd forgotten she was there. She touched his face with both hands, palms warm and dry. He realized he was sweating again, cold, chilling.

"Jesus, come on. Let's go inside. We've got to get you laid down."

He grabbed her arm with his hand, more firmly than he intended. She looked down at the contact point and then back up at his face. Her eyes started welling with tears and he knew that she'd overheard enough to know what had happened. She shook her head from side to side and mouth 'no'. He fell forward into her, head resting against her shoulder. She supported him, somehow stronger, wrapping her arms around his neck and burying him into her breast. She kissed the back of his head and sobbed into his hair.

It was overcast, threatening rain with deep growls and low brows of dense, heaping darkness. David could smell and feel the dampness on the air with his windows down, wind blowing his ruddy-and-grey hair enough that it didn't cover his receding hairline anymore. He was sloppily dressed, more than usual, his pants were hanging off without a belt, fly was down, shirt was buttoned all wrong, and he had his tie looped like he'd been drunk when he did it in the mirror.

Brannon was standing in the driveway of the farm when Polanski pulled up, long and lanky body like a scarecrow that you'd find in one of these fields. He was waiting on him, hands folded in front of him. David slammed the car into park, jolting forward and sliding in the gravel. He was surprised he didn't strip some gears.

He exited the vehicle and Brannon had teleported to stand just in front of him, putting his hands on his shoulders. The pale detective looked more pale than ever, dark circles under his eyes accented by both the dark pitch of his hair and the shocking lightness of his irises. He pursed his thin lips together, patting David on the chest.

"Take a deep breath, Polanski." Brannon said calmly, licking his finger tips and running it across David's wind-tousled hair.

"Fuck off, Jules," David breathed, voice having no volume or force.

"Do you want to look like shit?" Brannon asked, adjusting David's collar and undoing his tie. There was a mechanical and calming feel to the slowness of Brannon's movements and dialogue. David didn't know why he let him do it. Anything to put off walking over to Paltro, who he could see waiting for him out in the dried pasture.

Brannon nodded, giving the tie one tug downwards. "There."

He strode away without another word, approaching his vehicle on the other side of the drive. David now took it upon himself to walk across the field, his stomach aching.

Paltro turned at the sound of his approach and was, thankfully, composed. David needed that. Paltro nodded in greeting and then walked close to David's side, guiding him over to Emily's body with his elbow. David wanted to cry again, he wanted to scream, but Paltro went on, talking without giving him a chance.

"Realtor went out there to do a showing, noticed tire tracks, and then saw buzzards. When they were walking the perimeter they cut back through towards the house, just so happened to find her body. They didn't touch anything. They knew she was dead." He was professional and to-the-point as he took David on a tour of the grisly scene. "He hit her from behind, she fell. I assume unconscious instantly, probably dead soon after. Clear blunt force to the back of the head. Tire iron left over there."

"He left it?"

Paltro nodded. "I think he wanted him to know."

"Who?"

"Robichaud."

"Why would he want him to know? What difference does it make?"

"Her car is at her place of employment. She has a flat. I'm willing to bet my career that she tried to call him."

"Fuck."

"He left clear shoe prints. The ground is soft. Knee impressions here and here where he knelt over her. Dress cut open with some kind of tool after she was dead. Something sharp -he barely nicked her skin here above her navel when he cut the front... Looks postmortem. I'm still trying to map everything else out."

"Has anyone told him?"

Paltro looked up at him, dark brows pulled low over his eyes.

"Did anyone call Robichaud?"

He shook his head. "I didn't have it in me. I was hoping you would. I know that's unfair, but it's you or Brannon."

"I don't know if I can do this."

Paltro nodded. "I know. He'd rather hear it from you. I'm not good at this kind of thing."

He was pissed at Paltro for making him do this. But he also knew he was right. Quentin would rather hear it from David. He'd rather hear it from a friend, someone who was mourning with him. Someone who felt the pain too.

He pulled his phone out of his pocket, holding it in his shaking palm. His vision was white-hot, everything blown out and unbearable. He made himself breathe in and out, punching Robichaud's name with his thumb. He didn't answer immediately, and the ringing caused a vibration of pain in his skull with every cycle. Finally, David heard his voice on the other end: calm, unaware.

"Quentin, listen..." Polanski said, chest starting to ache again. "I need you to listen to me. It's Emily."

"What's going on? What about Emily?"

"I need you to breathe... I need you to listen."

"Is she okay?"

"Quentin..."

His voice began rising in panic, high pitched. "Fucking stop... Don't... Where the fuck are you?"

"I'll... just meet me at the station."

"I said where the fuck are you? You tell me where the fuck my wife is right now, David. Right now." David had to pull his ear away from the phone as he heard Quentin screaming into it. "I said where the fuck is she?"

"Please, Quentin, don't do this. Just meet me at the station and I'll get you to her as soon as I can. Just meet me there."

He couldn't handle this right now. He could feel his heart pounding in his chest, a little too fast and missing a beat now and again. Every too-long pause between beats made him breathless, like he was free falling to the ground right before being caught before impact. Avoid stress, they had told him. Avoid extreme stressors. He found himself talking, answering against his will.

"The old Lancaster farm."

"I'm coming there now."

"Quentin, please."

"I'm on my way. I'm on my way."

David needed a minute, more than a minute. He was never going to be ready for this. He paced back and forth as he tried to decide what he could do to make this easier. How was he going to help his friend? A man that he thought of as a brother, as family?

"Are we about wrapped up here?" David asked, voice cracking.

Paltro had squatted down beside Emily, taking photos from careful angles. He did not seem to hear David, and instead started setting out markers. Brannon and a few others also milled around, gossiping among themselves. David's mind was racing, thoughts spiraling out of control.

Time went by more quickly than he thought, and he heard Brannon whistle to him.

"Polanski!" He was motioning behind David, who stood still. He couldn't do this. He wanted to sink down into the ground beneath his feet.

Paltro, who rarely muttered a cussword in his life, breathlessly said, "What the fuck, Polanski? What the fuck is he doing here?"

David didn't want to turn around to see Quentin pulling up. He could hear the sound of the tall grass hitting the fender of the vehicle as it pulled through the field. Paltro would kill him for driving into the crime scene, he thought. David still had chunks of vomit sticking in his tonsils, and his breath was sour and sick. His jaws and head pounded with stress. He watched instead as Paltro jogged to his van to grab a black tarp and then came running back to try and cover Emily's body before Quentin saw it.

But it was too late, Quentin had already seen her lying in the grass, nearly pristine if not for the grass stains on her torn clothes where she had fallen, dead in her tracks. The back of her head was swollen, sticking out like it was trying to grow something: a new form pushing its way through her scalp like a plant through soil. Only feet away was the tire iron, with pieces of her scalp and hair still attached, made more noticeable by the yellow number four marker.

He was looking at her, beyond everyone else that stood there. David could tell that his knees were weak by the way he hitched each step that he made towards her. David met him in the middle, their bodies colliding forcefully as he pulled him to a tight embrace. They sobbed loudly into each other, ending up on their knees in the sea of green.

50
Quentin

Quentin didn't want to sleep in the bed. Even on all of the days that they had fought, they always shared the bed. It didn't feel right. He started the night sleeping on her side of the bed, face down in her pillow. He nearly suffocated but lay there until he could no longer smell the faint aroma of her shampoo. She always washed her hair before bed, falling asleep with it damp against the pillowcase as she read a book. He often took the book out of her hands, stuffing a tag or receipt into her place and putting it on the bedside table. The book lay there unfinished now, never to be continued. A story that she would never know the end of.

He couldn't turn on the radio or the television for background noise. The news reports were everywhere. Her name and her face were everywhere. Murder. Brutality. Horror. Another wildflower. Rape. Necrophilia. Mourning. Unthinkable. Prayers. Community.

He didn't want to hear any of it. He wanted to imagine that none of this had happened. In one moment, he wished she had never been here at all... and then he regretted it the next. He didn't want to think of her because when he tried to recall happy memories, they were interrupted by images of her lying dead in the grass. Just gone. Snuffed out. So *fragile* and temporary and simple. How could something that meant so much to him be taken away so easily? Why was it so hard to push the terrible moment out of his head and remember all of the good?

Quentin moved to the kitchen floor with his back against the refrigerator, wrapping himself in a quilt with his head propped on a pillow. He kept a flashlight with him, lying there until he found his sides aching, both from the stiffness of the floor and relentless crying. He then sat up, listening to every pop and crack and groan of their little house, shining his light across the linoleum in hopes that one of the obscure sounds might reveal her pale feet on the floor and her soft voice telling him it was only a nightmare, come back to bed.

51
Rion

Desperate times called for desperate measures.

Rion had never missed a day of work in his working life. *Ever*. He was on time, every time. Today, however, he needed to do something a little different. His shoulder was aching and sore. He needed medical attention. His neck was bruised where, he assumed, at some point Emily had grabbed a handful of his skin before he threw her out of the car. His knuckles were bruised. Someone, eventually, was going to ask what happened.

On his way to work, he veered over the rumblestrip and crashed his car into the nearest sign. He got out of the car to assess the damage, deducing that it was enough to cause an issue but not enough to cause serious damage. The car was still drivable.

Then he called the police and filed an accident report, and contacted his insurance. Mrs. Rice at Roots and Shoots was worried to death about him when he called on the phone. She insisted he stay home today and take care of himself. He told her he was fine to come in, but she told him she'd lock him out if he showed up.

Now he sat at home, having wasted the day staring at the ceiling as he thought about pretty little things. He watered his plants. He ate lunch and dinner. He jogged on the treadmill. He decided he would never miss another day of work again because this day had lasted *forever*.

He was about to fold his laundry when he heard a sound from down the hallway. He walked slowly over, trying to figure out what it was. It was a wet sort of sound, like a toilet that would not flush or a sink that had something stuck in the drain. The walls of the hallway seemed to distort, and his head started spinning.

Rion looked down the too-long stretch of hall. He could see himself in the mirror on the opposite end, socked feet set firmly on the carpeted floor as though he might take the opportunity to sprint away, anywhere else.

The sound came again: a gurgling groaning that evolved into a high pitched but harsh whine. His brain came up with logical explanations: a pipe, the sink was clogged. That was when he saw it, though. It seemed to be born of the shadow beneath the doorway, pulling itself out of the black as an inky form, fingers at the end of a slender arm that grabbed handfuls of the carpet in order to pull itself further into the light.

He took a curious step forward, squinting as the ink monster took on a more familiar shape: the girl he had killed in the shower. He found himself now stumbling backwards, falling over the coffee table and nearly cracking his skull against the entertainment center.

"No," he said out loud. "No, no, no. You're dead. You aren't real. Revenant? Where the fuck are you?"

Summer Glass did not appear.

The girl with the swelled, misshapen head, continued to come towards him, painfully dragging herself against the floor. Her wails were unbearable, not because he had any remorse, but just because the sound was *so* horrific. She sputtered against her puffy lips, teeth sticking out from the plump flesh like splinters.

"You aren't real," he said. "You're dead. You're dead. You are nothing."

He closed his eyes and then opened them again. She was gone. He got to his feet slowly, shaking all over. She really was gone.

A crunch from behind him had him spinning around to see the Revenant sitting on the back of the couch, eating a potato chip. She wiped crumbs on the fabric.

"She'll be back, Rion."

"Why is this happening?"

"That's a good question. Maybe they're here to help drag you to Hell."

"I'm not going anywhere... I'm not. I'm laying low for a little while. I killed Robichaud's wife, I just need to let things settle..."

She shook her head. "They still haven't found that little waitress. Remember her? This thing isn't going to settle anytime soon."

"It will. People will move on," he insisted.

"Can you resist the urge? When you get off on murder, there's not really a good way to scratch that itch in the mean time."

"I'll be fine."

"Not if Quinn Collins can get her hands on you. The things she's going to do to you, Rion... The things we are all going to do to you if we get the chance."

Rion went into his bedroom after turning on every light in the house, making sure that they illuminated every corner, and stuffed towels beneath the door cracks. While he lay in bed, awake because he could not sleep a single second, he could hear the painful wails of Quinn Collins from the dark recesses beneath his bed.

When he woke up the next morning, he could not scrub the phantom blood that she left behind off of the floor.

52
Quentin

People think about it, don't they? About skipping the funerals of loved ones? Quentin wasn't sure he could go, at first. The thought of seeing her dead again was not what he wanted, but the last image of her sprawled out in a field with her skull cracked open was also not what he wanted. At this point he didn't have control over how he remembered her and what he saw. He stood beside Brother Hodge, taking a deep breath as he prepared to enter the empty sanctuary.

"I know this is difficult, Quentin," Brother Hodge said, reaching out to put his hand on Quentin's back. "Everything has been taken care of for you, I just want you to see her alone before everyone else starts coming."

"I'm ready."

Brother Hodge guided him down the aisleway, and he looked at his feet as he followed. He couldn't watch her as he approached because he thought he might pass out. A woman in a beige dress was practicing music on the piano in the corner, but she swapped to a soft pedal as she saw them approaching in the mirror above the instrument. He stood now in front of the casket, and Brother Hodge took his hand, squeezing it.

Quentin looked up reluctantly. He found himself nearly in tears again when we saw how good she looked. He had leaned so heavily against the casket that Brother Hodge had to make him stand up to avoid tipping her over. They had parted her hair and placed her head on the pillow in such a way that you did not see the damage to the back. She was perfect, and he was okay for the first moment since it happened.

"What do you think, brother?" Hodge asked.

Quentin nodded. "She looks good."

"She does look good, doesn't she?"

Quentin choked, nodding. He wiped away tears as he leaned down to kiss her on the forehead. He seated himself at the first pew, crossing one leg over another as he took a deep breath. People started pouring in after a little while, the first being the Polanskis. David and his family settled down on the bench beside him.

"You alright?" Polanski asked, patting Quentin on the leg.

"Right now, yeah... Yeah."

"Leah made you something to eat on for the week. We'll drop it off after," he said awkwardly. They had talked about this before, how women always cooked for a widower like he was a helpless thing that didn't know how to use a stove. Being on this end of it, however, it didn't seem so funny anymore. In fact, he was thankful. The idea of having to prepare food without Emily, or shop for anything... it was exhausting. He would happily take something he could just warm up.

Quentin leaned forward to smile at Leah, who reached over and hugged him across Polanski's lap. "We're here for you, Quentin. Whatever you need."

Paltro entered, just a little later than everyone else, and took a seat behind them. He didn't say anything but simply nodded in greeting. He held the obituary in his hand, staring at it the entire time. A majority of his coworkers came, scattering themselves around the room, mingling with Emily's side of the family and her friends.

Quentin hadn't meant to zone out as the pastor gave a passionate sermon regarding Emily's life and about life in general. It didn't really feel right, since the man didn't know her. He had never been to a funeral without Emily, and this felt incredibly surreal. He wished he would have somehow cherished that moment, there... where she was still with him. Even though she was dead, and it was just her body, it was the last time he'd ever lay eyes on her again.

When everything was said and done, Quentin stood at the back of the church, greeting every single person that went through the door. Most of them he knew, at least in passing. Some of them just nodded, shook his hand, or offered him a hug. He was overstimulated, and every embrace was painful. He wanted people to stop touching him, but he stifled the desire to start snapping at every puffy, wet face that passed by him. These people were here because they loved Emily.

Pat came up to him, shaking his hand and looking at the ground between them. "Take a break, Robichaud."

"I'm alright, Chief. I need work. Distraction," Quentin said quietly.

"It's out of my hands now. You're personally involved, you're off the case, you've got to take some time. Use your vacation and... let me know if you need anything." She walked away briskly, and he felt a new wave of emotion take over him. He pulled it together for the next person in line, shaking their hand and thanking them for coming.

Finally the end was near, Brother Hodge. He hugged him, tightly squeezing, and whispered into his ear that he was praying for him. Praying for peace. Quentin was praying for something quite different.

A man stood up from a corner seat at the pew, coming down the aisle way behind Brother Hodge. Quentin didn't recognize him. He looked at Quentin like he knew him, however, so he smiled to pretend he wasn't a stranger.

"Thanks for coming," Quentin said.

"I'm so sorry about Emily... She was truly an amazing woman."

There was something weird about the way he said it. Maybe he was an ex-boyfriend, or a coworker with a crush. Maybe Quentin was just being paranoid. He'd always been a little jealous... usually prematurely.

"She really was... Do I know you?"

"I don't think we ever met," the man admitted, green eyes fluttering at him before averting to focus somewhere else. "I was an old friend of hers."

"Well, thanks again for coming. It means a lot to have you here."

"It meant... *so much* to get to be here for you."

Quentin extended a hand, but the man didn't shake it. Instead he rushed past him and abruptly exited the door behind Quentin into the parking lot.

53
Paltro

Deen was not a detective and he did not pretend to be. His place was with the dead, the quiet secret keepers. Fleshy puzzle boxes full of mystery and intrigue and challenge. He had never liked working with living people. He was made for his job.

He was making sacrifices today, though. He went into Roots and Shoots in person. He was wearing plain clothes: a t-shirt, a comfortable pair of shorts, and high top tennis shoes. He wasn't going in like he was on business, but this was *all* business.

He had called and asked one of the owners, a Mrs. Marissa Rice, if he could have a meeting with her. She agreed and they set it up. He walked through the door of the building, impressed by the vast displays of plants. He wasn't much of a houseplant person himself, but Tresa loved green things. He picked up a fox planter, holding it fondly in his hands as he stared down at it. She'd like that, he thought.

"Good afternoon!"

He looked up, nearly dropping the fragile pot if he hadn't caught it awkwardly against his thighs. An elderly woman, still bright eyed and lively, stood at the other end of the store inside an office door.

"Mrs. Rice, I'm sorry. I was just admiring this pot... I know someone who would really like it."

"It's a nice planter. Locally made and painted."

"I think I'll take it," he said, holding it under his arm as he walked into her office behind her. She had him sit down at the small metal desk across from her and she smiled warmly at him.

"I'm sorry to take time out of your day, Mrs. Rice. I just had a couple of questions that you might be able to help me with."

"Is it work related, Dr. Paltro?"

Deen shifted uncomfortably in his seat. It had been some time since anyone had called him that. He cupped the fox pot carefully in his lap.

"You could say that it has become more personal. I'm not asking you to do anything you're uncomfortable with."

She laughed, winking. "No one has ever made me do anything I was uncomfortable with."

"Do you have any male employees who are younger, brown or black hair, green or blue eyes. Probably attractive."

"We have a couple of good looking young men."

"Do they all do deliveries?"

"Whoever is free. I do them, James does them... Whoever's available."

"This guy probably doesn't have a steady relationship, takes work pretty seriously. Very tidy, neat."

He watched as she became very still, very quiet.

"Very easy to get along with. Never causes trouble. Drives a station wagon."

She suddenly, frighteningly, looked her age.

Deen leaned forward, "He's probably never missed a day of work, star employee. And his handwriting looks like this."

He slid one of Torres' cards with the man's handwriting on it across the desk.

Mrs. Rice settled back into her chair, crossing one leg over another. "Well. He'd never missed a day of work until this week."

Deen picked at the sticky residue left from the price tag on the fox planter as he toiled over what to do with the information that Mrs. Rice had given him. There was no guarantee, no concrete proof, that the name he had was the right guy. Torres thought it was him, and everything pointed in that direction... but what if they were wrong?

He sprayed glasses cleaner on the adhesive, using his nail to scrape the rest off after it was saturated. Satisfied, he set it in his passenger seat and took a picture to text to Tresa. He felt a flutter when the message sent, hoping that she liked it as much as he thought she would. Maybe he should have picked out a plant to go with it.

He knew he was delaying on purpose.

Should he tell Pat directly? Let her handle it, turn it over to the authorities who were leading the case now. Maybe tell Brannon so he could use the info instead to regain a little bit of faith in the department by cracking the case at the last minute. That would be the way of the law, justice at the hands of the court. They would arrest him, put him on trial. It would be the way things should be.

But nothing was the way things should be. Did he tell Polanski so that he could tell Robichaud? He could give him the chance to go after the guy. Give *him* justice, peace, revenge.

Revenge.

He thought about that concept. How barbaric, but how very human. It wouldn't bring Emily back, it wouldn't bring those girls back... but somehow, he knew it would feel good. It would be ice on the wounds of those families.

After a little more deliberation, he called Polanski.

He sounded fairly chipper, "Ye...hello."

"Hey, it's Paltro."

"Yup, I have caller ID, moron. What do you want? I'm getting a kielbasa."

"Not on your diet is it?"

"Shut your cocksucker. What do you want?"

Paltro took a deep inhale, blowing the air out into the receiver. "I got the bastard. I got an ID on him."

He thought he could hear Polanski choking on his sausage. "Shit! Gah... Dammit. Have you told Pat?"

"No... Listen. I'm telling you... and what you do with that information is up to you... but I think Robichaud deserves to know."

There was a long pause.

"He deserves to know."

"Paltro... You know he isn't okay right now."

"I know. He's never going to be okay. That's why I think he needs to know."

"You know he'll go after him. It'll be a shitshow. If anyone finds out that you told me... or that I told him..."

"Nobody is going to know."

"I don't know, Paltro..."

"I'm washing my hands of it. I'm done. This is it. Do you want the name or not?"

"Okay, give it to me."

"Theodore Orion Frey, goes by Rion. He works at Roots and Shoots in town. He's supposed to come in at five o'clock to pick up his paycheck, they still do paper."

"Got it. Gotta go."

Deen laid the phone down slowly, staring at the black screen for a long time. He could just barely make out his reflection on the dark screen, as he considered whether or not he had made the right decision.

54
Polanski

He was getting tired of this. The phone calls, the responsibility.

He sat in the driveway of his house with a cold kielbasa. It was his favorite, from a little local deli that served all kinds of sandwiches and sausages. It was covered in a sweet apple sauce with onions and tangy sauerkraut. Right now it was just nauseating. He had watched Leah peek out the window more than once to see if he was coming inside, but he didn't want to go in.

She finally came out to the car, knocking on the passenger side window with her knuckles. All he could see was her waist, the small gap between her jogging pants and her lounging tank top. She crouched down and peered in at him and he unlocked the door for her. She reached down and motioned to the sausage with a gag.

He threw it into the backseat, and she stared at him for a moment as though to silently ask what was wrong with him. She sat down inside the car and shut the door. They stared at the garage door together for a few minutes.

"Something else about the case?" she asked.

"Paltro called me and gave me the guy's name."

He looked over at her slowly. She had kept her face forward, towards the house and garage, but her gaze had drifted in his direction. She seemed to be fighting back emotion.

"He wants me to tell Robichaud."

She sniffled. "I know it's silly... a name mattering that much. But it seems like he's more... real all of a sudden. Because he has a name."

"Yeah, his first name is Theodore. Isn't that... juvenile?"

"Teddy," she mused. "Do we know him?"

David shrugged his shoulders. "Who knows. Probably ran into him at the grocery, or on the street. Just some guy. No criminal history, never been fingerprinted. Had the same job for... forever."

"What's he do?"

"He works at a garden center."

"A plant store."

David nodded.

"Are you going to tell Quentin?"

David shifted in his seat. "I don't know. I thought about just telling Pat. Letting her deal with it. Asking to be put on a post somewhere. Low stress. Maybe even evidence logging. Paperwork."

"David," Leah said, reaching over to clasp their hands together. Her tone was unusual, but one that he had heard before. That same voice she had when she was about to make hard decisions, irrevocable decisions. He knew what she was going to tell him, but he didn't know if he could do it.

"You've got to give Quentin the name."

"Leah..."

"You have spent your entire career watching his back, taking up for him, you've been taking calls and bending over backwards anytime he needed you to. It's his turn."

"This isn't for us... How does it help us? You know he'll go after him. He doesn't have anything left."

"You're right. He doesn't have anything left but this. It will give him the closure he needs... *and* it will give us some peace. We will never feel safe again and you know that. Not until this monster is put down. He came after Torres, he murdered Emily... How long before he really does come after Anna, or me, or you?"

David fumbled. "I can't send him out there alone. What if it kills him? What if that bastard kills him? I'll never forgive myself."

"He'll never forgive *you* for letting someone else have the satisfaction of taking him down. For letting that guy go to jail, avoid the needle because of insanity."

David knew she was right, Quentin was already gone. He was falling apart. He couldn't imagine losing Leah, not like Quentin had lost Emily. He couldn't imagine the nightmares he kept having of Anna being murdered coming to fruition.

He could give him the name and let him do what he felt like he needed to do. Whatever felt right for his soul.

David had always been there for him, always had his back, always made sure he would make it home... but not this time.

55
Quentin

"You don't have to be here today, Quentin."

Dr. Norrington leaned onto the arm of her chair towards him. She never before made a move towards him. She was always a solid and consistent figure that was never swayed. Today she was different, but so was Quentin. He was a heap in the chair, knees spread apart, each arm draped over the sides of the chair.

She spoke again, "How are you? Are you managing everything okay?"

All he could say was, "This is all my fault. All of it."

He could see it in her eyes, the way she wasn't saying what she wanted to say. She was never this nice to him. She was never this concerned about how he felt. She would have, on any other day, insisted that she was glad he had learned a lesson. Lessons were hard, but it meant that he could grow. Instead, she was coddling.

She sighed. "That's not true, Quentin. You can't blame yourself for the actions of a madman. They act and react irrationally, unpredictably."

"Why didn't I answer her fucking phone call?" he whispered.

"We are all guilty of ignoring texts, forwarding phone calls..."

Quentin shook his head, sitting up and leaning onto his knees. "You've been telling me it's my fault for a year now, and now... now I believe it."

"Quentin... I think you need to take some time off work. You need to heal."

"I am. FMLA. I don't know if I'll go back. They took me off the case, now that I'm personally afflicted."

She seemed puzzled, perhaps even frightened as her eyes moved to the personal gun at his waist. "Why are you still wearing your uniform?"

"I don't know how else to act. It's all I have anymore."

If he shed this uniform, like an old skin, what would be left of him?

"I think I'm done here... I just need to go home."

"Do you think about hurting yourself, or anyone else?"

He paused, looking her in the eye. He realized he didn't need to respond to her, because she was reading him. Could she see in his eyes how he had no desire to die because he already felt dead? Was there a way to explain how lifeless he felt, how empty? How he already felt passed on, like a ghost communicating with all of the warm bodies around him. Could she see how he wanted to kill the man that had taken Emily from him, so he could somehow bring him down to his level? Make him tangible, see him bleed, see him as the human he desperately needed him to be. Right now, it was just this force... this terrible, invincible force.

He shrugged his shoulders. "No."

Quentin had parked his car down the street to give himself something to do when he was done with his session. He needed the fresh air, to remind himself to breathe, to remind himself to move. As he walked down the cracked pavement, he was surprised to see a familiar figure leaning against the trunk of his vehicle. It was Polanski.

"David, what are you doing here?" Quentin asked, playing with his keyfob nervously. He hadn't been avoiding Polanski on purpose, but there was something about being around him that made him feel even worse.

"How are you, man? What have you been up to?"

"You know..." he muttered, motioning behind him. "Therapy."

Polanski shifted, awkwardly rubbing the back of his neck as he fought to speak. "Listen I'm not going to beat around the bush... Paltro got some info."

Quentin closed his eyes, putting his hand to head, "Polanski, I'm not in it anymore. I just... I need to let it go. I need to heal."

"Wait, Quentin. Wait. I know who he is, where he is... You don't have much time to make this move. I'm going to give you a headstart, then I'm telling the chief. Just... do with that... do what you want with the information."

Quentin nodded slowly. "Okay... Alright."

"His name is Rion Fray. He works at Roots and Shoots and he's going to be there at five o'clock. In and out, to pick up his paycheck."

"Thank you," Quentin said quietly, reaching out to put his hand on Polanski's arm. "Thank you. I've never told you how much you meant to me. You're my brother. I would have always done anything for you. I know that I have never been good at telling people what they mean to me, until it's too late. I want you to know now."

"Love you, man," Polanski said, pulling him snugly against his chest with his good arm.

He got into the car, watching as Polanski disappeared into his own vehicle and drove away. Was he going to do this? Without making a conscious decision he started driving to the garden center. He didn't think he'd ever been there. He had shopped at a few small florists, he never bought Emily anything more thoughtful than roses or whatever was on sale.

He pulled into the parking lot, stopping on the opposite side from the station wagon with the dented front fender. It was the car. His heart started pounding forcefully in his chest, he leaned against the window, fogging the corner with his nervous breath. He waited, and waited... and finally.

A man walked out of the store, and Quentin *recognized him*.

"That son-of-a-bitch!" he breathed to himself. "That son of a fucking bitch!"

He slammed his fists into the steering wheel over and over until his wrists were bruising. It was the man from the funeral, the last in line, the weirdo that refused to shake his hand. Rion paused, looking over at Quentin's car. Quentin took a breath and rolled down the window, just enough for him to see beyond the tint and confirm that they were looking at each other.

Rion sprinted to his car, and peeled out of the parking lot with squealing tires. Quentin followed.

56

Rion

"This isn't happening... This isn't how this was supposed to happen," Rion cried to himself, gripping the steering wheel in his hand.

"Between the lines, I don't want to die again," the Revenant said from the backseat.

Rion shook the steering wheel, screaming, "Fuck!"

"Calm down. Why are you so surprised?"

"What am I going to do... Where am I going..."

It was as though she was unaffected by the jostling of the car. Every turn, every lurch forward or backward, she was perfectly still. She sat leaning between the two front seats, watching him weave down the curving roads.

"Don't forget the gun," she said calmly.

"What?" Rion asked.

"The gun. My gun. It is in your glovebox. Make sure you take it with you."

"I'm going to try to lose him."

"You aren't going to lose him. Remember the gun."

She was suddenly gone.

He took a sharp turn down the winding road to the dam. It was the place that he had left Ji-su Cat, not far from the levee where he'd dumped Quinn Collins. There were people there, but he didn't know anywhere else he could possibly lose him. The building was falling apart, if he could get enough distance between them, maybe... just maybe... or...

His eyes moved to the glovebox, and it popped open as he slammed the brakes on the car in the parking lot. He grabbed the gun, shoving it into his pocket as he sprinted to the gate. The chain hanged uselessly, having been cut long ago by someone far less malicious than Rion. He shoved it open, going through the gaping opening and up the first flight of stairs. He heard Quentin's car outside. He thought he might have even heard the two cars collide with a loud *pop*. He stopped at a broken, stained window to see the former detective walking towards the building, gun drawn and ready.

Rion turned around and nearly collided with the Revenant. "You know how this is going to end, Rion."

"No. Stop!" he snapped, rushing past her and down the corridor to the next set of stairs. As he passed by a crumbling banister, he saw another woman standing on the edge. She saw him and started slowly following. He knew it was Olivia Brown. And then behind a pillar emerged Lisa York. They were all pale, bloated, deformed. The smell of decay had his eyes watering, throat constricted. He avoided a trail of maggots that Lola Simmons left in her wake. They reached for him, slowly, pursuing with a painful patience.

He would exit the service ramp. It was a fair drop to the ground, maybe ten or fifteen feet, but it was the only way out other than the way he'd come in. He jogged up the broken stairs, skipping over the rusted metal teeth. He skidded to a stop just as he entered the room. Elisa McBride came towards him, and he thought he could hear the echoes of her screaming dog with her. Just beyond her was the door, the exit. That drop to freedom.

The coolness that emanated from her had him scrambling away and back onto his feet, "Get away from me!"

The next room brought him face to face with Sharon Cook nearly immediately. She was still bound and gagged, dragging her intestines through the filth on the floor. She groaned at him, soft brows anchored over her eyes. He couldn't turn around, because Elisa McBride was already there. He spun around, finding that the girls had surrounded him in the middle of the room. Even the young waitress from the cafe, and Quinn Collins with her smashed face and broken fingers. They reached for him, all except the Revenant Summer Glass, who just stood staring with her arms crossed over her chest.

"Get away from me!" he demanded, spinning to speak to them individually. "You aren't real. None of this is real! You're dead. You're all dead!"

A gunshot filled the room. It echoed floors below them, all around. Crows screamed their protests. The girls disappeared. Rion looked down, side searing with pain, and he found blood gushing in a stream from his abdomen. He cupped his hands over it, jaw slack. He looked up slowly, and saw Quentin standing there, still poised from firing. They had trapped him here for him. They had him set up. This... this was it.

Rion gritted his teeth together, clamping his fist over the wound as he sprinted out of the room and to the last set of stairs: the stairs that would lead him to the rooftop. This wasn't the way he wanted it... sometimes though, things were out of your control.

Sometimes, there was a better way you hadn't even thought of.

Sometimes, there was a beauty and romance in serendipity.

57
Quentin

The stairs that extended haphazardly overhead precipitated rust and debris onto Quentin's face as he watched the bleeding man stumble in his ascent. Quentin had never been to the dilapidated dam before, but he knew that this flight of stairs was a dead end. Would the bastard jump and deprive him of his revenge? He needed this. He wanted to see him in the moment that he died, as that light that glowed and burned somewhere behind the eyes extinguished into a glazed and smoky haze. He had looked into too many eyes in his career as they went from animated and bright to something glassy and dull. From windows of the soul to dusty marbles in fleshy sockets. Many times those were innocent people, or people who made some bad decisions. Those eyes haunted him some nights.

He started up the stairs slowly, wrist aching from the way he clutched the Beretta in his hand. He could still smell the ashy aroma from the shot he had fired in the previous room, it lingered on his hand and around the barrel.

"Stop playing these fucking games with me, Fray," he yelled upwards, voice carrying to the ceiling and reverberating in the concrete room.

He didn't hear a response from above, only the sound of a breeze blowing through the now open door, the unearthly groans of the building, a distant boat engine, and the solitary call of a crow somewhere on the marina dock. His body was shaking now and the climb was becoming more difficult for him. His adrenaline was winding down and he found he was left with nothing more than the grim task at hand. He could take his time. This was it.

"It's over now," Quentin mused out loud, the building returning the warning to him with an echo. "It's all about to be over."

The sunlight was blinding as he exited the dark building onto the roof. He hesitated in the doorway, worried that the man would catch him off guard as his eyes adjusted to the brightness. Instead, he saw him standing at the opposite side of the roof, near the edge but not close enough that Quentin thought he might leap to his death. He was staring out over the water, stained pink and orange and a sickly chartreuse with the approaching sunset.

Quentin raised his gun again, hand finding its familiar steadiness even through the fatigue. He stared across the top of the glistening black weapon, waiting for the man to do something. Anything. He wouldn't shoot him in the back; he needed to see his face.

"Fray," he barked.

He didn't move, just continuing to stare out across the water. In the silence between them Quentin could hear the *pat, pat, pat* as blood dripped onto the asphalt roofing from the gunshot on Rion's abdomen. They could stand here all day, until he passed out from blood loss. He could maybe overtake him, beat him to death with his hands. The thought of it made him think of Rion's victim that he had beaten in the shower, the way her face had swelled and cracked from the fluid surrounding the fractures in her delicate bones. He didn't think he could do it, even with all of the hate and anger he had, he didn't think he could muster that much brutality.

"Look at me, goddammit!" Quentin yelled again, voice cracking in desperation.

Rion turned slowly, a look of solemn resolve across his face. Quentin didn't want him to look so calm. He wanted to see that same glimmer of fear he had seen when Rion had realized he was being followed. When he had been in the locker room below and he had been shot. None of that was there now, he seemed somehow… satisfied. His eyes were already dead and matte, like the surface of a dark button. Quentin wondered if they'd always looked this way, somehow without the gentle reflective quality of a soul.

The corners of Rion's mouth turned up, just the most subtle smile, and Quentin found himself pulling his trigger. He paused after the first shot, watching as Rion stumbled backwards, clutching the new wound. Quentin unloaded most of the Beretta into him, resisting the urge to keep pulling the trigger until it would give him nothing else. He saved a single cartridge in the magazine, mentally counting to allow himself that last shot. He started walking forward as Rion fell to his knees first, blood spouting from the holes in his torso, the tip of one finger had been blown off completely and lay somewhere among the broken glass and fractured shingles.

Quentin smiled, but the gesture held no joy. He felt a laugh erupt from him, and his chest ached. Rion collapsed onto his back, bubbles spewing from his chest as his lungs pumped valuable oxygen out the newfound orifices. He was drowning in his own blood.

"You're just a man," Quentin said, exasperated. "Just flesh… and blood. What did I expect? Why is this so… so fucking anticlimatic?"

He looked down as though he expected Rion to answer, but only the wheeze of his collapsing respirations could be heard. The man blinked up at him, as though he was listening quietly to what he had to say.

"When I was a kid, my grandmother would tell me about the boogeyman, and how he would hide under my bed and in the dark corners of my room. I always imagined him to have hundreds of teeth and nails like daggers, red eyes... I imagined this terrible monster. I asked my grandpa if he was afraid of the boogeyman, and he said absolutely. So I asked if he ever went away. He said when you get older... the boogeyman changes, but he's always there. I thought he'd get more teeth. He used to be a monster in the dark who stole army men and mismatched socks... Now it's just you. After all of this time, all this pain, all this fear... you're gonna die right here."

Quentin raised his gun again, but Rion's hand was already pulling a hidden revolver from his pocket. He lifted it and fired before Quentin had the chance to end his life, the bullet piercing through the detective's pale shirt and through his chest, lodging somewhere inside. His chest ached, heart throbbing erratically as his left arm went limp and numb. He dropped his gun, reaching up with his right hand to touch the spot as though to see if it had really happened. His fingertips felt especially cold against the warm blood that poured out of him in a dark, steady stream.

He dropped down, falling beside Rion on the ground. The killer's body had gone limp now, eyes staring unblinking into the darkening sky. Clouds overhead threatened rain in the dusk, appearing like blood-stained cotton on the pink backdrop. Quentin was reluctant to move as he lay there, not unaware that he was dying. The pain from the gunshot ached and burned, tightening until he wasn't sure he could breathe another breath. He turned to where Rion had been lying, but there through the haze of tears in his eyes he saw Emily.

She was wearing the same dress that she had on when they went on that date to Sugar's. He smiled, forcing himself to take another breath as he reached out to her. She clasped her hand around his, squeezing firmly as she gave him a soft smile. Quentin blinked, vision so unclear now that he wasn't sure he could see her at all anymore through the soft white film, but he kept his fingers curled where hers had been in his... sure that he could still feel her there. Numbness crept through his limbs and coolness started at his ears and moved down his throat.

He slipped into death like it was something natural, easy, and welcome: a little room of winter adjacent to this sweltering summer of life.

Printed in Great Britain
by Amazon